RETURN TO SENDER

Julia Alvarez

Alfred A. Knopf
New York

Library of Congress Cataloging-in-Publication Data
Alvarez, Julia.
Return to sender / Julia Alvarez. — 1st ed.
p. cm.
Summary: After his family hires migrant Mexican workers to help save their Vermont farm
from foreclosure, eleven-year-old Tyler befriends the oldest daughter, but when he discovers
they may not be in the country legally, he realizes that real friendship knows no borders.
ISBN 978-0-375-85838-3 (trade) — ISBN 978-0-375-95838-0 (lib. bdg.)
[1. Farm life—Vermont—Fiction. 2. Friendship—Fiction. 3. Migrant workers—Fiction.
4. Illegal aliens—Fiction. 5. Vermont—Fiction.] I. Title.
PZ7.A48Re 2009
[Fic]—dc22
2008023520

The text of this book is set in 12-point Goudy.

Printed in the United States of America
January 2009
10 9 8 7 6 5 4 3

First Edition

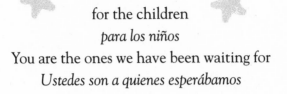

for the children
para los niños
You are the ones we have been waiting for
Ustedes son a quienes esperábamos

from *"La Golondrina"*

¿A dónde irá veloz y fatigada
La golondrina que de aquí se va?
¡O! si en el viento se hallará extraviada
Buscando abrigo y no lo encontrará.

Where are you going, swift and weary
Swallow, why are you leaving here?
Oh, what if you lose your way in the wind
Looking for a home you will never find?

—Narciso Serradel Sevilla (1843–1910)

CONTENTS

ONE
Uno

summer

(2005)

BAD-LUCK FARM

Tyler looks out the window of his bedroom and can't believe what he is seeing.

He rubs his eyes. Still there! Some strange people are coming out of the trailer where the hired help usually stays. They have brown skin and black hair, and although they don't wear feathers or carry tomahawks, they sure look like the American Indians in his history textbook last year in fifth grade.

Tyler rushes out of his room and down the stairs. In the den his father is doing his physical therapy exercises with Mom's help. The TV is turned on; Oprah is interviewing a lady who has come back from having died and is describing how nice it is on the other side. "Dad," Tyler gasps. "Mom!"

"What is it? What is it?" Mom's hand is at her heart, as if it might tear out of her chest and fly away.

"There's some Indians trespassing! They just came out of the trailer!"

Dad is scrambling up from the chair, where he has been lifting a weight Mom has strapped to his right leg. He lets himself fall back down and turns the TV to mute with the remote control. " 'Sokay, boy, quiet down," he says. "You want to kill your mom with a heart attack?"

Before this summer, this might have been a joke to smile at. But not anymore. Mid-June, just as school was letting out, Gramps died of a heart attack while working in his garden. Then, a few weeks later, Dad almost died in a farm accident. Two men down and Tyler's older brother, Ben, leaving for college this fall. "You do the math," his mom says whenever the topic comes up of how they can continue farming. Tyler has started thinking that maybe their farm is jinxed. How many bad things need to happen before a farm can be certified as a bad-luck farm?

"But shouldn't we call the police? They're trespassing!" Tyler knows his dad keeps his land posted, which means putting up signs telling people not to come on his property without permission. It's mostly to keep out hunters, who might mistakenly shoot a cow or, even worse, a person.

"They're not exactly trespassing," his mom explains, and

then she glances over at Dad, a look that means, You explain it, honey.

"Son," his dad begins, "while you were away . . ."

✦   ✦   ✦

In the middle of the summer, Tyler was sent away for a visit to his uncle and aunt in Boston. His mom was worried about him.

"He's just not himself," Tyler overheard Mom tell her sister, Roxanne, on the phone. "Very mopey. He keeps having nightmares. . . ." Tyler groaned. Nothing like having his feelings plastered out there for everyone to look at.

Of course Tyler was having nightmares! So many bad things had happened before the summer had even gotten started.

First, Gramps dying would have been bad enough. Then, Dad's horrible accident. Tyler actually saw it happen. Afterward, he couldn't stop playing the moment over and over in his head: the tractor climbing the hill, then doing this kind of weird backflip and pinning Dad underneath. Tyler would wake up screaming for help.

That day, Tyler rushed into the house and dialed 911. Otherwise, the paramedics said, his father would have died. Or maybe Dad would have been brought back to life to be on *Oprah* talking about the soft music and the bright lights.

It was amazing that Dad was still alive, even if it looked like his right arm would be forever useless and he'd always walk with a limp. His face was often in a grimace from the pain he felt.

But the very worst part was after Dad got home and Tyler's parents seriously began to discuss selling the farm. Mostly, it was his mom. His dad hung his head like he knew she was right but he just couldn't bear to do the math one more time himself. "Okay, okay," he finally said, giving up.

That was when Tyler lost it. "You can't sell it! You just can't!"

He had grown up on this farm, as had his dad before him, and Gramps and his father and grandfather before that. If they left their home behind, it'd be like the Trail of Tears Tyler learned about in history class last year. How the Cherokee Indians had been forced from their land to become migrants and march a thousand miles to the frontier. So many of them had died.

"Tiger, honey, remember our talk," Mom reminded him pleasantly enough in front of Dad. Tiger is what his mom calls him when she is buttering him up. Before his father came home from the hospital, his right leg and arm still in a cast, Mom sat Tyler and his older brother and sister down for a talk. She explained that they must all do their part to help Dad in his recovery. No added worries (looking over at Ben, eighteen going on I'm-old-enough-to-do-what-I-want). No scenes (looking over at Sara, fifteen with a boyfriend, Jake, and "Saturday night fever" seven nights a week, as his dad often joked, back when he used to joke). No commotion (looking over at Tyler, who as the youngest sometimes had to make a commotion just to be heard). They must all keep Dad's spirits up this summer.

But Tyler knew for a fact that selling the farm would kill his dad. It would kill Tyler!

After his outburst, Mom had another little talk, this time just with Tyler. She sat him down at the kitchen table again as if the whole thing were a math problem that Tyler was having trouble with. Dairy farms were struggling. Hired help was hard to find. And if you did find someone like Corey, he only wanted to work eight hours a day, five days a week. Problem was cows needed milking twice a day every day, and the milkings had to be spaced at least eight to ten hours apart. Tyler's brother, Ben, was helping out now. But he was off to college at the end of the summer, and not interested in farming once he graduated. Meanwhile, his sister, Sara, claimed she was allergic to most everything on the farm, especially her chores.

"What about me?" Tyler piped up. Why was he always being overlooked, just because he was the youngest? "I can do the milking. I know how to drive the tractor."

Mom reached over and pushed Tyler's hair back from his eyes. What a time to think about making him look presentable! "Tiger, I know you're a hardworking little man. But milking two hundred cows is impossible even for a big man." Her smile was tender. "Besides, you've got to go to school."

"But I could stay home and work. Just for this year," Tyler added. He was feeling desperate. Sure, he'd miss his friends and some things about school, like when they studied

Native American tribes or the universe or Spanish, which a new teacher was teaching them twice a week.

But Mom was already shaking her head. Tyler should have guessed. Never in a million years would she let him stay home. School was always what she called a priority. "Even if you end up farming, you never know what might happen . . ." Mom didn't have to go on with the sentence they could both now finish: look at what happened to your father.

"Tiger, honey, I know it's not easy. But sometimes in life . . ."

Any sentence Mom started with the words *sometimes in life* was not going to end in good news. ". . . we have to accept things that we can't change." She looked thoughtful, even a little sad. "But what we do with what we get makes us who we are." It sounded like a riddle. Like something Reverend Hollister might say in a sermon.

"But it'd be like Gramps dying all over again!" Tyler was crying, even though he didn't want to cry. Gramps's ashes were scattered up in the garden by the old house Grandma still lived in. How could they leave him behind? And what about Grandma? Where would she go?

His mom explained that the plan was to keep his grandparents' house, including a little plot beside it where Tyler's parents could build a new house. "We don't really have to leave the place," Mom added. Now it was Tyler shaking his head. Mom had grown up in Boston, a city girl. She didn't understand the way that Tyler did, the way Gramps and Dad did, what it meant to be a farm family.

How could he explain to her that the farm was not just Dad's, it was the whole family's, going all the way back before Gramps, as well as forward, his and Sara's and Ben's, even if they didn't want it?

Tyler remembered something the Abenaki chief who had come to his school for an assembly had said: "My people believe that our land is not given to us by our ancestors. It is loaned to us by our children."

"But it's not fair, it's not fair!" Tyler responded to his mom's explanations. And that was also what he said when she announced that Tyler had been invited to visit his aunt Roxie and uncle Tony for a month in Boston.

Now that *will* kill me, Tyler thought.

*　　　*　　　*

Aunt Roxie and Uncle Tony were peculiar in a way that Tyler didn't feel right complaining about. They were generous and always eager for adventure, and since they didn't have any children, they loved to spoil their niece and nephews. Sara adored them.

"Why can't *I* go for a month?" she asked as Tyler was being packed up.

"Trade you," he offered in a whisper. But his mom heard him and gave him that time-for-another-math-problem look. So Tyler shut up. Besides, he would never have wanted to hurt his aunt's and uncle's feelings. They were like two little kids, except they were middle-aged, so it felt weird that they were acting his age.

In fact, Mom hadn't always let her kids go off with her sister and Uncle Tony. "Don't get me wrong, I love Roxie to death," Tyler heard his mom telling Dad, "but she's a loose cannon, and he's not far behind, you know." Aunt Roxie and Uncle Tony had done wild, crazy things that Tyler wasn't supposed to know about. "Like what?" he asked Sara, who had a way of finding things out.

"Well, for one thing, how they met. Aunt Roxie worked in a roller-derby bar." Sara laughed, shaking her head, enjoying the thought. Tyler wasn't sure what was so funny. He was having a hard time putting the job together in his head: being on roller skates in a derby and serving drinks in a bar—all at the same time?

"How about Uncle Tony?"

"Ohmigod, don't even ask. He's done like a bunch of crazy stuff. He was the bouncer at the bar where Aunt Roxie was working." A bouncer, his sister explained, was a big, tough bodyguard guy who threw rowdy people out of bars.

"Uncle Tony?" Tall, goofy Uncle Tony who was always cracking jokes?

His sister gave him a deep, know-it-all nod. "Working at that bar is where they got the idea of throwing parties."

A couple of years ago, Aunt Roxie and Uncle Tony quit their night jobs to start a hugely successful party business, which, among other things, sold party products online. They were also party motivators, who flew to rich people's mansions and villas to help them throw the best parties, Christmas parties and wedding parties and birthday parties and I-just-feel-like-having-a-party parties. Party Animals, they called their company.

Mom was glad that she didn't have to worry about her baby sister anymore, and that her kids now had an aunt and uncle on her side they could count on.

Uncle Tony and Aunt Roxie came up for the Fourth of July dressed in matching red, white, and blue outfits, Uncle Tony sporting a top hat like Uncle Sam's, and Aunt Roxie a Statue of Liberty crown. On their drive back to Boston, Tyler thought he would die of embarrassment every time a car passed them on the highway. But drivers slowed down and honked their horns, giving Uncle Sam and Lady Liberty the thumbs-up. No wonder their company was so successful.

The month-long visit was actually okay. The Party Animals offices were in the downstairs of their condo, so while his aunt and uncle worked, Tyler entertained himself. He played video games and watched movies on the giant-screen TV. Every weekend, there was a party to go to or an outing to an amusement park or—Tyler's all-time favorite—a visit to the Museum of Science. He'd gaze up at the planetarium stars and think about the universe, forgetting his farm worries for hours at a time. On Fridays after work if the night was clear, his uncle and aunt would drive over to the museum so Tyler could look through the big telescope on the roof at the real stars.

But even though he was having fun, Tyler missed the farm so much. Often during the day, he would find himself thinking about what was happening right then back home—the cows were being milked or the back meadow mowed or the bales stacked in the haymow as the swallows dove in and out of the barn. Tyler could smell the fresh-cut grass, hear the mooing of the cows as they waited for the feed cart to come by their stalls. Then, without warning, the thought would pop into his head—*the farm was being sold, and that was why his parents had sent him away*—and he'd start to worry all over again.

At the end of his visit, Tyler's mom drove down with Sara, who would be staying on for her very own one-week visit with their aunt and uncle. On the way back to Vermont, his mom surprised Tyler with the best news ever. "Honey, we think we've found a way to keep the farm after all."

Tyler felt like his whole life had just been given back to him, wrapped up like a present with a big bow on top! But wait, did that mean Dad had regained the use of his arm? Was Ben going to stay on the farm instead of going to college? Had his dad's brother, Uncle Larry, who also farmed, offered to join their two adjacent farms together?

All these questions were popping up in Tyler's head like one of those video games where the dark invaders jump out at every turn. But Tyler was not about to let them take over his feelings once again. He'd grab the good news and run. However his parents had managed to save their family's farm, he was just glad they had worked this miracle in the month he had been gone.

"While you were away," his dad is explaining, "we found some folks who're going to help me with the work."

"I was wondering," Tyler admits. But he has promised himself not to ask a whole lot of questions and start worrying all over again.

"Those 'trespassers' are actually the reason we can stay on this farm," Tyler's dad goes on. "They're the best helpers a man can ask for." He smiles sadly. Tyler knows how hard it is for his father to ask for any help. Grandma always says that Dad should have been born over in New Hampshire, where the state motto is "Live free or die."

"They're from Mexico," Mom goes on. She is a far better explainer than Dad, for whom two and two is always four and that's the extent of it. Whereas Mom will go into how two is an even number, how if you multiply it by itself you get four, same as when you add it to itself. . . . The only bad thing about Mom's explanations is that they go on and on, and Tyler can't help feeling impatient.

"They came all the way from the south of Mexico, a place called Chiapas," Mom is saying.

"You mean you went to Mexico to pick them up while I was gone?" No wonder Sara didn't make more of a fuss about coming to Boston with Tyler!

"No, son." His dad shakes his head. "We didn't have to go to Mexico. They were already here."

"Your uncle Larry had some on his farm," Mom elaborates. "And he told us about them. Lots of them are coming up here because they can't earn enough back home to live on. Many of them used to farm. They're separated from their families for years." It sounds to Tyler like their very own Trail of Tears.

"Best workers," his dad asserts. "Put us all to shame."

"Well, Dad." Mom smiles fondly at her husband. "You do a pretty good job yourself."

"Used to," he mutters bitterly.

"So you see, they're most definitely not trespassers," Mom says, ignoring the dark cloud but pulling out the silver lining. "They're like our angels," she adds.

"I counted at least three guys," Tyler mentions. He doesn't like this angel talk. Not with Oprah still on the screen alongside close-ups of a mangled car in some horrible accident that's reminding Tyler of Dad's tractor tipping over.

Besides, *angels* are just one step away from ghosts and the spooky thought that maybe their farm is haunted with bad luck.

"And there's also three little girls," Mom adds. Dad looks up as if this is news to him. "They're going to be at your school," Mom continues. "One of them's your age. She'll probably be in your grade."

"You didn't say anything about little girls." Dad looks alarmed.

"I didn't know myself until I went to pick them up," Mom says, shrugging. Like Tyler, his mom probably didn't want to ask a whole lot of questions when angels came to their rescue, even if they were disguised as Mexicans.

"One last thing, Tiger," his mom says as Tyler is heading out the door. "We . . . Well . . . School's about to start." She hesitates. "What we just told you is not—I mean, it stays on the farm, okay?" His mom glances at the TV, still on mute. It's as if Oprah herself is following Mom's orders.

Tyler must look confused, because his mom goes on, explaining stuff that makes no sense. "You know like when there's a disagreement at home or we tell you something's private. You understand?"

Of course Tyler understands about privacy. Like the time his uncle Byron had his hemorrhoid operation. Or Uncle Larry's oldest son, Larry Jr., was caught with a girl in the barn. But why would hiring workers have to be kept private?

And then Tyler gets it. His father's pride! Dad doesn't want his farmer neighbors to know he needs not one but— Tyler counted them—three helpers. Not to mention that his parents are probably afraid some other farmer will hire these workers out from under them. Pay them more money, give them a house instead of a trailer.

"Okay." He nods, grinning with relief. "If anyone asks I'll just tell them we've got us some Martians." Actually, his classmates might just believe him! Back in fifth grade, Ronnie and Clayton, the two school bullies, used to chant "There's Ty, the Science Guy!" because Tyler was always talking about the universe and the stars in class. "We hired extraterrestrials," he'll report. "Excellent help. You don't have to pay them. You don't have to feed them. All you do is reboot them at night and they're ready to go in the morning."

It's only as he's headed upstairs that it hits him. If the girls are going to be attending Bridgeport, how can they be a secret? He's about to go back downstairs and confront his parents, but then he remembers the promise he made to himself. No questions. No worries. Let those girls come up with their own explanation. It should be easier being Mexican than being an alien from outer space.

But remembering his mom's worried look and his dad's bowed head, Tyler wonders if maybe being Martian is a lot easier to explain than being Mexican in Vermont. One thing's for sure. Sometimes in life he just has to accept stuff he'll never ever understand.

Queridísima Mamá,

If you are reading these words, it means you are back in Carolina del Norte! There would be no greater happiness for Papá, my sisters, and me than to hear this good news. We have missed you terribly the eight months and a day (yes, Mamá, I am keeping count!) that you have been gone.

By the time you get this letter, we will have moved north. "I thought we were already in *El Norte?*" Ofie asked when Papá announced we would be departing from Carolina del Norte to go to Vermont.

Papá laughed. *"Más allá en El Norte,"* he explained. A state even farther north in an area of the country where there are many farms. Tío Armando and Tío Felipe and Papá had heard from some friends from Las Margaritas who had found work there that the *patrones* are kind and need help on their farms.

At first, none of us wanted to move because we feared that you would come back and not find us where you left us. But since friends have taken over our apartment in Durham, and we left word where we are, and soon you will be receiving this letter, that worry has been put to rest.

Even so, it is difficult for Luby and Ofie to

leave the one place they have known as their home. The place they were born. As for me, Mamá, it is the place where I have been waiting. Waiting for you to return. Waiting for the laws to change so I can visit my birthplace in México and be able to come back into the United States again.

But Papá explained to us how our lives would be better in Vermont. We would all be together, living on the farm where he and our uncles worked.

Ever since you left, Mamá, he doesn't want to let my sisters and me out of his sight. And now, there are so many of us in Carolina del Norte that he could not always find work, and when he did, he had to go where the *patrón* sent him. The jobs were only for two, three weeks, and then back to a street corner with a crowd of other Mexicans, hoping he would be picked. And always fearing that *la migra* would pick him up first and deport him back home, where he'd have to find the money to pay for the dangerous crossing once again. Papá worries most about what would happen to my sisters and me if he was taken away, especially with you not around to at least be one parent in the family.

"Do not worry," Tío Armando reminds Papá. "I would take care of them like my own children." Our uncle has not seen his wife and kids since he went for a visit three years ago. His littlest daughter he hasn't even met. Papafón, she calls him, because she only knows him from hearing his voice on the telephone.

"And what if they take you, too?" Papá always replies. "What then?"

Our uncle Felipe strums his guitar to remind Papá that he can take care of us, too. Wilmita, he calls her. "I will treat them like *princesitas*," he sings as he picks a tune. "I will dress them in diamonds and pearls and take them to Disney World."

"How about we dress them in sweaters and boots and take them to a farm in Vermont," Papá says, smiling. Tío Felipe sure knows how to make us all laugh. Without him, we'd be a family of the well half dry, that is for certain.

Another thing that is for certain: Papá will be so much happier working on a farm! He often speaks of being a boy, helping our grandfather, Abuelote, farm in Las Margaritas. But that was before the family had to give up farming because there was no money in it. In Carolina del Norte, all he did was construction, and often the jobs were far away, and Papá could not come home for weeks at a time, and then just for a short weekend.

Don't worry, Mamá, I have taken good care of my little sisters when he is gone. You will not believe how tall Luby has gotten! She is up to my chest, and Ofie is almost as tall as me! A lot of people guess they are older than five and seven, which Ofie especially loves to brag about. Often those same people can't believe I'm really eleven going on twelve. "Good things come in small packages," they say to console me.

I understand why I am not very tall, because I resemble you and Papá. But where did my sisters get their height? In school, we learned about genes, how we become what our parents put in us.

"Genes?" Tío Felipe makes a joke when I explain it to him. "Jeans are to wear!" He says it is food, lots of it. When I was in your belly in Las Margaritas you were not eating as well as when Ofie and then Luby came along in this country. When he sees the sad look on my face, Tío Felipe tries to make another joke. "All those McDonald's and Coca-Colas!" He smiles his wonderful smile that is so hard to resist. Papá says that when Tío Felipe returns with his pockets full of money and his good looks, all the girls in Las Margaritas are going to throw themselves at him like girls do here at the movie stars. That makes Tío Felipe smile wider.

It is difficult to be the one different from my sisters. Some boys at my old school made fun of me, calling me an "illegal alien." What is illegal about me? Only that I was born on the wrong

side of a border? As for "alien," I asked the
teacher's helper, and she explained that an alien
is a creature from outer space who does not even
belong on this earth! So, where am I supposed
to go?

Even at home, I feel so alone sometimes. I
cannot tell Papá about the boys making fun
because he would pull us out of school, especially
now that he is so protective after you left. I cannot
speak to my little sisters, as I don't want to worry
them any more than they are. Besides, Ofie has
such a big mouth, I am afraid she would tell Papá
whatever I tell her. And how could any of them
understand why I feel so lonely? I am not like my
sisters, who are little American girls as they were
born here and don't know anything else. I was
born in México, but I don't feel Mexican, not like
Papá and my uncles with all their memories and
stories and missing it all the time.

If only you were here, Mamá, you would
understand. Now that you are gone, Papá says I
am to be the mother to my little sisters. "But who
will be my mother?" I ask him. He just bows his
head and gets so quiet for days on end. I'm not
going to make him more sad by asking him that
again.

That is why I am writing, Mamá. Not only to
tell you where we are moving to, but also because
I have nowhere else to put the things that are in

my heart. As you always used to tell Papá when he found you writing letters, or just writing in a notebook, *"El papel lo aguanta todo."* Paper can hold anything. Sorrows that might otherwise break your heart. Joys with wings that lift you above the sad things in your life.

Mamá, you know what I have missed most of all? Your stories! What wonderful ones you always told my sisters and me even before they could understand why you and Papá had come from Las Margaritas to Carolina del Norte, the dreams that drew you here so you could give us a better life and help our grandparents and aunts and uncles back home.

Since you left, Mamá, I have continued to tell them those stories. Luby and Ofie do not have as many memories of you as I have. So I am always adding mine to theirs so that you will not be a stranger when you come back. And I write you for the same reason, so you will know me through these words. So when you see me I will not be an alien to you, too, Mamá. For that would break my heart, even if I also write it down.

> I love you with all my heart and with
> my *corazón*, too,
> Mari

Queridísima Mamá,

I am writing to tell you that we arrived safely. I hope by now you have returned to Carolina del Norte and will find this letter as well as the first one waiting for you.

We have not yet gotten our own telephone number, but you have the number of the *patrón* we left for you and I will write it down here, too: 802-555-2789.

Our journey to Vermont was not as long as our journey to this country. At first, the plan was to buy a used car and Tío Armando would drive us, a voyage of about three days. But Papá feared that the *policía* would pull us over and find out that there were four of us without papers, including one driver without a license, and two little American-citizen girls whom we had obviously kidnapped.

There was the added problem that Tío Felipe thought the police might be looking for him. No, Mamá, he did not do anything wrong. But the old lady he worked for had two little dogs, and part of Tío Felipe's job was to feed and walk them. Tío Felipe said those animals ate better than most of the people in Las Margaritas. Several weeks ago, one of those little dogs disappeared, and the lady was sure that Tío Felipe had sold it, as those *perritos* are very valuable. But as Tío Felipe said when he told us the story, "Then why didn't I sell them both?"

But Tío Felipe could not defend himself because he does not know enough English. He did understand when this lady said the word *police*. So, after she went back inside her house, Tío Felipe ran off, arriving home in the middle of the morning. My sisters and I were not expecting anybody until the end of the day. We got so excited when we heard a key in the lock, thinking it was you, Mamá, returning home. We tried not to look too disappointed when it was only our uncle at the door.

After that, Tío Felipe was afraid to go out on the streets and be picked up for a theft he had never committed.

I offered to call the old lady, since my English is almost perfect now. I would explain how our uncle never even takes something out of the refrigerator that he has not bought himself without asking first.

But Tío Felipe shook his head. That *viejita* was not going to believe a Mexican. My uncle hadn't meant to hurt my feelings, but it made me feel the same left-out feelings as when the children at school called me names.

"I'll call her," Ofie offered. "I'm American."

"I'm American too," Luby said. "I'll let her play with my doggie, Tío Fipe." Luby held out this little stuffed puppy our uncle had bought her at the Wal-Mart.

Even Tío Felipe smiled, though his eyes were sad.

(Later the same day—as I had to stop.
Sometimes I get so sad,
even if I'm just writing things down.)

Papá and my uncles decided we should travel by bus, just as for that first journey when we came from México. I was only four. So I do not know if I truly remember, Mamá, or if it is your stories that have become my memories.

I do remember how hard you cried when we left Las Margaritas. "I cried so much that for years I had no tears," you once told me. I do not understand how that can be, Mamá. Since you left, I have cried and cried into my pillow so as not to upset Papá or my sisters over your absence, and every night there are fresh tears.

Those last moments in Las Margaritas, you told me you clung to Abuelita, and your sisters and younger brothers clung to you, and Abuelito looked down at the earth that could no longer feed his family. "My daughter," he said in parting, "if we do not meet again in this world, we will meet again in the next life." This only made you cry harder.

You told me, or perhaps I remember that long bus ride for days and days until we reached the border with the United States. You had not known our own country of México was so vast and beautiful. Last year in geography class, I found Las Margaritas on the map at the very tip of México in the south, and with my finger I traced our route to the northern border at the very other end. What a long journey to make to a place that does not welcome us but instead sends us away!

Your face was pressed to the window of that bus, you told me, and so was mine. Sometimes when we passed a town and saw a child or an old person, we waved, and they waved back at us. Sometimes that made you sad, as it reminded you of your mother and father and the loved ones you left behind.

Those times when the sadness made you want to turn back, Papá would remind you that a new life was about to start for our family. We would be joining Tío Armando, who was already in Carolina del Norte and had sent money for our passage. Tío Felipe accompanied us, and sometimes, sad as you were, he could make you smile with his boasting: "I will come back a rich

26

man with a big car and throw a fiesta with piñatas full of dollars!" To think he was only fourteen and already beginning his life as a man, leaving school and his home to help support his family.

We arrived in the border town and found the smugglers that Tío Armando had recommended. "But where are the coyotes?" I kept asking. Papá had said *coyotes* would be crossing us to this country, and so I had expected animals dressed in clothes and speaking Spanish!

But they turned out to be men, not very kind ones, always barking at us as if *we* were animals. We were to carry only a small bag that would not slow us down or take up room in the van that would meet us on the other side. I remember you gave everything away to the poor beggars outside the cathedral where we stopped to pray before setting forth. Then the *coyotes* stuck us in a little room with dozens of others, waiting for darkness, to take us in small groups across the desert.

It was very dark. Sometimes I walked alongside you, but mostly you and Papá and Tío Felipe took turns carrying me. I could hear your heart beating so hard in your chest I was afraid it would burst out, and so I clung even tighter, like a bandage to keep it inside. That journey seemed to go on and on, for days. I remember the fear of serpents, the sharp rocks, the lights of *la migra*. And always, the terrible thirst . . . I am not sure even this paper can hold such terrifying memories.

But we arrived safely, Mamá, and that is what I wish for you now after eight months and five days of traveling. I know Papá blames himself for letting you go back to México alone. But the passage was too expensive to think of taking any of us with you when the phone call came that Abuelita was dying. My sisters and I didn't even know that night when you put us to bed that by morning you would be gone. I still remember how after you tucked in my sisters, you lingered by my bedside. "Promise me," you said, your voice so urgent that my sleepiness instantly faded away, "promise me you will always take care of your *hermanitas*."

"*Mamá, ¿qué pasa?*" I asked, sitting up. "What's wrong?" Luby was already snoring and Ofie complaining that we were making too much noise.

"Shhh," you whispered to me, pointing over to my grumpy sister. "Nothing is wrong, my heart. But you will never forget me, ever?"

I shook my head adamantly. How could you even wonder about such a thing and why were you wondering now?

"Whenever you feel sad or lonely or confused, just pick up a pen and write me a letter," you said, tucking my hair behind my ears.

"But why would I write you a letter if you are here, Mamá?" I had heard that Abuelita was sick, but neither you nor Papá had mentioned your going away.

You laughed the way people do when they are embarrassed at being caught making a mistake. "I mean . . . that it's good to write letters. When you write down your thoughts to anyone, you do not feel so alone."

I nodded, relieved by your explanation. Soon after you tiptoed out, I fell asleep. But that night I had nightmares. We were crossing the desert again. There was a serpent wrapping itself around and around your body like a boa constrictor. Then a huge pen came writing across the land, drawing a big black borderline. I woke up, startled. The apartment was so quiet. I thought of getting up and finding you and Papá, but the peaceful breathing of my sisters drew me back to sleep.

Next morning, what a shock when Papá delivered the news! Now I understood why you had said the things you had, Mamá. My sisters cried and cried, but I had to stay strong for them and for Papá. Still, I bit my nails down so far that they bled. Papá kept reassuring us that the journey home was no problem, as you would be entering your birth land on an airplane, not on foot through a desert.

The danger came with your return after

Abuelita's death to be reunited with us. Papá had sent extra money so you could reenter the United States the safer way, through a reservation, disguised as the wife of an Indian chief, sitting in the front seat of his car.

You called before starting back, and we were so excited! For days afterward, we cleaned every corner of that apartment; even Ofie helped without complaining. We wanted everything to look perfect for your return. Finally, every surface twinkled and every package and can and box in the kitchen cabinets looked lined up with a ruler. And then, we waited and waited, and waited. . . .

Papá could not notify the police because it was illegal for you to be trying to come in without permission in the first place. Finally, he decided to leave us with our uncles and retrace your steps. Tío Felipe tried to distract us with his songs and jokes, but this time it didn't work. Tío Armando took only local jobs so he could come home at the end of the day.

Every night, Papá would call. "Have you heard anything?" he would always begin, and we'd ask him the same thing back. But no one could tell him anything about your whereabouts. By the time he returned, Papá was almost crazy with grief. Nights, after everyone had gone to bed, I would find him in the kitchen, sitting in the dark, his head in his hands.

"Papá, she will return." I was the one now reassuring him.

"*Espero que sí, mi'ja*," he would say in an anguished voice. "I hope so, my daughter."

As the months have gone by, he has calmed down, Mamá. Sometimes he hears me telling my sisters, "When Mamá comes back," and a strange, pained look comes on his face. Like he half wants to believe it but can't let himself hope too much. If my sisters press him, he just says, "It is in God's hands."

But I know you will return. That is why I write you. It is like the candle that Abuelita promised to keep lit at her altar until we returned. To light our way back to Las Margaritas. Or now to light your way to Vermont, to a farm owned by a crippled farmer and his kind wife, who seemed surprised when she picked us up at the bus station.

"I didn't know that there were children," she said.

"*¿Qué dice?*" my father asked. "What did she say?"

"I thought it was just going to be the three men," the woman went on.

"They are my uncles and my father," I explained. Luby clung to her little dog and to Ofie, who clung to Papá, afraid they would not be allowed to enter Vermont, even if they were Americans.

The woman must have seen our fear. Her face softened, but still she looked undecided.

"They will not bother," my father said.

When I translated, the woman shook her head. "Bother? Are you kidding? You guys are lifesavers! Angels, really."

"¿Qué dice?" Papá asked again.

None of us three knew the word for lifesaver in Spanish. "It's like a candy," Luby tried.

"She says we are angels," Ofie offered in her know-it-all voice.

For the first time in a long while, Papá laughed. "Sí, sí," he said, nodding at the lady. "¡Somos ángeles mexicanos!"

Mexican angels, Mamá! How is that for being a special alien?

Soon we were piled in the lady's van with the windows tinted so you cannot see inside, but once inside, you can see out. Tío Armando and Tío Felipe sat in the backseat, and Papá and Luby and Ofie in the other backseat. And guess who rode in the front seat with the lady? Me!

We are now living in a house called a trailer beside the home of the farmer and his wife and their handsome son, who looks about the same age as Tío Felipe, and their daughter, Sara, who is so pretty and nice. (She says there is another son, who is away with relatives because he has not been feeling well.)

"This is your new home," the farmer's wife said when she brought us here. But a home means being all together, so until you are back with us, Mamá, we will never feel at home, not in Carolina del Norte, not in México, not here.

Soon after we arrived, the daughter Sara came over with a big box of her "old" clothes that looked brand-new to me. But they were all far too big for us. "Grandma can alter them for you. She can sew like a barn on fire."

My goodness! For a moment I wondered what kind of a strange grandmother would sew like that. But Sara explained she meant her grandmother could sew anything. Why didn't she just say that?

Along with other things at the bottom of the box there were some real pretty hair clips and a lip gloss and blush, which I got to keep. Sometimes there are advantages to being the oldest! Not that Papá will let me use makeup. Like I told you before, he has become even more strict now that you are not around to protect us.

When Sara was leaving, I asked her if she knew where I could mail a letter. I had the first one I wrote you because I didn't have a stamp or way to mail it on the road. And soon I will be done with this one, too. Sara said just bring it over to her mother, who could mail it when she went to town.

So, Mamá, I will say goodbye. As you can see, I followed your advice and I have written you not one but two long letters! And you were right. I have felt less alone as I write them. I think I will keep writing letters every day of my life.

Con amor and with love,
Mari

P.S. Mamá, I am almost too upset to write! I will not be mailing you these letters. Instead, I am to keep them until you come back.

What happened was that Papá saw me writing and asked who I was writing to. When I said you, he got that pained, strange look on his face again, but he did not say anything.

Then, last night when he came in from the evening milking and I told him I had found a way to mail you these letters at our old address, he looked scared.

"Let us converse, my daughter," he said, nodding toward the bedroom he shares with my *tíos*. When Ofie and Luby got up to follow us— my little tail, I sometimes call them—Papá shook his head. "This is a private conversation," he explained, shutting the door behind us. He sat on the bed and patted a place beside him.

"Mari, it is not a good idea for you to send those letters," he began. Then, very gently, he explained how we are not legal in this country. How Mexicans getting mail might alert *la migra* to raid a certain address.

"But, Papá, a lot of Americans have Spanish names! Look at Luby. Look at Ofie!"

Papá just kept shaking his head. I think that having to live secretly for years in this country has made him imagine danger where it doesn't even exist. "You can save them until you see your mother again," he said. "How wonderful it will be for her to sit down and read them over and know all the things that happened while she was away." For the first time in a while, my father's voice was soft and warm and his eyes glistened. I don't think he allows himself to miss you as much as he really does, Mamá, or we would all be too sad to continue, no matter how many jokes our uncle Felipe tells us.

"Promise me, my treasure, please," Papá said, taking my face in his hands. He looked so worried! "For everyone's safety, you will not mail those letters."

What could I do, Mamá? I couldn't go behind his back, and I didn't want to upset him by arguing with him. *"Te lo prometo,"* I promised.

He gave me a grateful smile and kissed my

forehead tenderly. "Thank you, my daughter, for understanding."

But I do not understand, Mamá. Never in a million years will I understand my father's fears.

I have to close or I will wash away the words in this letter with my tears.

TWO
Dos

summer into fall

(2005)

NAMELESS FARM

"I think it might be a good idea for you to go next door and introduce yourself," Mom greets Tyler at breakfast. It is his first morning back at the farm after being away. Tyler has missed the farm terribly, but one thing he has not missed is his mother's good ideas.

"Mom," Tyler groans, "I already met them!" Early this morning before breakfast, Tyler slipped into the barn to check on Alaska, his favorite show cow. The three new Mexican workers were there hard at work, but they looked up, curious, when Tyler entered. He waved hello and then hung out, even helping one of them, who can't be any older than Ben, put the milker on the skittish Oklahoma.

"I meant say hi to the girls," his mom explains.

Tyler puts his head in his hands so he doesn't have to see anything but his bowl of cereal. Too late he remembers his mother has told him this is rude. Horses have blinkers, not humans. But sometimes, Tyler hates to tell her, sometimes he would just as soon see less, not more, of the world around him, a world full of accidents, bad luck, and Mom's good ideas.

But maybe because he just got home yesterday, his mom doesn't say anything about his blinkers. Instead she starts in on the sappy stuff that always makes Tyler cave in to her good ideas. "They don't seem to have a mother and they're cooped up in that trailer. It'd be really nice if you maybe just popped in and made them feel welcome."

How's he supposed to make three girls feel welcome? He should have borrowed a clown costume from Aunt Roxie and Uncle Tony! Furthermore, Tyler hopes his mom is not suggesting that he has to be friends with three girls just because their father works on the farm.

"I have a really good idea," Tyler says, sitting up. "Why don't I go help the guys with the milking? One of them didn't even know how to adjust the milker when it got loose on Montana."

Mom folds her arms and looks at him with that math-problem look. "First, Tyler Maxwell Paquette, remember these guys come from farms back in Mexico where there aren't any machines, so it's going to take them a few weeks to learn how to work all the equipment. Second—"

"That's why I should go help."

Mom is shaking her head. "Second, I'm sure they can handle the milking. They've caught on quickly. And third . . ." Mom always numbers her reasons when she wants to make a point, but often, like now, she forgets the point she was trying to make. "The oldest one is eleven and she's going to be in your grade at school."

"But I thought you said they were a secret!" Tyler blurts out. He has kept mulling over why he's not supposed to talk about the new workers being Mexican.

His mother looks unsure. He has obviously caught her in a contradiction, which usually means he's going to get scolded and sent up to his room.

Instead, his mom tries to explain. "It's not really a secret. Everyone around here is hiring Mexicans, so we're all in this together."

Tyler waits because there's got to be more, but there isn't more. "So, if they're Mexicans, how can they go to school?" After all, you can't vote if you're not American. Tyler's not real sure of the rules. He wishes now he'd spent more time paying attention when Ms. Swenson went over the Constitution last year.

"Of course they can go to school. In fact, I already checked with Mrs. Stevens and she said any child who wants to learn is welcome at Bridgeport.

"This is why this is a great country," Mom goes on. She

seems relieved to drop the subject of keeping the Mexicans secret. "We believe in public education. And many of us who still remember what it really means to be an American welcome outsiders, especially those who have come here to help us."

Good thing his mom added that last part about coming to help us. Tyler hates to admit it, but after September 11, he's a little scared of strangers from other countries who might be plotting to destroy the United States of America. It'd be worse than losing the farm, losing his whole country! Where would he and his family go?

"So, Tiger, would you please just say hello? Maybe take them some of your old board games and stuff."

Great, now Tyler has to be not only a friendly American but Santa Claus.

"Sara mentioned that they had some letters to mail, so if you could pick them up, okay?"

And also, the postman . . .

"Those brownies by the door—"

"M-o-o-o-m!" Tyler draws out her name.

"Don't worry, I kept some for us." She smiles, as if that's what Tyler's reluctance is all about. "Remember, if it hadn't been for them coming . . ."

"Okay, okay," Tyler groans. Next thing he knows, his mom will start in on how they are angels sent by God. Tyler might as well face it: he's going to have to be grateful for a long time for being able to stay on their farm.

"Knock, knock," Tyler says instead of knocking on the door of the trailer. They know he's here. He saw three faces peering through the window.

It seems like forever before the door finally opens. Standing before him is a lineup of three girls, the tallest one directly in front of him. They look a lot alike, very tanned with black hair and big dark eyes, each one slightly smaller, like those dolls Aunt Roxie once gave Sara: one inside the other inside another.

"Hi," Tyler says. He knows for a fact that his mom is watching out the kitchen window. He has got to put in at least five minutes of welcome or he is going to be sent back for more. But these three girls aren't making it easy. They look scared of him. In fact, the oldest is staring at him like he's some creature from outer space. "I live here," he tries again. "My name's Tyler." When she doesn't offer her name, Tyler wonders if any of them speak English. "¡Hola!" he says, remembering the greeting from Spanish class. "Mi nombre es Tyler."

"You speak Spanish?" the girl before him asks in pretty good English.

"I speak Spanish, too," the littlest one chimes in. "In Spanish my name is Lubyneida—"

"María Lubyneida," the second one corrects. "I'm María Ofelia. But everyone calls me Ofie. And everyone calls her Luby," she adds, pointing to the littlest one. "She's María Dolores, Mari for short." She points to the tallest, though not by much.

"So you're all María Something," Tyler observes smartly.

In Spanish class Ms. Ramírez said María was a real popular name in Spanish. But this is ridiculous. Even the cows without names get their very own ear-tag numbers. Tyler's just glad his mom didn't insist on naming him Abelard like his dad. He's got too many hand-me-downs, being the youngest, to have to put up with a worn-out name also. "So what's Mexico like?" He can't think of anything else to ask.

"I've never been," the middle one says.

"Me either," says the littlest. "Only Mari."

So much for them being Mexicans.

"We came from North Carolina," the little one explains.

"We've got a cow named Carolina," Tyler offers, to make up for the fact that he has never been anywhere except Boston. "We actually name all our cows after states. Well, we used to." Back when the herd was a lot smaller, many cows had names. But now with two hundred head, it's only the show cows that have names. The rest just have numbers on ear tags.

"How come you do that?" the middle one asks.

"Give 'em ear tags?"

"How come you name the cows after the United States?" the middle one persists. She seems to be the big mouth in the family.

Tyler shrugs. Many of the things that his family does were decided long before he had a vote. "That's the way it's always been done," he's always told if he questions why. But in this case, anyway, Tyler thinks it's kind of cool naming cows after states. It makes up for the fact that their farm doesn't have a name. Everyone just calls it the Paquette farm, but since there are a lot of Paquettes, that can get confusing. They've tried out a bunch of names—Happy Valley Farm, Sunset View Farm, Windy Acres Farm—but by the time Dad has gotten around to having a sign made, everyone's grown tired of the agreed-upon name. Only one of Tyler's choices ever made it to a final round: Milky Way Farm, which Sara vetoed on account of it sounded too much like a candy bar, one she didn't especially like.

Out of the blue, the oldest, who seems to be the shyest, asks Tyler, "How are you feeling?"

"Fine." Maybe it's a custom for Mexicans to ask after your health? Ms. Ramírez has said that they are very courteous.

"So do you have two Carolina cows, one for North and one for South?" the middle one asks. She is headed for the honor roll at Bridgeport, Tyler can see that. But just like that, she's giggling. That's a joke?

"In Spanish, you have to say Carolina del Norte." The little one is explaining partly to Tyler, partly to a scruffy stuffed puppy she holds under one arm. It's like she just figured out there are two languages and she has to match them up.

"We were born there," Ofie, the middle one, adds, pointing to her little sister and herself. "Mari was born—" Before she can finish, the oldest one has clapped a hand over Ofie's mouth. End of that conversation.

"I wasn't going to say anything!" Ofie says, pulling her older sister's hand away.

"Yes, you were," little Luby pipes up. And before anyone

45

can stop her she says, "You were going to say that Mari was born in Mexico."

"Thanks a lot!" Mari cries. She turns on her heels and runs down the hall of the trailer. A moment later a door bangs.

"What happened?" Luby asks, her bottom lip quivering.

Ofie shrugs. "She's just sensitive. Want to come in?" she asks Tyler, stepping to one side of the door.

Tyler isn't sure he wants to come into a house where three girls are having a fight over something silly like where they were born. "I better go," he says. "Gotta help milk the cows."

"Which one?" little Luby wants to know.

It takes Tyler a moment to figure out what the little girl is asking. "Boston," he says. It's the first name that pops into his head, probably because he's just been there. It's only on his way back to his house with Life and Candy Land still under his arm that he remembers that Boston isn't really a state. But then, he can't recall ever naming a cow Massachusetts.

*   *   *

"How did the visit go?" his mom asks Tyler at dinner. Sara is still down in Boston until the weekend, when Uncle Tony and Aunt Roxie will bring her back. Ben's supposed to start classes at the University of Vermont on Monday, so he has a few days left at home. After Dad's accident on the heels of Gramps's death, Tyler's older brother considered delaying college for a year, but his mom insisted he continue with his plans. The Mexican workers are helping them stave off having to sell the farm while they decide if Dad is going to recover enough to be able to manage, even if he doesn't do the actual work. Meanwhile, Mom has already started her service days at the high school, where she is a math teacher.

"They're such sweet girls, don't you think?" His mom obviously is not satisfied with Tyler's shrug as enough of a description of how the visit went.

"They're okay," Tyler says. If he makes them sound too okay, his mom will be sending him over there often. But if he complains, she will consider it a good character-building challenge for Tyler to befriend them. Maybe, hopefully very soon, now that Tyler's entering sixth grade, his mom will realize that he is not a little baby whom she has to keep improving or hiding things from.

"In a few years, Tyler bro, you'll be glad if Mom's throwing you at three pretty girls." Ben reaches over to ruffle Tyler's hair. Tyler bats away his brother's hand. He'd feel even more annoyed at Ben's disgusting comment if it weren't that his older brother will be moving into a dorm in a few days. Ben's still planning to come home on weekends to help out at the farm, but it won't be the same. Leave-taking is in the air. The swallows in the barn haven't yet left, but Tyler knows any morning now, he'll go into the barn and feel an eerie silence that will make his heart ache.

"I was thinking . . . ," Mom sighs. Tyler braces himself. He can tell when his mother is about to have a good idea, just like he can tell when a hen is about to lay an egg.

47

"Maybe, what do you think"—the question is addressed to the room in general, but Tyler knows he's going to be stuck with the consequences of his mom's brainstorm—"I was thinking of maybe inviting the girls over on Saturdays to help me around the house, pay them a little spending money?"

"You know what would really be great?" Ben adds. "If they could go over and visit Grandma. She's so lonely." Most every night when she isn't at Uncle Larry's or Aunt Jeanne's in town, Grandma comes over for dinner or at the very least dessert and a visit. Any little memory sets her crying.

Tyler looks down at his plate, not offering an opinion. He is thinking that with Ben away at college, and his dad often half asleep on the couch on pain medication, that means it'll be just him, Tyler, the sole boy, and three little girls, plus Mom and Sara and often Grandma as well. He's going to feel totally outnumbered.

"They had a fight," Tyler offers. He wasn't going to bring it up until now, when his mom might balance her good idea for company against commotion in the house.

"A fight fight or a disagreement?" His mom would make that distinction.

"The older one ran off crying and locked herself in the bedroom."

That piques Mom's interest. "What about?"

And now Tyler's curiosity takes over. Why did Mari get so upset? He explains that the two little sisters were telling how they were born in North Carolina and then when they

48

told him the oldest was born in Mexico, she started to cry. "They're also all named María." He doesn't know why he threw that in. For the first time in his life, he has met people who are really different. It doesn't exactly upset him so much as make him realize he's just one of a zillion people. Like finding out in Sunday school that God loves everyone the same, whereas Tyler was hoping that maybe God had reserved a special place in his heart just for Tyler. "He has," Mrs. Hollister, the minister's wife, told Amanda Davis in Sunday school when she asked the very thing Tyler was thinking. "God's heart is vast enough for everyone to have a special place in it."

"I think I understand," his mom is saying. She exchanges a look with Dad and Ben.

"What?" Tyler wants to know. He hates this feeling that the grown-ups are keeping some secret from him. In a couple of weeks, he's starting sixth grade, for crying out loud. "What's wrong with her being born in Mexico?" But Mom is suddenly busy removing the serving dishes from the table.

Ben takes pity on him. "Nothing's wrong with her being born in Mexico, little bro. She just probably didn't want you to know that she's not an American citizen."

"Ben, I think maybe we'll discuss this later," Mom says in her company voice, which is a waste of manners with no company in the house. "Tyler and María are going to be in the same class, you know." In other words, there are some private matters that Tyler should not know about his classmate because he might blab to the others.

Ben lifts his eyebrows at Tyler as if to say, She's the boss.

Tyler looks over at Dad, hoping he'll stick up for the underdog, like he often does. But Dad's still working on his half-full plate. Now that his right hand is out of commission, he has to feed himself with his left, which means eating dinner takes him twice as long.

Mom sets down the brownie platter and nods at Dad's plate. "Are you done with that?" she asks, all brisk business.

Dad puts his fork down. "I'm done," he says in a resigned voice, as if he's giving up on more than his chicken stir-fry.

*　　*　　*

That night, Tyler lugs his telescope out to the barn. Whenever he's feeling upset, it helps to look up at what Gramps used to call the bigger picture. In the hayloft, away from the lights of the house, Tyler can see the sky more clearly. And away from his parents and the sounds of their conversations and phone calls and TV programs, he can think more clearly, too.

He feels stumped as to why his mom is suddenly so cautious. Could it be the same reason she sent him down to Boston to visit Aunt Roxie and Uncle Tony? Does she seriously think Tyler's not right in the head and can't be told the truth about anything?

He climbs up to the loft, his flashlight throwing skewy beams this way and that as he tries to hold on to it and to the telescope while also keeping a footing on the ladder.

"Can I help you?" a girl's voice calls from overhead. It's the oldest Mexican girl. She has preceded him to his secret place in the hayloft, something Tyler is not happy about. "Here," she offers, grabbing hold of the telescope just in time.

"You can lay it down," he says, brushing off his jeans. He hates to admit he almost lost his grip on it. He doesn't want to even think what a drop from the hayloft to the barn floor would do to the lens of a telescope.

She lays it carefully between them. "What is it?" she asks, crouching down to inspect it more closely.

"It's a telescope," he explains, shining his flashlight on it.

"What's it for?"

Tyler can't believe someone his age doesn't know what a telescope is for. Maybe it has to do with her being from Mexico, a subject he will not bring up. Last thing he needs is a girl crying in his secret spot. Bad enough she has intruded into it. "It's for seeing into the far reaches of the universe," he says. Okay, it doesn't see that far, but Tyler loves to pretend that his is a powerful telescope, as powerful as the one at the Museum of Science. Maybe some night he'll discover some new star cluster or spot a spaceship zipping around the stars.

"My gramps gave it to me last Christmas," he explains as he sets it up by the opened hayloft door. The half-moon casts only a faint light inside. Without Tyler even having to ask, Mari takes the flashlight and shines it wherever his hands are screwing together the parts.

"See that star there, that bright one?" He takes the flashlight from her and uses it as a pointer. "Now take a look." He invites her to kneel down and peer through the telescope. A

51

way of thanking her, even though he didn't really ask her to help him.

"Amazing!" she gasps.

Tyler feels his heart soar proudly as if he has arranged this incredible night show himself. And his is a piddly telescope. Wait till she looks through the one at the Museum of Science! "That's the North Star. It always points north. That's how when there was slavery, people would escape and follow that star all the way to freedom in Canada."

"Like the Three Kings," she says in an awed voice. "And what about those ones that look like a scooper?"

"That's the Big Dipper. And those that are like a little upside-down house, that's Cepheus. And then, see the cross right overhead? That's the Northern Cross."

Tyler teaches her the most prominent constellations, first pointing them out, then having her look through the telescope. She is surprisingly quick for a girl.

"Did your grandfather teach you?" she asks when they are through.

Tyler nods. He doesn't trust his voice to explain that yes, Gramps taught him the most important things. As a matter of fact, Gramps would have been the one looking at the stars with Tyler tonight if he were still alive. "My grandpa died this June," he finds himself saying, although he hadn't planned to mention it even at school to his friends. Talk about private.

"I'm sorry," she says simply, which strikes Tyler as just the right thing to say. No clumsy consolations, no asking for the gory details. Then she tells him her own grandmother died last December.

"What about your mother?"

"My mother is alive!" she says, so quickly and sharply, it kind of surprises Tyler. "She is away on a trip. She is coming back soon."

So much for Mom's sappy idea that the girls don't have a mother. Tyler suddenly remembers the letters he was supposed to get from her. Mari was probably writing to her mother. "My mom wanted me to pick up some letters from you?"

It's her turn to fall silent. "My father . . . he took care of them."

Tyler follows her gaze out the loft door toward the small lit-up trailer. In the silence, he can hear the twittering of the swallows perched on the beams overhead. It strikes him that the loft of a barn is not a usual hanging-out place for a girl, even a girl who is good at learning the constellations. "So why did you come up here?"

"The birds," she tells him. "I come to visit them. I watch them all day flying in and out and in and out." She waves her hands in the air. "Like a dance."

"Those are swallows," he tells her.

"Swallows!" Mari seems delighted. "We have this song about swallows in Spanish. We call them *golondrinas*." It's her turn to teach Tyler something.

"I took Spanish," he tells her. But among the words Ms. Ramírez taught his fifth-grade class, Tyler doesn't remember *golondrinas*. "Any day now they'll leave and won't be back till next spring."

"Where do they go?" she wants to know.

"Mexico," he says before he even thinks that's the same place Mari is from, the place he's not supposed to mention or she might burst into tears.

But instead she seems delighted. "They fly all the way to Mexico?" When Tyler nods, she adds, "Just like the *mariposas*."

"*Mariposas?*" Tyler vaguely remembers learning that word in his Spanish class.

"Butterflies," she explains. "They're those little orange and black butterflies and they go to Mexico in the winter. I saw it on TV. They have another name."

"You mean monarchs?" Tyler offers.

"Yes!" Mari's face lights up again.

Tyler loves how every word out of his mouth seems to surprise her. It's wonderful to be the teacher for a change. And he's also learning some Spanish words from her, which is sure to impress Ms. Ramírez this fall. "Butterflies, birds." He counts them off. "I guess everybody wants to go to Mexico."

Mari beams proudly. She gazes out the loft door as if she is looking for something. "Which way is it to Mexico?" she wants to know.

"Thataway," Tyler says, pointing southwest. "But it's not like you can see it from here," he teases, because she is leaning out the window like she might catch a glimpse of it.

She pulls back. "I know," she says, sounding embarrassed.

"Mari! Mari!" a man's worried voice suddenly calls out.

"My father," Mari says, hurrying toward the ladder. "Please don't tell!" she calls out as she climbs down out of view. A minute later, Tyler spots her running across the backyard to the dark figure standing at the lit-up trailer door.

* * *

Coming in from the barn, Tyler is surprised to find his parents still sitting at the kitchen table, having a serious conversation.

"Tyler, son," his dad greets him. "Come have a seat, will you?"

Uh-oh, what now? Tyler wonders. He's allowed to leave the telescope in the loft of the barn as long as it's out of the way. The flashlight is back in its cubbyhole by the door. It's almost as if he's giving himself a once-over to be sure there's nothing incriminating on his person. All these secrets people are asking him to keep are making him feel like he's living in a scary universe.

"Son, I know you're wondering why we asked you not to go telling folks that we got some Mexicans working for us."

Tyler sits down, feeling relieved. Finally, the big mystery will be explained to him.

But his mother is shooting glances at his father. "We haven't yet decided how we're going to approach this," she reminds him.

"I think the boy should know. What if there's a raid or something?"

A raid?

"Are we doing something wrong?" Tyler is shocked. All his life his parents have taught him to obey the laws and respect the United States of America. In fact, one of the names they toyed with for the farm was Patriots' Farm, another name Sara vetoed on account of it sounded too much like a football training camp. Just as well they don't have a name. That way it won't be all over the paper: PATRIOTS' FARM RAIDED FOR BREAKING THE LAW.

"It's not wrong in God's eyes," his dad explains. Sometimes, a country has these laws that have nothing to do with what's right or what's best for most of the people involved. Turns out Mexicans need a certain document to be working in this country. "They all say they have it and that's all you need to know, legally," his dad adds. "These three Mexicans showed your mom and me their cards with Social Security numbers. So your little friend—"

She's hardly his friend. But Tyler has to admit, the lesson tonight just flew by. He hasn't had this much fun stargazing since Gramps died. Even looking through the big telescope in Boston was kind of lonesome with no one to share his excitement. Aunt Roxie and Uncle Tony would hang out downstairs in the café drinking wine while Tyler waited upstairs in line.

"Her reaction this afternoon, about being born in Mexico, well, that tells me that, no, they're likely not legal," Dad goes on.

"So what are we going to do?" Tyler asks. This is upsetting. Illegal people are living on their farm. "Should we call the police?"

Dad uses his left hand to hold up his limp right arm. "How badly do you want to stay on the farm, son?" His voice sounds bitter. His face looks suddenly as old as Gramps's. He pushes back from the table and limps out of the room.

Tyler puts his head in his hands. But it's no use. The image of his father's pained walk lingers in his head. He has never liked being the little kid in the family. And yet, if being a grown-up is this confusing, he wishes he could go back to that happier country of childhood. But it's sort of sad how the minute you realize you've left it behind, you can never go back again.

Esteemed Mr. President,

My name is María Dolores, but I can't give you my last name or anybody's last name or where we live because I am not supposed to be in your wonderful country. I apologize that I am here without permission, but I think I can explain. My teacher at my new school, Mr. B., said for our first big writing project we could write anything we wanted. So I decided to write to you because I understand you are the one in charge of the United States.

Most of my classmates are writing stories about what they did over the summer. My new friend, Tyler, is writing about seeing the stars through a very powerful telescope in a museum in Boston. Another boy in class named Kyle said he was writing a shopping list of everything he wants his parents to buy him! Mr. B. said that was fine as long as Kyle told a story about the importance of each item on the list. You can't trick Mr. B. for anything, although this boy, Kyle, always keeps trying.

I couldn't think of what to write about my summer, and the list of things I want is so long it could stretch all the way to Mexico! Mr. B. came around, checking on our first paragraphs. When he saw my blank paper, he suggested I write about my family and our culture.

But I am too afraid to call attention to our family being from Mexico because my classmates might turn us in. And it is not as simple as all going back to our homeland, because there is a division right down the center of our family. My parents and I are Mexicans and my two little sisters, Ofie and Luby, are Americans. It is just like the war of slavery in this country we learned about. Mr. B. explained how sometimes in one family, a son would be fighting for one side, another son for the other. I love what one of the presidents before you, Mr. Abraham Lincoln, said: "United we stand, divided we fall."

Mr. B. explained that this statement is now true for our whole world. He is always teaching us about saving the planet. We are all connected, he says, like an intricate spiderweb. If we dirty the air here in the United States, it will eventually blow over to Canada and maybe kill a bunch of people there. If some factory poisons a river in Mexico, it will flow into Texas and people will die there.

I even thought of my own example! Those swallows that Tyler says fly to Mexico for the fall and winter. Just a week ago, they all left. Suddenly, the backyard was so quiet. I miss them so, and I worry that something might happen to them on the way to Mexico.

"Our earth is already in trouble," Mr. B. tells us. Something else I worry about. What if it gets so bad that everyone on the earth will be like Mexicans, trying to get to another planet that won't let us in? But Mr. B. says no other planet in our solar system has the water and air we need. "We earthlings have to get our act together *pronto.*" He winks at me when he says this Spanish word.

Tyler says that is why he is glad he lives on a farm whose name I can't give you even if I could give it to you as the family still has not decided what to name it. Sometimes they all sit around the table trying to agree on a name. This is the way a democracy works, where every person has a vote. My sister Ofie, who is always asking questions, asked Tyler what happens in a democracy when no one can agree. Tyler said, "Then you try to get a majority."

I have seen you on the television, Mr. President, saying that you want democracy for this whole world. I sincerely hope you get your wish. But that will mean that if everyone in this world gets a vote, the majority will not be Americans. They will be people like me from other countries that are so very crowded and poor. We would be able to vote for what we want and need. So this letter is from a voter from that future when you would want to be treated as fairly as I am asking you to treat me.

Please, Mr. President, let it be okay for my father and uncles to stay here helping this nice family and helping our own family back home buy the things they need. Every week, my father and his brothers each contribute forty dollars to send to our family in Mexico. This total is more than their father used to make in a whole month. He was a farmer, working from sunrise to sunset. But now he is an old man, Mr. President, as old as you are—although he looks much older. But the companies that buy corn and coffee did not pay enough for him to be able to even buy the stuff he needed for the next planting.

I know this must seem like an untruth because coffee costs so much in this country. The other day Tyler's mother took us to Burlington, and after she bought us ice creams, she stopped by a shop where all they sell is different kinds of coffees. A big cup was almost two dollars! Mr. President, please believe me that those two dollars are not reaching my family. In fact, as Tío Armando says, we have come north to collect what is owed to us for our hard work back where we came from.

I wish I could be that bold in thinking I have a right to be here. Most of the time, I am just afraid of *la migra*—that is what we call the immigration police, Mr. President. What if they find me and separate me from part of my family?

I would also feel bad if we brought any trouble to this nice family who treats us like we are related to them. Most every day when Papá begins his afternoon chores, my little sister Luby, who only has school a half day, goes over to the grandmother's house, and when Ofie and I get home we go pick her up.

This grandmother lives all by herself in a big house because the grandfather died not too long ago. Every time she remembers something about him, she cries, and tears start in my own eyes, remembering my own grandmother who died and my mother who has been gone for nine months and one day. When she sees my tears, this grandmother throws her arms around me and says, "You are a sensitive soul, María." Ofie makes fun, saying that I cry so much because my name is María Dolores, which means Mary Suffering. But Mrs. S., the principal at our school, told us that Ofie's name comes from a lady named Ophelia who went crazy and drowned herself in a river because her boyfriend went crazy, too. My sister better be careful not to spit in the air, because like our father says, it will fall in her very own face!

This idea of a crazy boyfriend makes me think of Tyler. No, he is not a boyfriend, which I am not allowed to have until I am way older. But Tyler is a friend who is a boy. I have watched him carefully since his older sister informed me that her brother has not been well. A few times, I even asked him how he was feeling, and he looked annoyed that I would think there was anything wrong with him. In fact, the only time he seems worried is when Mr. B. starts talking about the future of the planet, which is enough to worry anybody.

The other day in class, we learned how the ice caps are melting and the poor penguins and polar bears have nowhere to go. Riding home on the bus, I looked out the window at all the red-leaved trees that looked like they were burning up with fever. "Are you sure they're okay?" I asked Tyler, who just sighed because this wasn't my first time asking.

"Mari, it happens every year."

In North Carolina, where we used to live, the trees changed color in the autumn, and the leaves fell, but here everywhere you look the trees are on fire.

"Tyler." I lowered my voice. I didn't want the other kids to hear. Tyler might get impatient with me, but he keeps being my friend. "Do you think what Mr. B. says is going to happen to the world will happen?"

"Sure, only like a hundred times worse." The way he said so, it sounded like he was looking forward to the opportunity to be brave. "But not till we're really old."

"How old?"

"I don't know. Maybe like Grandma." Then he unzipped his backpack and showed me a notebook with his plan. According to Tyler, if the planet gets into trouble, farms will be the best place to be. In fact, farmers are going to be the most important people in the world because they will be in charge of the food! But since on this farm I only see cows, I think we will all get very tired of milk for breakfast, lunch, and dinner. But Tyler says that out of milk we can make cheese, and the dead cows will be meat, and from the garden we will have vegetables. As for dessert, we will make a syrup from a tree called the maple. I am so glad Tyler has a plan. I feel even more lucky that we have landed on his family's farm.

Also in his notebook was a list of all the people who would be allowed on the farm in case there's an emergency. My family's names were on it, but also the names of some classmates who are not so nice, Clayton and Ronnie. "How come you're inviting them?" I asked. "I'm inviting everyone in our class," Tyler explained. Later, I was shocked to think I wanted to leave those two boys out . . . just like I'm being left out of this country.

But, Mr. President, I would not ask you to let in any criminals, and these boys are like criminals. They pick fights and say mean things.

They behave themselves in class but when we are out at recess they turn nasty. I've tried asking Mr. B. if I can just stay inside when the others go out, but when he asks if I feel ill and I say no, he says that fresh air is very important for the human body. These boys say the very same things as the kids in North Carolina used to say about me being an "illegal alien" who should go back to where she came from.

Usually an older brother picks up these two boys at the end of the day. But yesterday for some reason, they rode the bus home. I was sitting with Tyler, who was drawing the night sky and showing me where all the different constellations would be in the next few nights.

"¡Hola, buenos días!" a voice called out. I could tell it was Clayton without looking up. But Tyler was so absorbed in his lesson that it took him a moment before he realized Clayton was talking to us.

"You got yourself a little Mexican girlfriend." Clayton and Ronnie had ducked back a few seats and squeezed in with Rachel and Ashley in front of us. The two girls were giggling into their cupped hands like these bullies were funny. Meanwhile, Mr. R., who drives our bus, is so hard of hearing that unless he happens to catch troublemakers in the rearview mirror, they can get away with making somebody's life very unhappy.

"Stop it," Tyler said, but instead of continuing with his lesson, he put his notebook away in his backpack.

"Stop it," Ronnie imitated in a whiney girl's voice. "Hey, María, how do you say *stop it* in Spanish?"

If Luby had been there, she would have remembered. But I was too frightened to think of anything except how I could get away from these two boys and still not break the rule of staying in your seat while the bus is moving. Across the aisle several rows up, Ofie had turned around, and her eyes were as big as the roll-around eyes on Luby's little dog. I just hoped she would keep her mouth shut and not tell the whole bus that these bullies shouldn't make fun just because I was Mexican.

"You don't know how to say *stop it* in Spanish?" Ronnie put on this shocked face like he couldn't believe anybody was that stupid. "Hey, Clay, this girl's not just illegal, she's a dummy!"

Clayton must have thought that was funny, because the two boys rocked with laughter. They got so loud that up front Mr. R. glanced in his mirror. "Simmer down back there!" he hollered.

Clayton leaned over so his face was real close to Tyler's. His voice was an ugly whisper. "Your dad's breaking the law! You should all be thrown out along with them!"

This time Tyler didn't say a word. His face just reddened the way white people's faces do when they get upset.

Meanwhile, my sister Ofie was breaking the rules and marching up the aisle toward Mr. R. But instead of getting upset with her, Mr. R. pulled over and came lumbering toward the back of the bus. The minute he saw four kids squeezed into a seat for two, he knew who the troublemakers were. "You and you!" He pointed to Clayton and Ronnie. "I want you up at the front of the bus. Now!" There was no arguing with Mr. R., who might be hard of hearing but is tough on kids who cause trouble. Tyler says he used to be the wrestling coach at the high school.

The rest of the ride was so quiet that you could hear every shift that Mr. R. made in his driving. The whole time, I was hoping that Tyler would look up and maybe smile to show he was sorry for how mean the boys had been. But instead he ignored me like he wanted me to disappear. Finally, when Mr. R. dropped us off, instead of walking with Ofie and me up the driveway like usual, Tyler ran ahead without even saying goodbye.

"He must really have to go to the bathroom," Ofie said. She always thinks of something smart to say.

Of course, we both knew why Tyler was upset.

I was upset, too. "I wish you'd just keep quiet!" I yelled at Ofie. "You made things worse!"

My sister stopped and faced me, a hand on each hip. "Mari, those boys were being bullies, and Tyler should have told them to stop!" We both knew she was right, but it was easier to be upset with her than with Tyler.

Later, when we were returning from the grandmother's house with Luby, I saw Tyler in the distance coming out of the barn. I waved. At first, he pretended not to see me. But I called out to him and hurried over. Of course, my tail followed. I turned and told my sisters to please go wait for me in the trailer. "This is private."

"We have to protect you," Ofie said.

"Doggie too," Luby chimed in, holding up her little puppy.

"Please, *por favor*," I pleaded. We always say it twice to be extra nice when we want a favor. "*Dora* is on. Go, hurry, so you don't miss the beginning. I'll be right there." I knew this was bribery, but I desperately wanted to speak with Tyler alone. My sisters love the cartoons, especially the one about this little girl who speaks Spanish but is American like them. The television is a gift from the grandmother, who no longer needs two. I guess when her husband was alive, he always wanted to watch sports, and the grandmother preferred other programs, like one where a black lady like our Cristina talks to people about stuff that makes them cry. When she told us about the two TVs, the grandmother herself started to cry.

Once my sisters had left, I walked toward Tyler, who just watched me, no smile or greeting. His face reminded me of the black holes in outer space he has told me about that just swallow stuff up. I slowed my steps as I got close, afraid I would disappear forever inside his frown. I wondered if maybe Tyler was falling ill again with the malady that his sister mentioned was the reason he had been sent away over the summer.

"Tyler, can we do a star lesson after supper?" Several nights in the attic of the barn we had looked through his telescope at the stars.

"Nah, not tonight. It's gonna cloud up," he said in a voice that was almost as unfriendly as the first time I met him.

I looked over his shoulder at the clear evening sky. He was not giving me the real reason. But then, I wasn't asking him the real question I wanted to ask him. I pushed myself to be bold and brave. "Are you my friend?" I asked in a trembly voice that was the opposite of brave and bold.

Tyler just shrugged, which I knew meant he

wasn't sure anymore. I felt a black hole where my heart used to be. "It's because of what the boys said on the bus, right?" I was acting as nosy as my sister Ofie.

It took him a moment to look up. In his blue eyes I saw little pieces of the beautiful blue summer sky that was now gone until next year. "Just tell me one thing, okay? Do you have the documents my dad said Mexicans have to have to work here?"

Mr. President, I could not tell a lie, just like another of the presidents who went before you, Mr. George Washington, after he cut down the cherry tree. I told Tyler the truth. And then I added many of the things I am writing in this letter. That it was not my fault that I was here. That my parents brought me to this country when I was four years old. That I didn't have a vote like you do in a democracy.

He was quiet for a while before he spoke up. "I know it's not your fault, Mari," he began. "I know that if your dad and uncles hadn't come, we wouldn't be able to stay on the farm. But still"—Tyler's voice suddenly sounded like he was going to cry—"I'd rather lose the farm than not be loyal to my country.

"I'm sorry," he added because tears had come to my eyes. "I'm sorry because I really like your family." And then he walked away.

There have been a lot of sad moments in this country, but that moment of a new friend walking away was one of the saddest.

That is why I am writing you, Mr. President. I can't share my sadness with anyone else, because if I tell Papá about the boys on the bus, I am almost sure he will pull us out of school.

I also know you can't even write me back as I can't give you my full name and address. Please believe me, Mr. President, that I would if I could. I just don't want to worry anyone. That is why I am not telling my father that Mr. B. is planning to mail this letter. Mr. B. explained that without last names or an address, I won't get anybody in trouble. He is the one who says that you need to know what is going on in your country. How even kids who would otherwise be friends have to turn away from each other.

Tonight at midnight, Mr. President, when it turns into the 16th of September, it will be our Fourth of July in Mexico. It is the date when our country first became independent. And guess how the revolution started. A priest rang the bell to wake up all the citizens to freedom. So now, every 15th of September at midnight, our president in Mexico comes out on his balcony overlooking the huge square in our capital, full of hundreds and thousands of people like we have seen on the television for the New Year's Eve in New York

City. All over Mexico, people are waiting for the sound of liberty.

At the stroke of midnight, our president rings that original bell that has been carried to his balcony for this special night. Then he cries out "*¡Viva México!*" which means "Long live Mexico!" The crowd cries back "*¡Viva!*" Then the president says it again and again, three times in all, and the people cry back, each time louder, "*¡Viva!*"

Tonight, Mr. President, I am going to stay up until it is midnight. Then I will tiptoe through the trailer and come outside and lift my arms just above my shoulders to find the North Star the way Tyler has taught me to find it. I will turn in the opposite direction, facing toward my homeland. "*¡Viva México!*" I will cry out in my heart. Three times, "*¡Viva México! ¡Viva México! ¡Viva México!*"

But because, as Mr. B. says, we are all citizens of one planet, indivisible with liberty and justice for all, I will also turn toward where you live in your beautiful white house, Mr. President.

"*¡Viva los Estados Unidos del Mundo!*" I will cry out to myself. "Long live the United States of the World! *¡Viva! ¡Viva! ¡Viva!*"

Very respectfully yours,
María Dolores

THREE
Tres

fall

(2005)

WATCHED-OVER FARM

Sometimes when Tyler is looking up at the night sky, he thinks he sees his grandfather's face. It doesn't always happen because his mind automatically wants to connect the dots into a constellation, but sometimes if he stares long enough, a star will wink. Or a shooting star will go by. Or a meteor shower. Gramps! It gives Tyler a brief warm feeling to think his grandfather might indeed be watching over him.

If he mentions these visitations to his mom, there might be another trip down to Boston to visit Aunt Roxie and Uncle Tony. Actually, it's almost Halloween, which is one of

Party Animals' busiest times of year. So Tyler will probably not be sent anywhere but to the counselor at Bridgeport. Tyler doesn't even want to imagine what Ronnie and Clayton will do with that piece of information. Looney Tunes Tyler, he can already hear them chanting.

It still hurts not to have Gramps around. Everything on the farm, from Ben's daily absence to the silence in the barn now that the swallows are gone, to the rolling pastures covered in frost and mist in the early mornings, to the bright stars that seem to grow brighter as the cold sets in—everything feels doubly empty without him. But no one, except Grandma, wants to talk about missing Gramps. The best way to get over his grandfather's death is not to dwell on it, Tyler's mother has told him.

But Tyler doesn't want to get over Gramps's death. Forgetting about his death means also forgetting about his life, and then Gramps would really be dead. On the other hand, Tyler doesn't want to upset Grandma, and at any little mention of Gramps, she melts into tears. There's got to be a happier way to stay in touch with Gramps. And the stars are the closest Tyler has come, even though they are millions of light-years away.

It makes sense that his grandfather would want to communicate using stars. After all, Tyler's grandfather was never a big talker. It's amazing how much he taught Tyler without a whole lot of explaining, stuff about farming and fishing and finding your way using the stars. Last Christmas, it was Gramps who gave Tyler a telescope. On the gift tag, he'd written some words that Tyler now treasures: *Anytime you feel lost, look up.* So many times this summer and fall Tyler has done just that!

As for the telescope, Tyler has moved it back to his bedroom, since it's getting too chilly to be stargazing from the barn loft. But that's not the only reason. Moving the telescope lets Tyler off the hook. He doesn't have to feel bad about not inviting Mari over to watch the stars. In fact, she never asks anymore about the next stargazing lesson. Her father is super-strict, and if it's not okay for a girl to be with a boy in a barn with two hundred cows and two uncles plus her father going in and out, then it's definitely not okay to be alone with a boy in his bedroom at night.

Tyler knows it's not Mari's fault that her parents snuck her into this country. He doesn't like being mean to her, but he also doesn't want to be friends with someone who is breaking the law, even though that law, according to his dad, needs changing.

In school, he can't avoid her since they are in the same class. But in the morning at the farm, when they board the bus together, it's trickier. A few times Mari has headed to where Tyler is sitting, but then there's a little hesitation, and she goes and sits with her sister Ofie and sometimes with Meredith and Maya, some classmates who have sort of made María their project. These are the same girls who are most active in Earthlings, the new club Mr. Bicknell has started for saving the planet.

But Tyler has to admit that watching the stars by himself makes him miss Gramps even more. Especially now that Tyler feels so confused about how his parents are maybe breaking the law. He can't talk to Mom, who would just lecture about freedom and justice and liberty for all, and Dad would feel bad that he can't do all the work himself, and Ben is never around anymore, and Sara is a blabbermouth, and Grandma would get upset that Gramps can't help out because he's dead. That covers all the adults in his family, and Tyler wouldn't dare mention what's going on to anyone who isn't related. As it is, he thinks the farm is already being watched by Homeland Security. Recently, someone has been calling, then hanging up when Tyler or Sara or Mom answers. Sara is sure it's her ex-boyfriend checking to see if she's home.

"Stop being a pest, Jake!" she sometimes hollers into the phone, and Mom has to remind her of her phone manners.

"But he's being rude."

"Two rudes don't make a right," Mom says. "Besides, I think it's someone trying to reach the Cruzes." Even though the Mexicans have their very own phone in the trailer, the only number they had when they moved from North Carolina was the Paquettes'. "I just wish whoever it is wouldn't hang up so I could give them the right number." A lot of times now, Mom just lets the call go to the answering machine, where callers are cheerily invited to leave a message and have a nice day. Sometimes, Tyler will play and replay the blank pause before the hanging up, for clues. But all he can make out in the background is a bunch of static and maybe the sound of traffic on a freeway. Meanwhile, his dad is sure the calls are from bill collectors wanting to talk to him. And since Tyler's dad would never think of picking up a ringing phone if anyone else is in the house, there's no way to find out if he's right.

What Tyler is hoping is that his dad will soon be one hundred percent recovered. According to the doctors, Dad is a miracle case. He can now move the fingers on his right hand, and though he still limps, he's getting around much better. Best of all, his sense of humor is slowly coming back. If he keeps improving, Dad will be able to do a lot of the farmwork himself, with help from Corey and some part-timers and Ben on occasional weekends and Tyler whenever he doesn't have to be in school. Then his dad will be able to send the Mexicans away before he gets into trouble.

Tonight, a clear night, Tyler studies the stars, thinking about Gramps. This late, Mars is out, big and bright, the closest it's been to Earth in two years. As he watches, the outside light comes on at the trailer next door. A figure emerges, too small to be one of the men and too tall to be little Luby. It's either Ofie or Mari, but something about the way the shadowy figure moves, not perky and sure of itself, makes him guess it's Mari. Tyler has turned off the lights in his bedroom to see through the telescope better, so when she looks up in the direction of his window, he is almost sure she can't see him watching her. Still, he pulls to one side be-cause suddenly he wants to spy in case she is up to some-thing illegal.

Mari walks up the slight incline behind the trailer to the field where the cows graze. The moon is on the wane, but it's still a pie with half its pieces left, so there is enough light to watch her by. Midfield, she stops and gazes up at the sky, slowly turning west, south, east, full circle. She must be cold, because she pulls up the hood on the parka that Mom got her at Neat Repeats, but it keeps falling when she throws her head back. After several slow circles, she stands very still, looking at something in the night sky. Tyler angles the telescope up, searching for what she might have spotted above the farm. The North Star, the Little Dipper, the Dragon, the Swan. No meteor showers. No fireballs. Nothing unusual.

But then, gathering stardust and moonbeams, a face begins to form. Gramps! He is smiling down . . . at the girl in the field as if it is someone he is looking after. Clearly, his grandfather thinks it's Tyler behind his house late at night. Tyler wants to call out, Over here, Gramps!

But as Tyler is wondering how to catch his grandfather's attention, the girl in the field lifts her hands as if waving goodbye. Then she turns back to the trailer and Gramps's face disappears from the sky.

*   *   *

The next day after the three Marías have returned to their trailer, Tyler heads for his grandmother's house. She might not be the best choice to talk to about the Mexicans, but at least she's willing to talk about missing Gramps. Maybe Tyler can indirectly ask if Gramps ever broke the law besides the one time he got a fifty-dollar ticket for driving at night without a reflector on the hay wagon. Gramps could have gone to court and argued that the darn thing must have fallen off as he was driving home from the neighbor's field. But he couldn't hold up his cows' milking schedule to go to town to swear on a Bible that he hadn't done anything wrong.

Tyler lets himself in the back door. "Grandma!" he calls out.

"I'm up here, honey." Her voice is coming from one of a warren of little rooms that form the upstairs part of the house, which she hardly ever uses anymore. The stairs have gotten to be too much for her arthritis. In fact, Grandma has moved her bedroom downstairs to what used to be the sewing room, so it's surprising that she has ventured upstairs. But then, Grandma is big on decorating for holidays. She probably went up to the attic to bring down her plastic jack-o'-lantern, which she'll be wanting to plug in to let kids know they're welcome to drop by for her homemade cookies and candy corn from Wal-Mart.

Tyler still remembers the day Grandma brought the jack-o'-lantern home. Gramps's only comment was "We got a whole patch in the backyard."

But Grandma said that with her shaky hands she was liable to cut off a finger carving a grin in one of those small pumpkins. "Besides, I'm saving them for pies." That shut up Gramps, who loved all of Grandma's pies, but most especially her pumpkin pies.

Up in his grandparents' old bedroom, Tyler finds his grandmother in a rocking chair, facing a dresser covered with a white tablecloth. On top are trinkets that Tyler recognizes as belonging to Gramps. Several of his grandfather's favorite fishing lures are lined up by his John Deere cap, as well as his army medal and a pipe he stopped smoking but would still stick in his mouth from time to time. There's also a little dish with pistachios, which Gramps really liked, plus a plate with a slice of pumpkin pie. In the middle of this array, sitting on the big family Bible, is the framed picture of Gramps taken only last year, when he turned seventy-six.

Beside the Bible, there's an envelope with some writing on it. The whole thing reminds Tyler of an altar at church except piled up with all of his grandfather's favorite things. Tyler has been worrying that his family is forgetting Gramps, but this is the weirdest thing he has ever seen.

"Isn't it nice?" His grandmother is smiling fondly at the picture of Gramps. Tyler is not sure what his grandmother means, but he nods. One thing that is nice is that his grandmother is talking about Gramps without crying.

"I knew you'd understand, dear." Grandma rocks happily, as if pleased to have proven herself right. "We decided to put it up here because, well, the others might not understand."

Tyler is not sure he understands, either, especially when Grandma says "we decided." Who is "we"? Tyler is afraid to ask and find out that his grandmother has gone loony with grief and is talking to Gramps the way people do in the movies. But then, Tyler himself has been seeing his grandfather watching over the farm from the night sky. And he knows he isn't crazy.

"Every time I'm missing him, I come up here now and visit with him," Grandma goes on, rocking herself cheerfully. Just last night, Mom mentioned that Grandma seemed to be doing a lot better. But Tyler's mom thought it had to do with Grandma's relief at seeing her son's recovery. "If you'd like to add something"—Grandma nods toward the altar—"I think Gramps would like that."

The first thing that pops into Tyler's head is his telescope that Gramps gave him. But if he brings it over, he won't be able to look at the stars from his own room or spy on the Mexicans.

"Pull up one of those chairs there," Grandma is saying. For some reason seeing three chairs lined up against the wall makes Tyler think of the three Marías. Do they know his grandmother has gone a little batty? If so, they have been really nice about not telling anybody or making fun, but instead visiting her daily. Tyler feels a flush of gratitude but also shame, thinking about his own behavior toward them.

"Our little neighbors told me all about this," Grandma is explaining as if she can now read minds. "Did you know, in Mexico, they don't celebrate Halloween like we do?"

Tyler nods. He does know all about it. Ms. Ramírez has been doing a unit on the Day of the Dead. It's a big holiday in Mexico, and it's not just one night but three days, starting with Halloween. Whole families go to the cemetery and have picnics with their dead relatives. Very creepy stuff.

"Our dead are always with us," Ms. Ramírez told the class. "We take them their favorite foods, sing their favorite songs. We even write them letters, telling them what they've missed in the last year." She showed pictures of little sugar skulls with the names of everyone in the family, even those who are still living.

As Ms. Ramírez spoke, Tyler's gaze was drawn to Mari's face, which seemed suddenly lit up from inside like a jack-o'-lantern. Some memory was making her look radiant. Tyler found himself staring, and when she glanced his way, he couldn't help himself, he smiled. But instead of her smiling back, her face darkened as if the light inside her had gone out. Next thing he knew, Ms. Ramírez was calling on Mari, asking her if she'd tell the class some more about the Day of the Dead in her native land.

Mari had looked down, shaking her head, embarrassed. But later when Ms. Ramírez asked the class to each write a letter to a loved one who had died, Tyler noticed that Mari started writing right away. Most of the class was complaining that they didn't know any dead people. Clayton flat out refused on account of his family didn't believe in voodoo stuff. "We're Christians," he bragged. That was when Ms. Ramírez went into a long explanation about how most Mexicans are Christians and the Day of the Dead is actually an example of how the Church took Indian beliefs and gave them a Christian spin. But Tyler could tell Clayton wasn't buying it.

"The girls told me about how they build altars to their relatives who have died, most especially the ones who've died in the last year," Grandma is explaining. "So I asked them if they'd help me do one for Gramps. I don't call it an altar," Grandma adds quickly as if she might get in trouble with Reverend Hollister at church. Tyler's grandmother is the most churchgoing person Tyler knows. Both his parents go to church—though Dad often misses because of some farm emergency—and they insist their kids go, too, as long as they are living at home. But Tyler's grandmother will actually go to church all during the week, as she is on every committee you can think of where cooking and flowers are involved, which kind of covers most of them.

"I call it a memory table," Grandma goes on. "It's just been so nice to be able to do this and talk to the girls about Gramps, you know?"

Tyler feels a knot in his throat. Of course he knows.

"María told me all about her grandmother who died last December. Her mother traveled back home to Mexico and got to see her right before she died. She's on her way back— the girls' mother, that is," Grandma adds, letting out a sigh.

Tyler feels bad all over again that he didn't get to spend Gramps's last few hours with him in his garden. Gramps died right before summer vacation, on Tyler's last day of school. Gramps had gone out midmorning to check on his peppers and tomatoes, and by the time Grandma called him for lunch, there was no bringing him back. Grandma found Gramps stretched out in the pathway as if he'd waited to have his heart attack until he'd laid himself carefully down so as not to fall on top of his fragile seedlings. Tyler came home that June day to find his mom standing by the mailbox, waiting with the news. Besides the day of Dad's accident, the day Gramps died is the worst day of Tyler's life so far.

Sometimes, Tyler will find himself thinking, What if? What if it had been one day later and classes were done?

What if he had been helping plant the garden when Gramps had his heart attack? Tyler would probably have been able to call for help in time to save Gramps, just like Tyler helped save Dad's life after his accident. These are the kinds of what-ifs that make Mom say Tyler mustn't dwell on Gramps's death. Best to move on.

"So anyhow, dear, I'm glad you dropped by so I could show you before we take it down in a few days." Grandma suddenly looks bereft, like she might be losing Gramps all over again. "I don't know . . ." She hesitates and glances over at her husband's picture, trying to decide something. "Maybe I'll just take away the perishables like the pie on account of ants. But leave this little spot for us to remember him." Grandma looks relieved. "Anytime you're missing him, Tyler dear, you just come over."

Tyler can't help feeling remorse. He has been avoiding Grandma's house so as not to bump into the Mexicans. But that doesn't mean that he hasn't been feeling a big black hole in the center of his life. "I've really been missing Gramps," he admits, and then, as if that admission uncorks the rest of his feelings, he tells his grandmother how Gramps is watching over him. How sometimes the stars seem to form his grandfather's face. Other times, Tyler'll see a shooting star just as he's thinking, Gramps, are you there? As he talks, his grandmother keeps smiling and nodding, which encourages Tyler, so that he goes on to mention the phone calls and all the stuff he was not going to talk to her about. Like about the Mexicans.

"Gramps wouldn't have let Dad break the law, would

he?" Tyler glances over at his grandfather's picture on the table. It's as if Tyler is hoping Gramps will settle this matter for them all.

"Actually, dear, your uncle Larry's had Mexicans for a while over at his place," Grandma explains. "Your dad wouldn't hear of it, until, of course, the accident made him reconsider. But when your uncle Larry told us, you know what Gramps said? He said, 'We Paquettes came down from Canada back in the 1800s. Nobody but nobody in America got here—excepting the Indians—without somebody giving them a chance.' That's what he said. 'Course, he would have preferred that Uncle Larry wait till it was legal. But the cows can't wait for their milking till the politicians get the laws changed. They'd still be waiting."

Tyler can't believe his own grandfather might have been some sort of revolutionary rebel! Like that priest that Mari told about in class for Mexican Independence Day. How he rang the church bell, waking the whole sleepy town to fight for their freedom.

"So, honey, I think Gramps would understand," Grandma is saying. And that same tender smile she had when she was gazing at Gramps's picture she now has on her face as she gazes over at Tyler.

*　　　*　　　*

Before Tyler goes home that day, Grandma invites him to come to supper next Wednesday, November second—the actual Day of the Dead, the three Marías have told her.

"We'll have a little supper party for him," she tells Tyler mysteriously. "Just us remembering Gramps, that's all, honey," she adds, more normally.

"Should I bring my telescope?" Maybe after supper they can look at the stars like he used to with Gramps. It's also getting to be the time of year for the Taurid meteor shower.

"That's a lovely idea," his grandmother says. "We can set it up in the garden . . ." She doesn't have to say what Tyler is also thinking: on the very spot where Gramps died. It sounds crazy, but talking about Gramps is actually making Tyler feel as if his grandfather, while not exactly alive, is at least still a part of Tyler's life.

And so, Wednesday after school, Tyler lugs his telescope across the field and sets it up in Gramps's garden. That evening when Grandma lets him in the back door, Tyler sees he is not the only guest. Just as he suspected, the three Marías have also been invited to this special supper. They are helping decorate the table, but they stop when he enters. They look startled, maybe even a little scared, like that first day at the trailer door.

"This is María Guadalupe," Grandma says, picking up a framed picture that was keeping Gramps's picture company in the center of the table. At first, Tyler thinks this might be the girls' mother. But the photo shows an old woman about Grandma's age standing in a raggedy dress in front of a tumbledown shack that looks like it's made of cardboard. Incredibly, as poor as she is, she's smiling widely, revealing several missing teeth.

"That's our grandmother," Ofie explains. "She's dead."

"Abuelita," Luby says, but when Tyler looks over at her, she hides behind her oldest sister.

"We brought candles and lids to set them on, Grandma," Ofie says, pulling out tiny candles as well as a bunch of jar lids from a paper bag.

Tyler is surprised that the girls call his grandmother Grandma as if she is their family. Actually, he is the one feeling like the stranger in this company. But then, he has been avoiding them for weeks, though he has been spying on the family every night. If Homeland Security has also been on the watch, they must be awful bored with how little there is to report. TV sounds, some nights someone plays a guitar and everyone sings, other nights a girl goes out in the back field and stands there for a while looking up at the stars.

"I brought my telescope," he offers, feeling empty-handed, wanting to contribute something. "After dinner, we're all going to watch some stars." He says this to all of them, but of course, he means it for Mari. Finally, summoning all the courage he's been saving up for when the planet gets in trouble, Tyler looks over at Mari, and this time he is rewarded. She returns the smile he gave her in the classroom a week ago.

✳   ✳   ✳

Dinner is delicious—all of Gramps's favorite things, as well as Coca-Colas because Coke was one of the special treats that Mari remembers her grandmother, who died right before Christmas last year, really liked. Abuelita was too poor to buy Cokes except on her saint's day, Mari says her mother told her. Her grandmother also really liked mole, a sauce made with chocolate, so the girls have brought some Hershey bars Tyler's mom gave them for Halloween. They've piled them on a little dish by Abuelita's picture.

After dinner, they all put on their coats and go out to the garden. Tyler leads the way, guiding the group with a flashlight. Grandma tells the girls how much her husband loved his garden, how he had a green thumb, and when the girls gasp, Grandma laughs and explains how this expression means someone is a natural-born gardener.

They stand in the chilly air while Tyler points out the stars visible to the naked eye: Ursa Major and Ursa Minor, the two bears; Draco, the dragon; Cassiopeia, which looks like a W or an M on it side; Pegasus, the flying horse. Then they all take turns looking through the telescope.

"I don't see anything!" Luby keeps saying until they discover that she is closing her eyes instead of peering through the eyehole. "I see lots and lots of stars!" she exclaims at last. "I see a beautiful lady!"

"You do?" There is a thrill in Mari's voice Tyler has never heard before.

"Let me see! Let me see!" Ofie nudges her little sister over. But after a minute of looking, Ofie gives up. "You're lying!" she accuses her little sister. "That's not funny."

"I am not," little Luby says, sniffling. "I saw her. I really did. She was winking at me!"

"Liar—" Ofie begins.

"Shhhh! Listen!" Mari whispers. From the trailer comes

the sound of someone playing the guitar and singing, the saddest tune Tyler has ever heard. It makes him feel homesick even though he is already home.

"It's 'La Golondrina,' " Mari explains. "That song I told you about," she reminds Tyler. "You sing it when you are far away from your homeland and the people you love." And then she begins to sing and her sisters join in. Tyler doesn't understand all the Spanish words, something about a swallow looking for something. But for once, not knowing the words doesn't matter. Just listening to the lonesome tune captures Tyler's feelings when he is missing Gramps or Ben.

So this is what the three Marías feel, so far from home! And to think that Tyler has made them feel even more lonesome with his unfriendliness and spying. He wishes he had words that would let them know he is sorry, that they do belong here. Thankfully, his grandmother speaks up. "I know it's not your homeland, but you're here with people who love you."

This is far too sappy for Tyler to ever say himself. Like Gramps, he finds it easier to talk through the stars. And what a night for stellar conversation! Up above, a star shoots across the sky, then another, and another. "Look!" Tyler shouts, pointing up. A meteor shower. Mari sees it right away, but the two little sisters have to be aimed in the right direction.

"I see it! I see it!" little Luby screams with delight.

"Me too!" Ofie adds.

They stand for a while in the clear, cold night, watching the absent ones rain down their welcome light.

Querida Abuelita,

The letter I started for you in Señora Ramírez's class I had to hand in, so I am writing you another one that can be as private as I want.

First of all, thank you, Abuelita, with all my heart for sending down so many kisses of light on Day of the Dead night!

Some nights when Tío Felipe plays his guitar, Wilmita, and sings such beautiful songs that make my heart soar, I have felt you close. But after the shower of light I am certain you will never abandon us even though we have wandered far to a strange land like the swallow in the song.

Tyler, the *patrón's* son who is now our friend again, says that what we saw was the Taurid meteor shower, which comes in early November. I don't know if this is true. But every clear night, I continue to go out, and though the shooting stars have diminished, you always send down one or two to let me know you are still watching over us.

We have taken down the altar we made for you in the trailer, pouring your Coca-Cola on the ground. (Luby and Ofie ate your chocolate bars. "You always tell us not to waste," they defended themselves.) When I am done with this letter, I will put it behind your picture inside its frame.

Someday I hope to bury it at your graveside the way Señora Ramírez said her family in México used to do with their letters.

We took your picture to the supper in your honor at our American grandmother's house. She lost her husband, Gramps, only five months ago, so the supper was also in his honor. At the table and later in the garden, the grandmother told us so many stories about him that I felt as if I knew him. "He would have been tickled by you girls!" she repeated several times.

I did not want to correct her, but we would never disrespect an old person by tickling them! Often when I do correct something she says, she laughs and explains what she means. Then say what you mean, I feel like telling her. But I do not want to upset her as she is so nice and has made us feel that we do have family in this country. Grandma, she has asked us to call her, which is *abuela* in English.

So now we have three grandmothers, but only you are in heaven to watch over us. Abuelita, please ask God to keep it that way. Papá's mother, Abuelota, has not been well, which worries him and my *tíos* and me. Her blood pressure is up and the doctors have prescribed medicine that costs a lot of money. My uncles and Papá are now each sending sixty dollars a week, but even that does not cover the added expense.

I sincerely hope her health improves . . .
because if anything should happen, my *tíos* and
Papá will all want to travel back as Mamá did to
be with you during your last days. This time, Papá
would have to take us back with him, and,
Abuelita, I don't think my two sisters could get
used to life in Las Margaritas. They are like
American girls, preferring to speak in English and
not thinking about the cost of things, as if we
were rich people like the Paquettes.

Morning, noon, and night, they will drink
Coca-Colas and think nothing of leaving some in
the glass! "I'm full," they say if I tell them not to
waste. I put the leftover in the refrigerator for
later, and when I serve it to them at the next
meal, they complain, "It's not bubbly." I know
that now with the help of Papá and the *tíos*, our
family has built a concrete house with indoor
water and electricity back in Las Margaritas. But
that would not be special enough for my sisters.
They would want their own television, and so
many games and toys that they have to choose
which one to play with. They would expect to
ride a bus to school instead of having to walk the
five kilometers there and back. And if any of their
elders were to tell them what to do, my sisters
would reply that they don't have to if they don't
want to.

Ofie, especially, loves to argue. She is getting

so she won't obey me even though Papá has told her that she must mind me without Mamá around. "You're not my mother!" she answers back, her hands on her hips. Once she makes up her mind, there is no reasoning with her.

Like what happened as we were preparing for this Day of the Dead. Papá had come back from the evening milking, and we were all four setting up the altar to you. Suddenly, Ofie disappeared to the bedroom we sisters share and brought Mamá's picture from when we were in Carolina del Norte that we keep on the dresser. Just like that, she placed it on the altar along with yours. I couldn't believe that Papá said nothing. I snatched it right off. "She's not dead," I told her. "You can't put her here!"

"I can too put her there!" Ofie shoved me away and placed the picture back on the altar. Usually, I just let her have her way to avoid fighting as I know how tired Papá is when he comes in from milking. But this time, I had to prevent her. It wasn't just about getting my way, Abuelita, it was the fear that if Mamá's picture was on that altar for the dead, she would surely die. Wherever she was right at that moment, trying to find her way back to us, she would have a horrible accident, or get hit by a car, or bitten by a serpent, or die of thirst in the desert.

And so I snatched that picture off the altar,

and before I knew it, Ofie had grabbed one end, and we were yanking it back and forth. Each one was screaming at the other to let go. Finally, Papá swooped in and took the picture away from us both.

"Papá! Give it back, it's mine!" Ofie was partly right. It was her frame she had bought for a dollar at a sale our American grandmother took us to at her church. Very pretty with little seashells all around the border. But the picture itself belonged to all of us. Not only that, it had been my suggestion to use the frame for Mamá's photograph. Ofie had wanted to put a picture of the new American Girl doll from the catalog we found in the *patrones'* trash.

"I am going to keep the picture for now," Papá explained, raising a hand to his lips to quiet Ofie's protest. "We will sit down like civilized people and decide whether or not it belongs on the altar with your *abuelita*."

I know that this must be the influence of democracy on our father, just like the Paquette family deciding things by discussion and voting. But I found it incredible that Papá would even allow there to be a vote about this life-and-death matter.

We sat around our supper table, actually just the four of us, as Tío Armando and Tío Felipe, being in-laws, would not have a say in this matter. But very respectfully, they had turned down the television, where a bloody *lucha libre* was going on, just like the fight Ofie and I were having. Papá started off by saying that it had now been a year.

"No it hasn't!" I protested. "It's only been ten months, two weeks, and two days."

Papá winced as if it pained him that I knew the exact count. "It has not been a year, but it has been a long time." He went on to explain that the crossing was very dangerous. That the desert had many dangers.

"Did something happen to Mamá?" I gasped. Maybe this was Papá's gentle way of delivering horrible news.

"No, I'm not saying that." He stroked my hair for comfort. But I felt none as he went on. "I am only suggesting that after this much time"—he pulled Luby over to his side as if to protect his baby girl from what he was about to say—"after so many months, your mother is probably watching us from the other side of life."

Ofie narrowed her eyes at me as if to say, See, I was right! How could she be so coldhearted? Actually, I don't think she or Luby really understood that Mamá being on the other side of life meant she had died. "So we can put her picture on the altar, right, Papá?"

"Well, *mi hijita*," Papá said, glancing over at

me as if afraid he had already said too much. "I think we should wait until next year." I could tell he was saying this more for my benefit than because he was convinced that Mamá was alive. And by now, it didn't matter if Mamá's picture was on the altar for the dead. Her whole family had deserted her, except for me. It was as if she had really died.

I began to sob. I could not stop myself. Papá looked confused, as he had ruled in my favor. As for Ofie, willful as she is, she has a tender heart. When she saw me so upset, she came to my side and threw her arms around me as if she were my little mother.

"Don't cry, Mari. We won't put Mamá on the altar. Not even next year," she promised. But her sudden kindness just made me cry harder. She looked over at Papá helplessly, then reached for the picture of Mamá and gave it to me to hold.

"You can keep the frame, too," she added. And then, she, too, began to cry, and that made Luby cry, and Papá, and soon, Abuelita, we were all sobbing democratically around that table.

(Later the same day)

Abuelita, there is something else I wanted to tell you about that has been preoccupying me.

You know that when we left Carolina del

Norte, some new arrivals from Las Margaritas took over our apartment. The arrangement was that we would let them know if we were coming back. The Monday before the Day of the Dead, Papá had some minutes left on his phone card after calling Abuelote and Abuelota in Las Margaritas, so he decided to call our acquaintances in the apartment in Carolina del Norte and let them know that we were happily settled in our new home in Vermont, the work was good, the *patrones* nice.

Imagine his surprise when he got a recording that the telephone had been disconnected. He dialed again and put me on to listen to the taped voice to be sure he understood the English. He had heard correctly. The number had been disconnected and there was no further information.

"¡*Esa viejita!*" Tío Felipe exclaimed. He was sure the old lady with the two dogs had sent the police to the apartment and they had rounded up our acquaintances from Las Margaritas. "I should have warned them!"

"That *patrona* didn't know where you lived," Papá reminded him.

"But maybe she gave the other little dog something Tío Felipe had touched and the dog followed the smell," Ofie offered. We had all seen a program on television where the police had tracked down a missing girl by giving a dog some of her clothes to smell.

At first, I was just worried about our acquaintances in the apartment, but then I started thinking about Mamá. We had left them instructions as well as the Paquettes' phone number. But if our acquaintances had been rounded up by *la migra*, how would Mamá know where to find us in this huge country?

Maybe he had the same worry because Papá called a friend from Las Margaritas who was also working in Carolina del Norte. This time the friend answered. And yes, he told Papá, our acquaintances had recently been picked up at work and deported. The apartment had been taken over by other Mexicans, but not from our village. No one we knew.

We were all gathered around Papá, trying to reconstruct the news from the expressions on his face. "I see. I see," he kept saying. I was desperate to know what it was he was seeing. Finally, as Papá was saying *adios*, I reached for the phone. My father looked startled but he handed it over. "Please, *por favor*," I asked Papá's friend, "if you would do us a favor." And then I begged him to go by our old apartment and leave our new phone number here in Vermont for my mother, María Antonia Santos, if she should come back looking for us.

Papá's friend sounded unsure, but I must have been as insistent as Ofie because he finally agreed. He repeated our new number before the time was up on the card and we were cut off.

After that call, we were all very nervous as we always are when we hear news of someone being nabbed by *la migra*. It is as if a cloud hangs over our family and darkens our world. The very opposite, Abuelita, of your shower of light. So when the doorbell rang, we all jumped. For one thing, in the four months we had been living here, that doorbell had never rung. Everyone uses the back door. At first, none of us even knew what it was. One ring, and then another, another. It reminded me of the priest ringing the independence bell in México to wake up the people to freedom. But since we feared it was *la migra*, this ringing was more the sound of the end of our family's freedom.

On and on! Each time it was like a needle going through my heart. Papá lifted his hand and put a finger at his lips, just as he had the night before when Ofie and I had been fighting about Mamá's picture on the altar. Very, very slowly as if a fast movement would make noise, he stole over to the light switch and flicked it off. I heard a terrified gasp that I thought came from Luby. But a moment later an ice-cold hand clutched my own, too big to be Luby's, belonging to my brave and bold sister, Ofie!

Luby herself had begun to cry. "*Shhhh, tranquilita, tranquilita,*" Papá shushed her in a whisper that almost had no sound. Our visitors had now given up ringing and were banging and shouting at the door. Perhaps because we had already been spooked by the bad news about *la migra* and our friends, none of us remembered that this was Halloween. We knew from Carolina del Norte that children would dress up and come to our apartment door for candy. Papá and Mamá always locked the door and refused to open it for anyone. "You never know if it could be *la migra* in disguise," Mamá warned. As for us, no matter how much we explained the American tradition, my sisters and I were not permitted to go around begging for treats. "That is a lack of respect," Mamá explained. "With so many beggars who really need alms!" Sometimes, even if I had been born in México, I felt a huge desert stretching between my parents and who I was becoming.

Finally, the ringing and banging and shouting stopped. By now, Luby was sobbing hysterically, so Tío Felipe carried her to our back bedroom, where she would not be heard. After a moment's pause, we heard soft thuds as if something squishy were being thrown at our windows. Then silence, and the sound of laughter and hooting and shouting. Finally, doors banging and cars driving away.

We stayed in darkness for what felt like hours but was probably only minutes. "Can we turn on the lights?" Ofie kept asking. But Papá was unsure if we were still being watched. At last, Papá turned on the switch, and just as he did, the telephone began to ring as if one thing were connected to the other. "It's them," Papá whispered desperately, flipping off the lights again. He had every reason to be suspicious, as hardly anyone ever calls us, except sometimes the Paquettes or some of my uncles in California or a wrong number. And that phone kept ringing and ringing, even longer than the intruders at the door had rung our doorbell. Finally it, too, stopped, and we could breathe, though Papá still would not allow us to turn the lights on.

A little while later, there was a knock, this time at the back door. "Hello! *¡Hola!*" a voice called. "It's just me, Connie." We were so relieved to hear the voice of the *patrón's* wife. Papá hurried to the door and opened it.

Mrs. Paquette was dressed in jeans and a sweatshirt with the initials UVM, which stand for her older son's school. She was carrying a flashlight and a bucket of candy. She explained that she had heard the car doors and seen the kids banging at our door and then throwing eggs and rotten fruit at our windows, and she guessed what had happened. Halloween trick-or-treaters had not gotten their treats and so were playing tricks. But then, she also realized we might not understand. She would have hurried right over, but she wanted to be home in case the kids came to her door. Sara and Tyler were both out trick-or-treating with their friends, and it was too much for Mr. Paquette to be up and down to answer the door with his injuries. So she had tried calling us to explain and gotten worried when no one answered the phone.

"We knew it was Halloween." Ofie was showing off. Oh yes? I probably had several broken bones in my left hand to prove otherwise.

"Of course!" Mrs. Paquette laughed at herself. "What was I thinking? You would have known about it from North Carolina." Anyhow, she had brought over some extra candy for us to have and hand out. Even Ofie did not dare tell her we were not permitted to give alms to pretend beggars.

"Very kind of you to come and explain," Papá thanked her. He wanted to walk the *patrona* back home, but Mrs. Paquette wouldn't hear of it.

By this time Tío Felipe had joined us at the back door with Luby still sniffling in his arms. Somewhere in their dark walk to the back bedroom Luby had dropped her stuffed dog. So on top of being scared, she didn't have her faithful puppy to protect her.

Abuelita, even after all of us realized that we had not been in danger, there was an uneasy feeling in our family. In those ten minutes of terror, we had been reminded that we were living on borrowed kindness and luck. Most of all I thought about our mother, perhaps this very night, ringing the doorbell of our old apartment in Carolina del Norte. Perhaps just as we had never opened to strangers, the new inhabitants would not open the door to her. All I could hope was that as she went back out on the street, *la migra* could not be sure if the woman with the long braids and dark skin was a real Mexican or someone pretending to be one. Just as the children begging for treats were not real beggars.

Abuelita, before I close and put my letter behind your picture in its frame, I want to ask you a favor. Just as you sent down your shower of light to let us know you are watching us, please look out for Mamá. Guide her steps to the apartment after Papá's friend from Las Margaritas has delivered the new phone number. Put some dollars in her hands so she can buy a phone card. Let her call when one of us is home to answer. Because if she does not come by next year, I will be the one going to our bedroom and taking my

new frame down from the dresser and placing
Mamá alongside you on the altar for the Day of
the Dead even if Ofie begs me please, *por favor*,
not to.

Your blessing, Abuelita, *la bendición*,
Mari

FOUR

Cuatro

late fall

(2005)

FARM OF MANY PLOTS

"And thank you, dear Lord, for all the many blessings you have bestowed upon us," Grandma prays before the Thanksgiving meal. Then she asks everyone to say one thing they are especially grateful for before they all begin to eat.

Tyler sees several glances going around the table. Everyone is no doubt thinking that the meal is not going to stay warm through that much thanksgiving.

Grandma begins by saying how she has so much to be thankful for. All her children and grandchildren are gathered together: Uncle Larry and Aunt Vicky and their three sons, Larry Jr., Vic, and Josh; Aunt Jeanne and her husband,

Uncle Byron, who teaches at the nearby college, and their twin daughters, Emma and Eloise; as well as Tyler's whole family. And—Grandma insisted—the three Marías and their father and two uncles.

"I don't know," Uncle Larry said confidentially to Tyler's dad when he heard who all was at the back door. He hadn't invited his Mexicans. But no one wanted to raise a fuss with Grandma. This is going to be the first Thanksgiving without Gramps, so they're all poised for a lot of tears.

But everyone is pleasantly surprised by how upbeat Grandma is. Even though she mentions Gramps often, Grandma has not cried once. Mom's theory is that the three Mexican girls have filled her mother-in-law's life with company and someone to care for. "She's never happy otherwise," Mom has said, countering Aunt Jeanne's theory that Grandma is "losing touch with reality."

A few weeks ago Aunt Jeanne dropped in and found Grandma alone in the garden, having a full-fledged conversation with Gramps! When Aunt Jeanne confronted her, Grandma made some lame excuse about how she was just praying out loud. Aunt Jeanne pretended to go along, but the seed of suspicion had been planted in her. Then the car accidents. Minor fender benders, but still. Grandma should not be driving. She should not be living alone.

The week preceding Thanksgiving, there has been a round of phone-calling. Plots and plans tossed back and forth. According to Aunt Jeanne, the family should intervene and insist that Grandma either come live with one of them or go into an assisted-living facility. Uncle Larry

110

thinks their mother is just fine. It's Aunt Jeanne who's the challenge. Ever since she majored in psychology in college, Aunt Jeanne's always finding problems to solve. Dad is unsure, worried about his mother but inclined to agree with his brother that if something ain't broke, you don't fix it. "Or even worse," Uncle Larry clinches it, "break it so you can fix it!"

All week Tyler has been overhearing his parents discussing "the Grandma problem." What if Aunt Jeanne is right and something happens to Grandma? Maybe she should be persuaded to move in with one of her kids?

Tyler finally speaks up. "Grandma says she's only leaving home feetfirst." Both his parents are startled to find him standing in the doorway. Mom goes from surprise to annoyance at Tyler's "bad habit of eavesdropping." But it's not as if his house is posted with NO LISTENING signs! One thing Tyler knows for sure: if giving up the family farm would've killed his dad, moving Grandma out of her beloved homestead will kill her even quicker, sad and old as she is.

But now that they're seated together at the big table, "the Grandma problem" seems forgotten. Everyone has contributed a dish or two, including the thirty-pound turkey Tyler's mom cooked in their oven and drove over, since she was so worried about a spill. Grandma has baked all the pies, and the Mexicans have brought over some refried beans and tortillas. Of course, Aunt Jeanne and Uncle Byron made an entrance with some fancy cheeses that are so smelly Tyler wouldn't get close to them, much less put them in his mouth.

They go around the table saying their thanks, the

slowpokes being urged with coughs to move along. By the time it's Tyler's turn, everyone is too hungry to listen to one more thank-you. Tyler doesn't have to say much—something else to be thankful for. "Thank you for my dad getting cured." Next to him, his mom squeezes his hand gratefully.

The Marías and their father and uncles are all too shy to say anything. But after Mari translates what's being asked of the guests, her father says thank you to the Paquettes for making them feel like family. His two brothers chime in, "*Gracias.*"

"We call it Día de Acción de Gracias," Ofie tells the table.

"The Day of Saying Thank You," Luby translates.

"Well, thank you and *gracias* to each and every one of you," Grandma finally ends the round.

Before anybody can add anything else, Uncle Larry is carving up the turkey and telling everyone to hand over their plates before it's Christmas.

It's late by the time the meal is done and the Mexican workers head off for the evening milking. Mom convinces their father to let the three Marías stay a little longer. The two youngest have especially hit it off with the nine-year-old twins, who treat Luby and Ofie like real-life dolls, dressing them up in their hand-me-downs they brought in a bag. Meanwhile, Mari is busy helping Grandma with the dishes. "What a doll!" Aunt Vicky whispers to Tyler's mom, who agrees, "They all are."

Tyler heads for the front room, where Ben and his dad and uncle and boy cousins are all watching the football game. During a lull, Uncle Larry starts telling Dad how a pal in the sheriff's department dropped by to let him know that things are heating up for Mexicans in the area. Three were picked up just last week walking down the road to a milking barn. Two more were taken away after a trooper stopped them for speeding and the driver didn't have a license or a current registration for the used car he'd bought off another worker who'd left to go back to Mexico.

Tyler had stopped worrying about the Mexicans working on the farm, but, hearing Uncle Larry, he starts worrying again. Except that now he doesn't really want Mari and her family to go away. He wants the law to be changed so they can stay, helping his family as well as themselves.

"I tell Vicky, don't get too attached," Uncle Larry is saying. "It's just a matter of time."

"Did I hear my name being used in vain?" Aunt Vicky has come from the kitchen, where the cleaning up is winding down.

"Nothing, dear." Uncle Larry motions toward the TV, where some tricky play is in progress. His team messes up, and he turns his attention back to his wife. "Just talking about our friend's visit from the sheriff's department."

Aunt Vicky sinks into the arm of her husband's chair with a sigh. "I just don't see how we're expected to survive."

Tyler's mom has joined them in the front room. "Where's Jeanne?" she asks. They all know Uncle Byron is in the small front parlor reading the *New York Times*, which he reads every day to keep up with the state of the world.

"You and Larry, two peas in a pod," Aunt Vicky likes to say. Turns out Uncle Larry reads his weekly *Valley Voice* down to the classifieds. Every time Aunt Vicky says so, Uncle Byron's distinguished-professor eyebrows arch ever so slightly at the comparison.

"I think she went upstairs to check on the girls," Aunt Vicky answers Mom. "They're in the attic playing dress-up. Did you see their little faces when they saw that bag of clothes?"

Mom nods, laughing. "I know. They think we're rich because we have stuff to throw away. And we *are* rich, compared. I tell you, having these Mexicans has put a whole new spin on our lives, hasn't it, sweetheart?" Mom beams at Dad, who looks uncomfortable but nods in agreement.

"Enjoy it while it lasts, ladies," Uncle Larry says grimly. "Any day now, Homeland Security is going to pay us all a visit. I don't put it beyond them to just come on our property and haul them off."

Tyler is shocked that his uncle, a reasonable adult, would think this is possible. But if he's shocked, it's nothing compared to Mari, who has just appeared at the door, the cleanup over.

"Folks," Tyler's mother warns. But it's too late. Mari's face has tensed up with worry and fear, the way it gets when Mr. Bicknell starts talking about the future of the planet. "Honey, Uncle Larry was exaggerating," his mom explains. "Weren't you, Uncle Larry?"

Tyler's uncle looks unsure, but then gazes toward the door, where Grandma has joined Mari, her old, spotted hands on the young girl's shoulders. "Of course I was," he says. "You know me," he adds unconvincingly, "I'm one of those caught-a-big-fish kind of guys."

"I'll say," Aunt Vicky pipes up, and Uncle Larry pretends he thinks it's funny, too, when everyone—except Mari—bursts out laughing.

*   *   *

When Grandma goes up to check on the little girls, Aunt Jeanne, who has joined the group, closes the door.

"Larry, turn that thing off, will you."

"For crying out loud!" Uncle Larry grumbles under his breath. He is the youngest of the three siblings. "I know just how you feel," he has told Tyler. "We're the low men on the totem pole." But Tyler can't say he has noticed. In fact, Uncle Larry is the bossiest of all his relatives. Well, sometimes Aunt Jeanne is a close second.

"We need to decide about Mother," Aunt Jeanne begins.

"What now?" Uncle Larry says like he doesn't think there's a problem.

Aunt Jeanne crosses her arms. "Maybe you need to take a little trip upstairs."

"Maybe the kids need to leave?" Tyler's mom puts in. But Uncle Larry's boys protest. They want to watch the game, and no, they can't go to the other TV, since Grandma gave it away to the Mexicans.

Aunt Jeanne nods all around, as if this is further proof of what she has been saying. "In the kitchen, then," she directs. The adults rouse themselves from their chairs and file out for their summit meeting. The TV blares on.

Tyler tries to watch the game, but he feels distracted. For one thing, he can sense Mari's discomfort as she sits on her hands in a chair, feeling she has to be polite, but not understanding at all how football works. When Sara announces she's leaving, Mari decides it's time to go home, too. She heads upstairs to round up her sisters.

Tyler joins Sara in the hallway. He does not want to be around if there's going to be a big scene with Grandma. From the kitchen, they can hear Aunt Jeanne's voice, just some words here and there: "Like a voodoo altar . . . Three car accidents . . . Shouldn't be living alone . . ." Tyler wishes he could go defend Grandma, but then he'd be accused of eavesdropping again.

Soon Ofie and Luby are stomping down the stairs, upset that they have to go home. Mari follows, trailed by Grandma and the twins. The party is breaking up. "Bye, Grandma, thanks!" Tyler says in a loud voice to alert the closed-door kitchen meeting. He's hoping that if there has been a vote, two sons and daughters-in-law can prevail against Aunt Jeanne. As for Uncle Byron, he's still in the front parlor, reading his *New York Times*, keeping up with the world while a minor revolution is erupting right here in his mother-in-law's house.

Tyler invites the three Marías to come over and look at the stars through his telescope. Their father and uncles won't be done with the milking and feeding and cleanup for another couple of hours. And three girls all together must make it okay to be in a boy's bedroom even if it is nighttime.

"Do you think it's true what your uncle was saying about *la migra?*" Mari asks as they all walk over to Tyler's house. She has to explain that *la migra* is what the Mexicans call the agents from Homeland Security who try to catch them.

Tyler can't honestly say whether or not Homeland Security will raid the family's farms. But as with the possible planetary dangers in the offing, they should at least have a plan.

"What kind of a plan?" Luby wants to know.

"You know," Tyler offers, "like a fire drill at school."

"We all run out of the house?" Luby asks.

"We shouldn't run." Ofie is good at remembering rules. "We file out and . . . Then what?" She looks over at Tyler.

"We hide, right?" Luby thinks this might be a fun game after all.

"There's all kinds of hiding spots," Tyler agrees. He can't believe he is the same boy who several months ago wanted this family deported. Now he's plotting how they can escape capture. But maybe it's like the Underground Railroad: helping slaves find freedom. Besides, two of these girls are American citizens.

117

"Grandpa showed me where there's a cave," Tyler explains. "We can go exploring tomorrow when it's light."

By now they're at the back door and Sara's getting ready to call her new boyfriend, Hal, when the phone rings. She lets it ring three times before she picks it up. "Hello," she says casually. "Hello? HELLLOOOOO?! Will you stop it, Jake? I'm going to report you to the police!"

She slams the phone into its cradle. The three Marías are surprised at this outburst. So Tyler explains about the annoying caller who keeps hanging up when they answer.

Mari looks like she has seen her second ghost of the evening. "I think that maybe it's our mother," she says haltingly. She just recently gave their new phone number to their father's friend to take over to their former apartment. But it could be that their mother went by before the old tenants were deported and got the Paquettes' number instead.

Tyler doesn't get it. If the girls' mother went to Mexico for a visit, wouldn't the family call her so she'd know where they'd be when she got ready to return? "You mean she doesn't know where you are?"

Before Mari can reply, Ofie speaks up. "We don't know where she is." Then, in a rare moment of self-doubt, she turns to her big sister. "Right, Mari?"

"Papá said she went to the other side of life," Luby recalls. She is holding on so tight to her stuffed puppy, it'd be a dead dog if it were alive. "Right, Mari?"

Now Tyler is completely confused. *The other side of life* is the way people talk about Gramps's death. But how can the girls' mother be dead and be on her way back from a trip to Mexico? "But she's alive—right, Mari?"

Everyone has turned to Mari as the authority. Tyler notices just the teensiest hesitation—unlike her instant vehement assertion in the loft a few months back—before she replies, "Yes, our mother is alive."

As if to prove her right, the phone rings again.

Mari rushes to answer it. Tyler and her sisters and Sara gather around her. "*¿Mamá?*" she begins.

"*¡Mamá! ¡Mamá!*" The two little Marías are jumping up and down ecstatically.

Mari hushes them. "I can't hear a thing!" Then she turns back to the caller. "*Mamá, ¿eres tú?*" But it must not be her mother because her face drains of excitement. "I'm sorry. Yes, she's here."

Mari tries handing the phone to Sara. "It's Jake," she explains. Sara shakes her head and mouths, "I'm not home."

"She says she is not home," Mari tells Jake.

Sara and Tyler burst out laughing. But Mari doesn't understand what's so funny, even after Tyler explains. In fact, all three Marías have the same stricken look on their faces, as if they have just heard that their mother has vanished without a trace.

"Let's go up and look through the telescope, you want to?" he offers, hoping to change the subject to something that might make them happier. Instead of cries of "Yes!" the two little Marías again look over at their big sister. "I think we better go home now," Mari says, taking Luby's hand. Without prompting, Ofie reaches for Mari's other hand.

119

Tyler turns on the outdoor light, and he and Sara watch the three girls walk across the yard toward their trailer. "I want my mommy," Luby begins to wail halfway there. Ofie joins in. Mari must say something reassuring, because her sisters quiet down. Arms around their shoulders, Mari leads them home.

"That is totally weird," Sara says as the trailer door closes behind them.

Tyler is not usually in agreement with anything that comes out of his sister's mouth, but this time, he has to agree. It's clear the girls have no idea where their mom is. But how can you misplace your own mother, for heaven's sake?

It's a mystery Tyler could ponder all night, but trouble soon arrives in his own family. His parents return, long-faced from the confrontation at Grandma's house. Grandma has told her children that if they try to move her out of her house, she'll run away, which is kind of funny, Grandma running away from home to protest being forced to leave her home.

Except that it's not funny, Tyler thinks, wishing he could travel to another galaxy. He'd pick a planet with lots of farms and no borders or bullies bossing you around. His grandmother has told him that's what heaven is like. But Tyler doesn't want to have to die to go there, although it might be nice to be able to join his grandfather and get to eavesdrop on the rest of the family plotting and planning on the earth below—without getting in trouble with his mother.

12 diciembre 2005

Adorada Virgen de Guadalupe,

Today, your feast day, I write you with an urgent petition.

Please help Tío Felipe! He was picked up by *la migra* over a week ago, but there is still no word about where he may be and whether he will be released or sent back home to México.

Mr. and Mrs. Paquette have been calling the sheriff's office, where a friend of Mr. Paquette's brother works. But once Homeland Security is involved, the matter is out of the sheriff's hands, and so neither the sheriff nor anyone at his office has further information about my uncle.

"But people can't just disappear!" Mrs. Paquette says with temper into the phone. She is very upset with her son Ben for being so careless. "You get sent home with a warning. This young man is in prison and his life is ruined!"

Ben just bows his head. "I feel bad enough as it is, Mom."

"He is not culpable," my father tells Mrs. Paquette. Who can blame a young man for wanting a little fun? Sure, Tío Felipe should not have accepted the invitation of the farmer's older son, but what kind of life does he have, never going out, working almost every day? For what?

Unlike Tío Armando, who has his wife and children back in México, Tío Felipe has no one but his parents, whom he has been helping since he was just a few years older than me.

Ben and Tío Felipe were returning from a university party that Ben was kind enough to invite Tío Felipe to attend. They were stopped for speeding, and when the police officer shone his flashlight inside the car, he got curious about the Mexican fellow riding in the passenger seat. We heard the whole story from Mrs. Paquette, who heard it from the sheriff's deputy, who said he might just have slapped her son with a ticket for going sixty in a forty-mile zone, but then Tío Felipe made a big mistake. He panicked and opened his door and took off into the night. Before you knew it, the officer had notified Homeland Security, and by dawn, there were roadblocks everywhere and a helicopter combing the countryside on account of now Tío Felipe had become a fugitive.

Meanwhile, Ben had been escorted home by the sheriff, and Mrs. Paquette had come over to let us know what was going on.

"Will they come for us?" Papá asked her.

"I really don't think so," Mrs. Paquette reassured him. "But you all best lay low. We'll take care of the milking today."

But Papá was sure it was just a matter of time

before *la migra* came for him and Tío Armando. He stuffed his Mexican passport and some phone cards and cash in his pockets and packed a small bag with a few clothes. Tío Armando did the same. Then Papá told us to pack our most important things into the big suitcase we bought for coming to Vermont.

This did not go over well with my sisters, especially so soon after the disappointing phone call that we thought might be our mother. Then Tío Felipe's capture. Ever since his arrest, Luby has had to sleep with me, which means her little dog has to come, too. After she crawls in, the covers lift again. This time it's Ofie, but not Ofie alone. Wilmita is lonely for Tío Felipe! Three girls, one guitar, and one stuffed dog on a twin bed fighting for the blanket and pillow. I would laugh if it weren't that we're all so afraid and sad.

"But why do we have to pack our stuff?" Ofie protested to Papá. "Where are we going, anyway?"

I could tell Papá didn't know what to say. He was torn between telling my little sisters the truth and not alarming them. Only with me does he unburden himself. Because I am the oldest. Because, he has said, taking my face in his hands, "you are just like your mother."

"We all have to be ready," he explained to my sisters. To distract them, he tried to make it into a game. "Let's see how many things you can fit in this suitcase. Wilmita won't fit," he added, because Ofie was reaching for Tío Felipe's lonely guitar.

"Where are we to go?" I asked Papá in a low voice. For the moment, my sisters were entertained with their packing.

"You will ask the *patrona* to send you back to México, to Abuelota and Abuelote. You wait for us there."

"I don't want to go to México," Ofie declared. She had overheard us talking.

My father's face got a strange, hurt look on it. I think it was the first time he realized what it really means that two of his daughters are American. It isn't just that they are legal in this country. They belong here. This is their home.

"Tyler told us about a place," I whispered. "It's a cave where we can go and hide."

My father actually looked tempted. But then he shook his head. "Your uncle ran and now he is in worse trouble. We will just lay down low like the *patrona* said and wait." And then he took our blankets off the bed and we lay down on them on the floor in case *la migra* looked in the windows.

"Why are we lying down, Papá?" Luby wanted to know.

"Because we're going to tell stories," Tío Armando said in a calm voice like this was the most normal thing in the world: to throw

124

blankets on the floor in the middle of the day and have a story hour. He is the most quiet of all of us. "He misses his family so much," Papá once explained to me. But ever since Tío Felipe's capture, Tío Armando has been trying to keep me and my sisters from worrying too much. "Who wants to start?" He looked over at me, I guess because I am the one who is always writing.

"Tell the story of crossing the desert." Ofie loves that story. Especially if I throw in a few extra serpents and make the *coyotes* real coyotes.

"Not now," Papá said sternly, casting a glance at his brother. Instead, he reached over and turned on the television, very low, so you could hardly hear it. But thank goodness it was Dora heading for a fiesta with her friend Boots, an episode we had all seen several times. Still, my sisters lay on their stomachs in front of the screen, soaking up that happy world.

A little while later, there was a tap-tap-tap at the back door. Tap-tap-tap. Like someone who didn't want to be heard. We were all sure it was Tío Felipe, who had snuck back home through the fields. Of course, we wanted him to be safe, but by coming to the trailer he was leading *la migra* straight to our doorstep, and we would all be rounded up. Still, we couldn't just leave him locked out in the cold.

But when we peeked out the little window in

the door, imagine our surprise: it was the grandmother and she was carrying a little suitcase!

"I'm going to ask you a big favor," she began. And then she looked over our shoulders and saw the blankets strewn all around the living room floor. "What's going on? Are you having a slumber party?"

"No, Grandma," Ofie blurted out. "The police are looking for our uncle Felipe and we're supposed to lay low so they don't catch us."

"Oh my goodness." Grandma put down her little suitcase. "And I thought I had troubles."

It turned out she had not been told about Ben being stopped by the police and Tío Felipe running off and getting caught. "I'm the last one to know anything in this family," she said crossly. "They treat me like a total invalid!"

"They do not want to worry you, *señora*," my father said kindly after I had translated. "That is why they did not tell you." He had pulled up a chair for her to sit down. But Grandma waved it off, looking even more annoyed that anyone would think she needed to sit down. She was glancing all around the room now.

"I need a place to hide," she said straight out. None of us were sure we had heard her right. An old woman hiding from her family! "But why?" Luby asked finally, clutching her little dog as if it might also decide to hide from her. "Is the police looking for you, too?"

"I wish," Grandma said, and then her eyes were full of tears, and she began to cry. This time when my father took her by the arm and escorted her to a chair, she accepted and sat down with her little suitcase at her feet.

"What is wrong, *señora?*" Papá asked her. And that is when the grandmother told us the most unbelievable story. How Mr. and Mrs. Paquette and her other children were going to put her in a nursing home if she didn't agree to give up her home and go live with one of them. How they had taken away the keys to her car so she couldn't drive over to her friend's house.

Poor Papá was so shocked. He had been totally fooled by the *patrones'* seeming kindness. If they did this to their own mother, what wouldn't they do to us? "We don't believe in treating our old people that way," Papá told Grandma. "You can stay here for as long as you wish."

Grandma was shaking her head, like she didn't believe it herself. As for staying with us, she had called her friend Martha from church, who offered to come over that night to pick her up. "Under the cover of darkness," Grandma explained. "That'll show them. Martha's son tried to do the same to her last year." Just the thought of her friend's evil son made her start crying all over again.

So that is how the grandmother came to spend the whole day locked up in the trailer with us. Late that afternoon when Mrs. Paquette came to the door with the news that Tío Felipe had been caught in a whole other county—"To lead *la migra* away from us," Tío Armando guessed— Papá did not invite her in but spoke to her right at the door. She lingered awhile like she was worried about us.

"Everything all right?" she kept asking. "I mean, I know you must be worried to death about your brother." The sheriff's office had told her that usually an undocumented person would just have a hearing, then get deported. But because Tío Felipe had broken the law—defying a police officer—he would have to stand trial.

"Ridiculous, I know." Mrs. Paquette sighed. "But anyhow, you can rest easy as they won't be coming around to search for him here now that they've found him. So you can start back with the evening milking." She went on to mention a couple of cows that she thought might be in heat, and another whose milk shouldn't be sent to the tank because one teat looked infected.

As she talked, Papá stood at the door, not inviting her in out of the cold and risking the grandmother being discovered. Finally, Mrs.

Paquette turned to go. "Anything you need," she said so nicely that it really was difficult to believe that she would force an old woman out of her home and lock her up with strangers.

"Thank you," my father said, the door already half closed. Then he lifted the curtain to check and see that Mrs. Paquette was really gone.

"I think she is on her way to visit you," he said over his shoulder to Grandma. We all rushed to the window, and there was Mrs. Paquette headed up the hill to her mother-in-law's house. We watched as she knocked and knocked, then tried the knob and let herself inside the house. A little while later, out she came, her steps hurried, her arms swinging like a person on a mission. When I looked up at Grandma, there was a small triumphant smile on her face.

By evening there had been several trips up to the grandmother's house, Mr. Paquette with his limp, and Ben and Sara. I don't know where Tyler was, but he hadn't joined them, which was odd, as I knew he was home. I had seen him go into the barn to join my uncle and Papá for the evening milking.

Meanwhile, Grandma was worried that her friend might show up at the trailer and give away her hiding place. "I didn't think of that when I told her to pick me up here!" She tried calling but there was no answer. "Martha's probably on her way already. She drives like she's training for a funeral home. I like a little speed myself."

For the first time that day, Grandma laughed. Not a revenge smile, not a nervous hiccup of a giggle. She laughed. And for some reason, it was such a relief to hear laughter in that room that although I didn't really know what I was laughing at and my sisters didn't either, we just laughed along with her, until it was impossible to stop. But finally we did.

"I'm going to miss you girls so much!" Grandma said fervently.

"Can't we visit you anymore?" Luby wanted to know, her bottom lip quivering. She looked like she was going to cry.

"I don't see how," Grandma said. And just as suddenly as she had been laughing, Grandma began to cry. Again, we were infected by her mood, and soon we were all blubbering. I admit I was also crying about Mamá, how she might have been calling us next door, but now that Sara had mentioned the police, Mamá would never try that number again. Most of all, I was crying for Tío Felipe, imagining him locked up and looking out, his hands clutching the bars like prisoners do on television. We couldn't go visit him or we would be caught. Would they hurt him or torture him? What would happen to him?

"Maybe I should move to México," Grandma

was saying. "Only problem is I don't know any Spanish."

Soon we had all dreamed up a wonderful plan. Virgen de Guadalupe, may it someday come true! We would all move to México, and Grandma would build a house with a swimming pool and many, many bedrooms and we would all live together. "They want me to move out, I'll move out! Sell the house, use the money to suit myself."

At the front door, the bell was ringing. Grandma's friend Martha had finally come for her.

The next day, Papá did not want us to go to school. He was still worried that *la migra* would raid the farm and we would come home to an empty trailer. That morning—something that never happens as Tyler is usually running out at the last minute with his toast in his hand—he swung by so we could all walk together down the driveway to wait for the bus. Papá and Tío Armando were already at the barn, milking. "We're not going to school today," I explained to Tyler.

"On account of your uncle?" he wanted to know.

I nodded. The less said the better. All I could think as he stood there was this was a boy who would turn against his own grandmother.

As if he could overhear my thoughts, he

brought her up himself. He lowered his voice. "Grandma's gone. We're afraid maybe she just walked off and drowned herself in the creek." Tyler could be so dramatic. I almost blurted out: She'd do no such thing. Then he said something that made me realize he was against his parents' evil plan. "That's what they get for trying to force her to move. I just wish she'd told me," he added. "I'd have run off with her. It's awful at my house," he went on. "Ben's grounded for the whole Christmas break, and now Sara isn't allowed to ride around with her new boyfriend, Hal, 'cause he might do what Ben did. Everybody's in a really bad mood. And on top of it all, Grandma could be dead!"

The bus had come and Mr. Rawson was leaning on his horn. "I better go." Tyler heaved the hugest sigh, like he was off to a firing squad to be shot to death for a crime he never committed. "Come back after school!" I called to him. When he twisted around, he looked like I had just granted him a pardon.

During the day we watched through the windows as different members of the Paquette family came and went. They walked all around, calling and calling "Ma! Ma!" just like the baby calves do when they are weaned from their mothers. It made me sad because I understood what it felt like to be missing your mother. Midday as we were eating lunch, the *patrón's* sister, Jeanne, and her husband, Byron, came to our door. It turned out that this husband knew some fancy Spanish like in a textbook. First they said they were very sorry about Tío Felipe. Then they mentioned about the grandmother and how worried they were. Had we maybe spotted her walking in a certain direction?

Virgencita, we all looked down at our shoes like they were suddenly the most interesting things in the world. And though a second later Papá shook his head, the lady knew we knew something. Her eyes were all wet and worried. "It's all my fault," she explained. "You see, I've been worried to death about her, and I'm afraid I pushed the envelope."

The husband translated everything the lady said for Papá and Tío Armando into his fancy Spanish, which made it hard to understand. But then I hadn't understood this lady's English, either. Why would pushing an envelope make her mother run off?

"I just want to know Ma's safe," Jeanne explained, dabbing at her eyes.

Tío Armando spoke up.

"He says your mother is fine," Mr. Byron told his wife. "I told you so."

"Oh thank you, thank you!" Jeanne sobbed. "I've been so worried. Please tell us where she is, please. We're not going to hurt her."

"You must promise not to send her from her home," my uncle went on once the husband had translated. "We know what that is like," he added to soften the fact that here he was telling the *patrón*'s family what to do.

Virgencita, to bring this letter to a close, by the time Tyler came back from school, heading straight for our trailer without even stopping at his own house first, we had seen Grandma unloaded up at her house from her daughter's car. The brother Larry's car was up there, too, and the Paquettes had walked on over. As soon as we gave Tyler the news, he flew out the door, calling for us to come, too. But Papá and Tío Armando were in the barn milking and we had the strictest orders to stay indoors. All I could think as Tyler raced up the hill was how sweet it is when a family is reunited and the lost ones brought back into the fold.

Which brings me back to my petition, Virgencita de Guadalupe, that you help deliver Tío Felipe out of prison, even if he has to go back to México. Perhaps because we helped them find their grandmother, the Paquettes have promised us they will do everything they can to help our uncle.

I do have one more petition. In two days it will be a whole year since Mamá left us. It's not that I've stopped believing she will come back. But that moment in the *patrones'* kitchen when the phone call was not from Mamá, I began to feel a tiny bit of doubt. I have to keep believing or that little candle at the window will go out! So, *por favor*, Virgencita, return Mamá and our uncle so that we can be a united family in the United States or in México, it does not matter anymore, as long as we are all together.

Now that I am getting ready to close, I have begun wondering how I will deliver this letter to you, Virgencita. In México, and even in Carolina del Norte at the church Mamá always took us to, there was a statue in your honor. People always left you petitions and letters and photographs of their sons or daughters who were sick or sad or in the military. But here, we do not have such a church. The grandmother has wanted to take us to her church but Papá has refused. "They are Protestants," he explained. "They do not worship our Guadalupe." I was surprised to hear Papá say so, as unlike Mamá, he has never been a churchgoer.

But then, right after Thanksgiving, on our way to school on the bus, I noticed a big Nativity scene set up outdoors in front of a big church that might be Catholic. I am going to ask Mr. Rawson if I can run up and say a real quick prayer while the town kids are getting off and crossing the street. I will bury this letter under Mary's robe, as Mamá always said you were one and the same Virgin.

Meanwhile today for the first time since she came back, we visited the grandmother. She embraced us and told us that her children have promised her that she will be carried out of her house feetfirst. I'm not sure why she would want to be carried out that way, but, Virgencita, when the grandmother wondered out loud how her family found out where she was hiding, I told her we had made her daughter promise that she would not force her mother to move.

"So I owe it all to you!" she said, smiling and hugging us.

No, I told her. She owed it all to the Virgin of Guadalupe, who has a special place in her heart for mothers and grandmothers—and, we hope, for our uncle, too.

> Please, *por favor*, Virgencita,
> grant both my petitions,
> María (named after you!)

FIVE

Cinco

winter

(2005–2006)

CHRISTMAS TEARS FARM

It's going to be the worst Christmas ever! Tyler is dreading what lies ahead in the two weeks that school will be out.

One eighteen-year-old brother grounded and the keys to his car that he paid for himself taken away. One fifteen-year-old sister not allowed to ride around in her boyfriend's car. One-third of your workforce in prison and the other two-thirds on pins and needles every time the milk truck pulls up to the barn to collect the day's milking, thinking it's the police coming to haul them away. All the ingredients of a holiday from hell without even adding the fact that it'll be the first Christmas without Gramps.

At least, Grandma is back. "I'm sure glad I'm somebody's silver lining," Grandma says when Tyler tells her how happy he is to have her next door, given how bleak things are over at his house.

Another thing Tyler feels bad about is the closing down of their Christmas tree farm. It isn't really a whole farm, just three acres that Gramps set aside to plant evergreens in rows, now going on ten years, which means some of the trees are sizeable, candidates if not for the White House at least for the statehouse down in Montpelier. Blue spruces and balsam firs and Scotch pines.

Every year, folks have come by and left their fifteen bucks in a can by the shed, where they've picked up a saw and gone off to cut down their very own tree. One year, some guys from a fraternity at UVM came by on a Saturday afternoon with a twelve-pack, and before they left, they'd cut down Gramps's prized tamarack that had nothing at all to do with Christmas. That was when Gramps took down the sign on the road that read CUT YOUR OWN CHRISTMAS TREE—$15. Then it was only word of mouth: neighbors and friends for whom cutting down their Christmas tree at the Paquette farm had become a part of their holiday tradition.

But this year, not only will there be no sign on the road, there also won't be a coffee can on the picnic table or saws in the shed. Grandma and Tyler's parents have decided it's too risky having a whole lot of folks coming on the farm and maybe spotting their Mexican workers going in and out of the barn. Not with one of them already in jail.

Of course, Aunt Jeanne and Uncle Larry have come to

get their trees. At the last minute, Grandma decides to put up a tree for the girls, who otherwise won't have one. Grandma has always been big on decorating for holidays and has boxes of ornaments up in the attic, as well as a file folder full of recipes for every kind of Christmas cookie you could think of. The church always holds a Christmas bazaar, stocked primarily by Grandma and her friends: baked goodies and caps and stockings and stuff they've made. This year Grandma has invited the youth group to come and cut down a whole bunch of trees to sell. Afterward, the field looks so forlorn, it reminds Tyler of a tree version of the French Revolution his class read about when lords and ladies got their heads cut off on a guillotine.

But the saddest of all is how the Cruzes next door are worried sick about Felipe, the younger uncle, whom Tyler likes the best of the three men. Felipe plays the guitar and knows more English than he lets on, plus he loves making jokes. Like the one about having a girlfriend, Wilmita, that turns out to be his guitar! Tyler's mom has called the sheriff's office so often that now no one is available to take her call except the operator, who has to since it's her job. Finally, through Larry's friend, they find out that Felipe is in a pickle of trouble, as Grandma calls it. Not only is he going to have to go through a criminal trial on account of he fled from the authorities, but after he's convicted and sentenced and served his time for that offense, he'll have to go through a deportation hearing as well.

"He'll be middle-aged by the time he gets out of there." Mom is beside herself. She calls a group of lawyers up in

Burlington who help poor people in trouble for whatever they can afford to pay. She finds one who is willing to donate his services for free to see if they can't get Felipe deported without having to make him into a criminal first.

But even with a lawyer on board, it's the holiday season, so cases are stacking up and everything is moving a lot slower than it normally would. But the good news in all this bad news is that Felipe is actually being held in the local county jail, where prisoners can receive visitors on Saturdays and Sundays from ten to three, one-hour slots, first-come, first-served. Mom signs them up for the only slot left open, ten o'clock Saturday morning.

"But we can't go see him," Mari reminds Tyler when he gives her the news. They're in the kitchen, helping Grandma make her gingerbread house. Going to the county jail without papers would be basically like turning themselves in.

Tyler never thought of that. Still, somebody will have to translate for Mom and the lawyer. "I know!" Tyler says. "How about Ms. Ramírez?" Their Spanish teacher was born in Texas, but her parents came from Mexico. It's a brilliant idea except her number isn't in the phone book.

"We could just go house to house asking for her," Grandma suggests as she lays another wafer shingle on the roof of her gingerbread house.

Mari thinks Grandma is serious. "It'd be just like the *posadas*." Mari goes on to explain how for a whole week before Christmas, Mexican kids have a kind of trick-or-treat where they go from house to house pretending to be Mary and Joseph. At each house, they ask if there's any room at the inn. Everyone turns them away until the last house of that night, where they're let in and have a party and break a piñata with candy and treats for all the kids. The very last night of the *posadas* is on Christmas Eve and the last house that night has a really big party because it's the actual night the whole story happened. Grandma thinks *posadas* are a great idea, which she's going to bring up at the next church committee meeting as something the youth group can do right here in Vermont.

Although Ms. Ramírez isn't in the phone book, Mrs. Stevens is. Mari doesn't want her principal to know that her uncle's been picked up by the police. So Grandma calls Mrs. Stevens and tells her an elaborate story about how she wants to give her friend Martha Spanish lessons for Christmas, as their youth group is considering going to Mexico on their service trip next summer, and so can she please have Ms. Ramírez's phone number? For a churchgoing person, Grandma sure knows how to tell a good lie.

By the next night, it's all set, Ms. Ramírez and Tyler's mom and the lawyer from Burlington are all going to visit Felipe on Saturday, which happens to be Christmas Eve day. But get this. Visitors cannot bring any packages or presents or clothes or food or anything to the prisoners even though it's the day before Christmas!

"I feel just like Mary and Joseph at all the *posada* stops where they're turned away," Mari says, tearing up. "No room for us in this country."

"But there's room for you here on our farm," Tyler tells

143

her. They are outside while Ofie and Luby help Grandma finish up the lawn on the gingerbread house. Tyler is teaching Mari the winter constellations. Orion, the hunter, wears his belt of three stars. To the west, a bunch of little stars glitter like teensy blue diamonds. "They're the Pleiades, the seven sisters," Tyler says.

Mari is momentarily distracted. "Seven? I only count six."

"You're not supposed to see all seven," he explains. "One of them is so dim you can only see her with a telescope. She's supposed to be missing or hiding out or something."

"Why?" Mari wants to know. Tyler has noticed this before, how Mari is always so intrigued when the subject of someone missing comes up. The day Mrs. Stevens and the school counselor talked to their class about missing children and the appropriate behavior if a stranger approaches you, Mari, who never asks questions, wanted to know all about what to do if someone was missing in your family. Mari has told Tyler that one of the things she likes the most about astronomy is how you can use the stars to guide your way, so you never ever have to be lost. "How come that sister star got separated from the others?"

Actually, Tyler can't remember. It's some Greek myth. He'll have to look it up in his star book.

"I know," Mari proposes. "She's crossing the sky to get back to her six sisters. But when she gets to the Milky Way, there's no bridge. So she asks that constellation that's the charioteer."

"So does she get across or what?" Tyler is now the one intrigued. Maybe astronomers should hire Mari to make up new stories about the constellations. Hers would probably be a lot better than all those dumb Greek gods falling in love with mere mortals. Suddenly, Tyler is aware that Mari is not looking up anymore, but looking straight at him.

"Can I tell you something, Tyler?" When he nods, Mari goes on. "You know how I said my mother might be calling us?"

Of course he remembers. He and Sara both thought it was weird that the girls' mother wouldn't know where they are.

"My mother, she went to Mexico last December," Mari begins. "And then when my *abuelita* died, my mother left Mexico to come back, but she never showed up, and my father, he tried to find her, but no one could tell him where she was." Mari pauses to catch her breath, as if she might drown in the torrent of words tumbling out of her mouth.

"We've waited and waited. A whole year now. My father, I can tell, doesn't think she's going to come back. And my sisters, too. But how can somebody just disappear?"

"You think maybe something . . . happened to your mom?" Tyler hates bringing it up, but it's clear Mari really wants to talk about it.

Instead of going ballistic like she usually does when Tyler has suggested her mother might be dead, Mari begins to cry. Tyler has no idea what to do when a girl cries— except get her to stop. "But maybe it's like the seventh sister, Mari. Maybe your mom is just lost and trying to find her way back to you." Just saying the words, Tyler has himself half believing it could be so.

And Mari is believing it, too. The sobs turn into sniffles. "You think so? Oh, I think so, too. But sometimes . . . sometimes, I just worry. And I can't talk to my father or my sisters and worry them more."

Tyler knows all about how hard it is to talk to adults. "Gramps is the only one I can really talk to. I mean, when he was alive," he corrects himself. "Gramps used to tell me to look up when I felt down."

"Fell down?" Mari doesn't quite understand.

"*Feel* down, like when you're really, really sad."

"Look up when you feel down," Mari repeats, looking up.

Looking up with her is what gives Tyler the idea. Tomorrow night, he's going to bring the telescope over to Grandma's. He can't give Mari her mother, but he can at least show her the seventh star reunited with her sisters.

His mom and dad and grandma are determined that the girls will have a nice Christmas. Especially now that the whole story is unraveling that their mother has actually been missing for a full year and probably died on the dangerous border crossing. There is a small chance, a chance Tyler is really hoping for, that the mother is alive and trying to reach the family. But the calls have stopped. That's what comes of an older sister with a big mouth threatening the caller with the police.

"How was I supposed to know?" Sara defends herself

when the whole Cruz situation comes up. Everybody in the family is feeling the tug of guilt: Mom and Dad for hiring them and enabling a sad situation, Ben for getting Felipe into the mess he's in, Sara for possibly scaring the mom away from ever calling again, Tyler for shunning them when they first came to the farm.

"What do you think we should get them for Christmas?" Mom wonders. Tomorrow she has a trip planned to the big-box stores across the lake. Since the Christmas tree farm is closed down this year, Tyler doesn't have the cut that Gramps always gave him for helping run the operation. So a group present would be great, especially with three girls and three men to shop for. Actually, two men. The third isn't even allowed a phone card.

"Have the girls mentioned anything they might want?" Mom asks Tyler. You'd think he was the resident expert on the three Marías.

Tyler shrugs. The one time he asked the girls what all they were getting for Christmas, they explained that there'd be no gifts this year. Money is tight now that there are only two sons working to send the same amount home. Besides, their father can't risk going off the farm to shop. Tyler's mom used to take them all once a week to the Wal-Mart across the lake. Now they just make a list and Mom gets them whatever they need.

But that same morning in the milk barn, Mr. Cruz pulls Tyler over. He unfolds some pages torn out of a flyer and points to a stuffed dog that could be the rich, glossy cousin of the scrappy puppy Luby carts around, a cardboard dollhouse with a sack of teensy furniture, and a very pretty purple backpack with pink butterflies. He counts out five twenty-dollar bills from the zippered pocket in his jacket. "María, Ofelia, Lubyneida," he says. "Santa."

Tyler understands. The backpack is probably for Mari, since she's too old for a stuffed animal or dollhouse. But what will his own family get her and her sisters? Tyler drops by the trailer, hoping to tease out something else the girls might want.

No problem getting Ofie and Luby to rattle off a list a mile long. But Mari shakes her head like she's too proud to ask for what she knows she can't get. Tyler says nothing about the money in his pocket. Although Mr. Cruz didn't say so, Tyler assumes that the gifts are meant to be a surprise. "Santa might just want to leave you presents at our house. Come on, Mari," he coaxes. "There must be *something* you want?"

Mari gives him a fierce look, tempered by the tears glinting in her eyes. "Okay, I'll tell you what I want. I want my mother to come back. I want my uncle Felipe to come back."

"Me too," says little Luby. "That's what I want, too."

Ofie looks torn. She doesn't want to give up the dollhouse or the Strawberry Shortcake Fruity Beauty Salon or the new Barbie in a skating outfit. "I know," she pipes up, her face brightening. "We can ask Santa for presents and then we can ask the Three Kings to bring both Mamá and Tío Felipe back." She looks hopefully at her sisters.

"We're not going to get anything from anybody," Mari reminds her in a scolding voice.

"You are too!" Tyler puts in.

For a moment, a look of yearning comes on Mari's face, like a break of sunshine on a cloudy day. She hesitates. "Maybe . . . maybe if we could just know my mother is okay, my uncle is okay . . ." Her voice fades away. She bows her head, trying to keep her tears to herself.

If only those were things Tyler could give her! Instead, that afternoon in the crowded store, Tyler helps his mom pick out a little boxed set of stationery, as Mari is always writing letters, and for Ofie and Luby, a puzzle with puppies and coloring books and crayons. He finds the gifts Mr. Cruz asked for, and from himself, he decides on a packet of glow-in-the-dark stars Mari can paste to the ceiling in the trailer. That'll bring a smile to her face. Christmas tears are just the worst unless they're the kind that spring to your eyes when you are so touched, your happiness has to borrow from your sadness. As he stands in the checkout line with his mom and Sara, Tyler is amazed how thinking of making Mari happy has lifted the dark cloud that was hanging over his own holiday.

Early Christmas Eve morning Mari comes over with a letter for Tyler's mom to deliver to her uncle. Mom glances at it a long moment, sighs, then hands it back. "I'm sorry, honey, but we're not allowed to bring anything in. They're no-contact visits. But tell you what," Mom adds, because Mari is looking just like Mary and Joseph every time the door bangs shut in their faces on those *posada* nights. "What I can do is tell him whatever you want, okay?"

"Tell him we miss him," Mari says in a quivering voice. "Tell him we love him."

"I will, I promise. Please, don't be sad." Mom puts her arms around the young girl. "We're going to do all we can to get your uncle home as soon as possible, either to Mexico or here."

Mari manages a small smile that Tyler can tell costs her a big effort to muster. It makes him feel even sadder than if she'd burst into tears. When she heads outside, he follows. "Give me the letter." Tyler doesn't know how he's going to do it. But it's one thing he knows Mari really wants for Christmas. "I'll get it to your uncle, promise."

Mari hesitates. "But your mother said . . . ," she begins. Then that hopeful look comes on her face again as she hands over the folded-up pieces of notebook paper. It goes through Tyler's mind that it's too bad that Mari didn't have the box of stationery the Paquettes are giving her tomorrow for writing her uncle a letter today.

"Tyler," she calls after him. "Thank you."

Don't thank me yet, he feels like saying. But then, he has until tomorrow to make good on his Christmas promise.

Tyler must have inherited his grandmother's storytelling genes, because he tells his mom a pretty good tale about why he has to visit Felipe in prison this morning.

"I promised Mari to bring her back a personal report."

"I can do that," Mom says, eyeing him closely. "Besides, I'm not sure they let in kids."

"I'm not a kid," Tyler declares.

"I know you're not." Mom smiles fondly. The thin edge of the wedge is in the door. "But they're going to take one look at my little man in his boy disguise and say no."

"Please, Mom." Tyler can see that his mother is struggling to find reasons why he can't visit. Before she can begin numbering them, he goes on. "Remember how you asked me to find out what the Cruzes wanted for Christmas? This is what Mari told me she wants."

His mother considers, then sighs, giving in. "I guess there's no harm in trying. Worst comes to worst, you can wait in the car."

Ms. Ramírez arrives with the lawyer. At first, Tyler thinks the redheaded man in jeans with a teensy earring in one ear must be his Spanish teacher's boyfriend. But no, it's Caleb Calhoun, the free lawyer from Burlington. When Mom asks him if it's going to be okay to bring Tyler along, Mr. Calhoun just shrugs. "It'll depend on the deputy, if he's having a good day." What kind of a lawyer answer is that? No wonder he's free!

But at the county jail, they're in luck. The deputy in charge today is Uncle Larry's friend. What's more, he's in a holiday mood. He doesn't say a thing about Tyler being a kid. As for the rule about each prisoner being allowed only three visitors at a time, the deputy can't see any harm in this foursome, as one's a lawyer and another's the translator. "That makes two visitors by my count."

He leads them up some stairs and down a long hallway to the visitation room. "Anything on your person you got to leave behind in one of them," he says, pointing to a row of tiny lockers lining one side of the hallway. On the other side are small high windows with bars. It's the first real sign that this is a jail instead of a hallway at the high school or the boys' locker room at the gym. To enter the room, they have to walk through a metal detector. Mom has to leave her car keys in a little basket, but Mr. Calhoun is allowed a pen and pad. Thank goodness letters don't set off any alarms, Tyler thinks as he goes through the doorway with Mari's folded-up letter in his pants pocket.

The room is small, with a glass wall at the far end. In front of it are two chairs and a narrow counter with a phone on top. On the other side of the glass, the same arrangement. It turns out that prisoners and visitors talk by phone, looking at each other through that thick, probably bulletproof glass. Now Tyler understands what his mom meant by a no-contact visit. There is no way he's going to be able to hand over Mari's letter.

"Just call me when you're done," the deputy says, nodding at a wall phone by the door. As he leaves, locking them in, Tyler feels a jolt of fear. And here he's just *visiting*. Imagine what Felipe must be feeling.

After a few minutes, the door on the other side of the

glass partition opens. The same deputy leads Felipe out and nods to where he's supposed to sit. Felipe looks around warily like he might have been dropped off in some room where he's going to be tortured. When he spots Tyler and Mom standing on the other side of the glass, his face breaks into a huge grin. Tyler waves to him and he waves back.

First Mom introduces Ms. Ramírez and Mr. Calhoun. They sit in the two front chairs, handing the phone back and forth, Mr. Calhoun explaining, Ms. Ramírez translating. They tell Felipe what all is in store for him. The criminal hearing once the holidays are over. The sentencing. Then the deportation hearing. Even though Tyler can't hear what Felipe is saying at his end, he can tell that the poor guy is getting more and more heavyhearted with the news.

"Please do assure him that I'm going to try to get this criminal stuff dropped. Ask him if he's got any kind of a record."

Felipe shakes his head when Ms. Ramírez translates. But then he hesitates and tells some crazy story about a little dog in North Carolina that a lady he worked for thought he stole. Maybe she reported him to the police. Mr. Calhoun takes notes.

When it's finally Tyler's turn, he feels awkward and shy, like when he has to talk on the phone to Aunt Roxie and Uncle Tony. "*Hola, ¿cómo estás?*" he starts. Behind him, he can feel Ms. Ramírez beaming at how good his Spanish pronunciation has gotten.

Felipe seems genuinely happy to visit with Tyler. He

rattles off some stuff in Spanish, but every once in a while he switches into English. How're Mari, Ofie, Luby? *¿Mis hermanos?* which Tyler knows means his brothers. Please give them my greetings. And Sara and Tyler's dad? And Ben? Tell Ben not to feel bad. How's Oklahoma, Wyoming, Nevada? And Wilmita? Is she very sad?

Tyler laughs. Even behind bars, on the other side of bulletproof glass, Felipe hasn't lost his sense of humor.

"I have a letter for you," Tyler finally says, reaching into his pocket. He can't read it because, of course, it's in Spanish. Somehow, he knows having Ms. Ramírez read it over the phone won't be the same as Felipe reading it himself. So he unfolds the letter and holds page after page flat against the glass, half expecting some alarm to go off.

Tyler doesn't know what the letter says, but as Felipe's eyes move across each page, his face softens with feeling. When he is done with the last page, he puts his palm on the glass where the paper is, then rests his head on the back of his hand. Tyler tries to hold his own hand steady, willing himself not to cry.

When Felipe drops his hand, Tyler can see he, too, is fighting back tears. He really is just a kid, no disguising it, with man-sized troubles.

"Thank you, my friend," he tells Tyler in English over the phone. "My Christmas today."

This is what Christmas is all about, Tyler thinks as they drive home. What Mary and Joseph must feel at that last *posada* house when the door flies open and there's room for them inside after all. Tyler can't wait to tell Mari exactly how he delivered her letter. In fact, he decides to write down everything that Felipe said and put it in a card and give it to Mari as a present tomorrow.

Back home, he is writing away when the phone starts ringing down the hall. It's probably Mari calling for the Cruzes to find out how the visit went. But no, the minute they arrived, his mother and Ms. Ramírez and Mr. Calhoun headed for the trailer with their report. They did promise not to tell Mari about Tyler's surprise.

Down the hall in the kitchen, Sara is saying, "*Un momento, por favor.*"

And then she is calling for Tyler in this excited, house-on-fire voice. "Tyler!!! Tyler!!! Run next door and get one of the Cruzes. I think it's the mother!"

Tyler bolts out of his house like it is on fire. But the only thing burning is the happy tears in his eyes, borrowed from his sadness. He can't believe it himself, but merry Christmas! Mari may be getting every one of her wishes after all!

Querido Tío Felipe,

We have been so worried about you since that horrible night three weeks ago when the *patrón*'s wife came over with the news that you had been stopped by the police.

(Although this letter is in Spanish, I don't want to mention any names and get anybody in trouble. My family's won't matter since nobody at the jail knows us anyhow.)

Neither Papá nor Tío Armando realized that you were going off the farm when you accepted the invitation from the *patrón*'s son. They assumed the party would take place at the *patrón*'s house. But they say that they don't blame you. You deserve a little fiesta now and then after the hard way you have been working to help the whole *familia* since you were fourteen and came to this country! And before that, Papá has told us, when you were even younger than little Luby, you were already helping Abuelote farm in Las Margaritas.

Finally, thanks to the Virgen of Guadalupe, to whom I made a special petition, we have found out where you are. We feel so much calmer knowing you are close by, even if you are behind bars. I don't think any of us in the family could stand someone else we love disappearing, like Mamá has disappeared. (Ten days ago marked one whole year since we last saw her. I cried so hard. . . . But I don't want to make you any sadder.)

Papá and Tío Armando want me to send you special thanks for running *away* from the farm rather than leading *la migra* here by returning home. "That brother of ours has courage!" Papá and Tío Armando have both said many, many times.

So, even though this country is treating you like a criminal, you are our hero! I speak for all of us, including my little sisters. We want you to know what we have asked for from the American Santa Claus and from the Three Kings: your safe and quick return to our family, either here or in México.

Early this morning, as I was writing this letter, Ofie asked what I was doing.

"Writing to our uncle. I will give the letter to the *patrón's* wife to deliver."

"What are you writing about?" she kept pestering. You know how nosy Ofie can be!

I wanted to scold her to leave me alone so I could finish the letter before the *patrón's* wife left for the jail. But it being the day before

Christmas, I tried to be patient and explain that I was telling our uncle that what I wanted for Christmas was news of his safe and quick deliverance.

My sister stood by like she was debating something with herself. I knew because she was biting her fingernails (which is what all three of us do when we are nervous, and Papá is always telling us not to). Finally, she said, "Tell Tío that's what I want for Christmas, too. I'm going to pray right now to Santa. I'll ask the Three Kings for my dollhouse and my Barbie and beauty salon and lip balm instead."

Poor Three Kings, loaded down with all of my sister's gifts! They will definitely need another camel.

Meanwhile, dear Tío, you will get nothing as we are not permitted to send you food or a gift or even a phone card. But thank goodness Santa has a whole team of reindeer to carry all the hugs and kisses we are sending you!

xoxoxoxoxoxoxoxoxoxoxoxoxoxoxoxoxoxo
Each one is *un besito* (x) and *un abrazo* (o),

Mari

31 *diciembre* 2005

Querido Tío,

This is the last day of the old year, and as
Papá says, good riddance. May the new year bring
you safely home! I hope that you can stay in the
United States because our family is not the same
without you, Tío. How we miss your beautiful
guitar playing and songs and your great stories
and jokes.

I know you miss your guitar, too. The *patrón's*
younger son told us that you asked if you could be
allowed to have your Wilmita with you, but it is
not permitted. It made me wonder what I would
miss the most if I were locked up in a jail. Besides
my family, it would be my letter writing (though I
think this is permitted) and then very small
things like catching snowflakes on my tongue or
looking up at the stars on a clear night.

Maybe it just makes you miss your freedom
more to hear me mention these things? But
sometimes, Tío, like when you sing *"La
Golondrina"* and feel transported back to México
through the song, something similar happens
when I write. Mamá once told me that just
writing a letter to someone would make me feel
less alone, and she was right! I have written to
her, and even to Abuelita, and while I am

writing, I feel they are back. Also, when I write you these letters, it's as if I am talking face to face with you again. And not only that, Tío, but I am able to tell you things I never could in person.

The *patrón*'s wife told us that you are in jail with seven other men, and a half-dozen jailers, none of whom speak Spanish. She said that one of the deputies told her everybody feels sorry because you have no one to talk to. Which is why they allowed the *patrón*'s wife to bring you that box of cookies my sisters and I made with the grandmother just for you. I'm sorry the parrots came out looking like socks with beaks.

We also met your lawyer, who came over with the *patrón*'s wife and our Spanish teacher after their first visit to introduce himself. He doesn't look like a lawyer—don't you agree? Maybe it's his red hair or how he wears jeans and a little earring in his ear like a girl. (I know pirates wear them, too.) But he is very smart and has told me a dozen times he wants to learn Spanish so he can defend the rights of oppressed people from the impoverished Americas. When he talks like that I feel embarrassed that I have a brand-new backpack and a tummy full of parrot cookies and a warm bedroom with stars on the ceiling that I'll tell you about later in this letter.

First, I have very exciting news: we think Mamá called! While we were meeting in the trailer after that first visit, the *patrón*'s younger son came racing over to report that our mother was calling us on their telephone. We all ran out of the trailer like it was in flames, across the yard to the *patrón*'s house. The sister was standing in the kitchen, clutching the phone to her chest like she was afraid it might run away from her. Papá grabbed it and cried out, "*¿Mi amor?*" When he kept repeating the same words over and over, my heart sank. I knew what must have happened. The call had been disconnected.

We did not know what to do! Then Sara remembered that you could hit a certain number to call back the caller, but by the time she'd gotten the phone back from Papá, who didn't want to let go, it was too late. The phone on the other end just rang and rang.

After we got back to the trailer, we called Abuelota and Abuelote to see if maybe Mamá had called them. But no, Abuelota said, they had not received any calls. Then every one of us got on quickly to wish them a merry Christmas. "*Feliz Navidad,*" they wished us back. As we were saying goodbye, Abuelota asked, "What about Felipito? Are you not going to put him on?"

Papá made an excuse that you were still at work, as he did not want to worry her. But he is already wondering how we are going to handle your absence when we call again tomorrow to wish them a happy and healthy and prosperous new year.

The lawyer is trying to see if the jailers can allow you a phone card. He said that prisoners are only permitted to make collect calls on the jail phone, but we explained that Abuelota and Abuelote don't own a phone, and the grocery store where they receive their calls would never accept a collect call. But the jailers have been putting aside many rules as you are a "special case." Most Mexicans are sent right down to Boston or New York to big deportation centers, but because you have a criminal charge, you have to stay in the friendly neighborhood jail until that's cleared up. Lucky-unlucky, as Papá always says about you.

Before I close with all our best wishes for next year, I hope that you have noticed the beautiful stationery this letter is written on, a Christmas gift from the *patrón*'s family. Now that you can receive letters, this one will be in your actual hands, not on the other side of the bulletproof glass, as the *patrón*'s younger son described in a card he gave me for Christmas. And guess what else he gave me? Some beautiful little stars that you paste on your ceiling and they glow in the dark. I told the *patrón*'s son that they must have been invented by a prisoner who missed seeing the night sky.

I am slipping one of them inside this
envelope. She is like the seventh sister of the
Pleiades that you can't see with just your eyes the
way you can her six sister stars. But the *patrón's*
younger son showed her to me with his telescope!

Keep this lucky star until you can look at the
real ones in the night sky once you are free.

Muchos besitos y abrazos,
Mari

7 *enero* 2006

Querido Tío,

Yesterday was Three Kings Day and we had a
special dinner at the grandmother's house.

We had told her how on Three Kings Day,
Mexican people make a special cake that has nuts
and fruits, which she said sounded just like
fruitcake. The only thing is the American
fruitcake doesn't have the little baby Jesus inside.
In México, whoever gets the baby in their slice
has to throw a big party on February 2nd, which
is Día de la Candelaria, or Day of the Candles,
when Jesus was baptized.

"Why, that's our Groundhog Day," the
grandmother said, shaking her head. She

explained how on that day Americans wait for the groundhog to tell them if winter is over. "If he comes out and doesn't see his shadow, that means an early spring. If he does, six more weeks of winter. It's ridiculous," the grandmother agreed when she saw the look on our faces. "You know, I think I must be a Mexican at heart. I like your holidays so much more than ours!"

So the grandmother decided to have everyone to supper and celebrate Three Kings the Mexican way. Only thing is they don't sell baby Jesuses to put in your fruitcake here in the grocery stores. But Ofie offered to let the grandmother borrow the teensy baby that came with her dollhouse family. Guess who got the piece with the baby inside it? Me!

But I won't throw a party unless you are free, which I am hoping will be soon so we can celebrate Candlemas all together.

Now that we're back at school, I worry that these two mean boys in my class will find out about you being in prison and make fun of me. It is not that I am not proud of you, Tío, just that I don't know how to defend myself against them. I am writing their full names here so the police know to look out for them, Ronnie Pellegrini and Clayton Lacroix.

My Spanish teacher has promised not to say anything about your capture. She says it's nobody's business. We think of her as our *madrina* because she has been like our godmother in this country. "And you are *las hijitas* I never had," she told us the other day. I didn't dare ask her why she hadn't had any kids, but you know Ofie, how bold she can be. Our *madrina* replied that until very recently, she had not found the right man. "So why don't you have one now?" Ofie asked. Can you believe her rudeness? Thank goodness Papá was not around to correct her. Ofie might as well have said, You are getting too old, you know. Our Spanish teacher is about Papá's age, or older.

She just laughed and told Ofie, "You better talk to my gringo about this!" That's what she calls her boyfriend, "my gringo"—to his face! She says he just laughs and calls her right back "my hot tamale"!!!!

Last Monday, the government offices opened again after the holidays, so the *patrón*'s wife says your criminal hearing could happen as soon as next week. We know that the deputy is getting permission for you to call Abuelota with the phone card we sent. She still just thinks you have gotten work at another farm and that is why you are calling separately. Papá says to please play along. When you are released, that is soon enough for her to know what has happened.

We have not heard again from Mamá, but

Papá called his old friend in Carolina del Norte, the one who had promised to deliver our new number to the people now living in our old apartment. He said he had been delayed in his promise as he had been down in Florida picking oranges. But as soon as he got back a few weeks ago, he did drop in, and one of the men now living there said that before they disconnected the apartment phone—they all just use cell phones—several people had called for us and he had given them the number we had left taped to the wall. Papá's friend said he gave the new tenants our correct number with an urgent message that if a woman with Mamá's name dropped by, to please tell her to call us immediately.

Papá warns us that we must not let ourselves hope too much, but as you yourself say, Tío, hope is the poor man's bread. So I'll eat as much as I can stand with butter and sugar and jam—butter for your release, sugar for Mamá's return, and jam for the big party I'm throwing once we are all reunited as a family!

With hope and *esperanza*,
Mari

Querido Tío,

This is a quick note because I did not think anyone would be visiting you today. The *patrón's* whole family went to Boston for an aunt's birthday party this weekend.

Papá and Tío Armando were just returning from the morning milking when we heard a car on our driveway. We always get nervous when that happens, especially with the *patrón's* family gone, but it was our Spanish teacher on her way to visit you. She wanted to know if we had any news or letters or packages to send. The sheriff is now allowing you to receive books and clothes as well as letters. They have to be left at the front desk to be checked out first to make sure there is nothing illegal hidden inside a pocket or a hollow book like we saw in a movie.

So while Papá and Tío Armando quickly make up the package that accompanies this letter, I am writing to say that we heard already from the lawyer that your hearing is set for next Friday, January 20th. It might be that you are out in time for Candlemas, after all, and I will get to throw my party!

Speaking of parties: the other letter I am sending along is one the *patrón's* older son brought over. It's from some girl you met that night you went to the party with him. She heard what happened and she wanted to write you. The *patrón*'s older son said this girl also wants to visit you in jail if you will allow it.

When he heard this, Papá just scratched his head and laughed. "There's that lucky-unlucky brother of mine again!" Papá claims that you have always had the worst luck and the best luck, often side by side. "He'll come out of jail with a big fine *and* a girlfriend!"

I have to close as my Spanish teacher says she doesn't want to miss her visiting time slot at the jail. But please let us know if your gringa comes to visit you. Tío Armando says to tell you that he hopes that even if she is American, she is also a hot tamale!

xoxoxoxoxoxoxoxoxoxoxoxoxoxoxoxoxoxo,
Mari

21 enero 2006

Querido Tío,

We were disappointed by the news the *patrón*'s wife brought us last night. We thought the hearing yesterday would decide things once and for all. But it turns out that it was just a hearing, like the word says, for the judge to hear the charges. Next Thursday, you are to return to this same judge, who will then sentence you.

The other disappointing news is that the sentence for your offense is usually no less than three and no more than six months, but you have only served a little over a month. Still, the lawyer said the judge might decide to set you free. That would be the lucky part. The unlucky part is that you would then go right into *la migra's* hands!

I know I should not worry you, Tío, but if as Mr. B. said in class, the truth will set you free, then perhaps this truth I am telling should get you out of jail and into México next week.

Abuelota and Abuelote now know that you are in jail. We didn't know how on earth they had found out. But it turns out that Tío Armando had told his wife, and Papá says telling her anything is like broadcasting it on the radio. Abuelota is so worried that you are being tortured and going without food. Papá told her that American prisons are like country clubs compared to the ones in our country. But I've never been to a country club with bars on the windows! In fact, I've never been to a country club at all. I've only seen some on TV. Papá, of course, once worked on the grounds of a fancy one in Carolina del Norte, which he said hired a lot of Mexicans.

So please, if you can use the phone card we are putting in this envelope, please call poor worried Abuelota and Abuelote and tell them how much you are enjoying your country-club jail with its swimming pool and excellent food and wonderful service provided by Mexicans.

Lots of love and *mucho amor*,
Mari

28 enero 2006

Querido Tío,

We know you have two good reasons to be happy! Your lawyer reported that the judge at your hearing on Thursday said that you had suffered enough, especially being locked up during the holidays with no family to visit you. She would not insist you serve another two months.

Now you are in the hands of Homeland Security and your deportation hearing is next week. I know that this part is not welcome news as it means more waiting without knowing your fate. But at least the judge asked that the process be "expedited," which means rushed, so you can get on with your life.

"Are you married, young man?" the judge asked you. "Do you have children?"

You seemed unsure why the judge wanted to know such personal information. But you shook your head and explained that you had been working since you were a boy helping your parents and six sisters and brothers. You hadn't had any time to court a girl, much less marry one and have kids.

"I hope your *tío* didn't tell them about Wilmita," Papá said. I love it when he makes a joke. Usually, he is so sad and hardly talks at all. "Maybe now in prison, Tío Felipe will have the free time to court this *americana*," Papá added. Last Saturday, the *patrón's* younger son said their visiting was cut short as another visitor had also signed up to share your hour.

His mother and your lawyer and our Spanish teacher were all very surprised, as they thought they were the only ones you knew in this area besides your family, who can't visit you for reasons I won't go into.

When they came downstairs, they found the second reason you must be very happy. The mystery visitor waiting to go up was an American girl, about the older son's age, who spent last summer working in an orphanage in México, so she speaks a whole bunch of Spanish.

I asked the *patrón*'s younger son what she looked like. He shrugged. "Normal."

That was no help at all. So I had to go piece by piece: What color is her hair? Is she tall? Short? Is she thin?

But it was hard to fit all his piecemeal answers into a whole picture. Finally, I gave up and just asked, "Is she pretty?"

The son shrugged again and said he didn't know!

But then when the older son came for the weekend to pick up his car that his parents are finally going to let him take back to school, he dropped in for a visit. So Tío Armando asked him if this girl was *bonita*.

"*Muy, muy bonita*," the son said. "A real knockout!"

Knockout? I know from the *lucha libre* fights my uncles watch on TV what a knockout is, but it doesn't sound like something you'd want a girlfriend to do to you.

The son was laughing. "*¡Muy, muy caliente!*"

Very, very hot?! Knockout?! Why doesn't this older son speak regular English or Spanish? Isn't he supposed to be in college? But my uncle and

Papá seemed to understand because they couldn't stop laughing.

So even if you are deported to México, Tío, this girl already knows her way to México and can visit you in Las Margaritas. It should be a lot more fun than visiting you in jail.

Buena suerte and good luck,
Mari

4 *febrero* 2006

Querido Tío,

Candlemas came and went and I didn't throw my party as you still are not free. Your deportation hearing was yesterday, but it won't be until next week that you will be on your way to México.

Papá says that once we get the call from Las Margaritas that you have arrived, we should invite the *patrón's* family and your lawyer and our Spanish teacher and her gringo and the grandma for a special meal to thank them for all the ways they have helped us during this difficult period.

I know I should be happy that you are finally going home, but it is not very welcome news for my sisters and me.

Without you, who will make us laugh, Tío? And we could sure use your help right now as Papá has made a new rule: only Spanish TV in this house.

It started when Ofie announced that she was not moving to México. This came up when you were caught and Papá was preparing us for the eventuality that we might all be deported.

Papá seemed to be waking up from a long dream that started eight years ago when he and Mamá and I came to this country. His shoulders slumped as if he were carrying a heavy load.

The very next morning, Ofie asked, "Papá, *necesito dinero* for my lunch *porque hoy sirven* grilled cheese sandwiches."

Papá was on his way out the door to start milking. He stopped in his tracks. *"En español,"* he reminded her. He already knew that Ofie wanted money to buy her lunch instead of taking leftover tortillas and beans. But he wanted her to ask him in Spanish.

Ofie folded her arms and stood her ground. "I'm American. I speak English."

Papá gave her several slow nods. *"Bueno, americanita, tendrás que comprar tu almuerzo con tu propio dinero."*

"That's not fair," Ofie cried. "Why should I buy lunch with my own money that I already spent!" The little American girl had understood every word of Papá's Spanish!

Papá put on his *no comprendo* face that he wears when an American approaches him speaking a mile a minute. He finished zipping up his jacket and walked out the door. That night, when he and Tío Armando returned from the evening milking, he turned the TV to a Spanish channel. "*Se terminó la televisión en inglés,*" he announced. No more English or Spanglish in the house. We had to practice our Spanish.

What an outcry from Ofie! Luby, who always starts crying when someone else does, joined in. Off they both went in a huff to our bedroom. I followed to counsel and comfort them. I guess by now with Papá always telling me I'm the little mother, I have become one.

"I have an idea," I proposed. "Why don't we all try speaking just Spanish for a few days."

"But we're American," Ofie countered.

"Nobody can tell us what to do." Luby added her two cents she'd borrowed from Ofie.

Not a good start. "You *are* Americans," I agreed, trying a different tack. "But remember, America is the whole hemisphere, north and south. We are *all*-American! *Raíces méxicanas y flores norteamericanas.*" I made believe I had a bouquet of flowers, with Mexican roots and North American flowers. I took a whiff and offered them each a little invisible bunch. They giggled.

Finally, they were listening. As you used to say to me, Tío, I would make an excellent lawyer because I know how to move the heart with words—if only I were bolder.

"*¿Bueno?*" I asked. "How about it?"

Luby looked over at Ofie, who nodded reluctantly. "Okay," she agreed.

"You have to say *de acuerdo*," Luby reminded her.

"I'm not starting till tonight," Ofie snapped. She always has to have the last word. Maybe *she* should be the lawyer!

So that night we had our first all-Spanish supper in a long time. Only once did Ofie mess up. "Please pass the milk," she asked Papá.

Papá had picked up the jug, but now held it in the air, waiting for Ofie to correct herself.

"I mean, *por favor, pásame la leche.*"

Papá laughed and passed her the milk. I guess he decided to allow Ofie two words in English!

And, Tío, I think my plan is working. Already, Papá says that this weekend, Ofie and Luby can watch their cartoons in English, provided they switch the channel to Spanish during commercials.

By the way, while we were eating our supper

en español, the telephone rang. It was the visitor Papá and Tío Armando are already calling your girlfriend. She was calling to tell us that she is going to Chiapas during her spring vacation. If we want to send anything to our family, she will carry it down for us. Right away we asked if she would take your Wilmita. She hesitated until we explained Wilmita was your guitar.

"In that case, sure!" She laughed. "I thought one of you sisters wanted me to sneak you across."

On Candlemas Day, I asked the grandma about the groundhog, if he had seen his shadow or not. "I'm afraid he did, dear. As they say, if Candlemas is bright and clear, there'll be two winters in the year. So we've got some more winter left."

I didn't need the groundhog to tell me that. Just the fact that you won't be coming home means that winter will be with us for a long time.

That same night, we lit candles, and Papá and Tío Armando told us how back in Las Margaritas on Candlemas the priest blessed all the seeds for planting in the spring. "It was always a time of looking forward to the promise of the future," Papá reminded us. "Not anymore," he muttered bitterly.

But I am looking forward to something in the future: seeing you again, Tío. Until then, I will be like that groundhog and crawl back into the hole in my heart to sleep out the long and lonesome winter of your absence.

xoxoxoxoxoxoxoxoxoxoxoxoxoxoxoxoxo,

from Luby

xoxoxoxoxoxoxoxoxoxoxoxoxoxoxoxoxoxo,

from Ofie

xoxoxoxoxoxoxoxoxoxoxoxoxoxoxoxoxoxo,

from me!

SIX
Seis

and more winter

(2006)

FARM FOR THE LOST & FOUND

When Tyler asks the Cruzes what they think of their first Vermont winter, they just shake their heads as if there isn't a word in Spanish for how cold it gets in Vermont in winter. In class, when Mr. Bicknell talks about global warming, Mari's eyebrows shoot up.

"María?" Mr. Bicknell calls on her, guessing she has a question.

But Mari just looks down, too shy to speak up. Later, she asks Tyler how it can be getting warmer when it's gotten so cold outside.

"It's not that cold, Mari!" Tyler tells her how some years

181

the temperature has gone down to thirty below zero. "Gramps used to have to wipe off the cows' teats or else the milk would freeze where it dripped."

Now they both look down shyly. For some reason Tyler can't quite figure out, talking about certain body parts with a girl has become embarrassing. Even if the private body part in question happens to be on a cow.

Maybe it's because he's about to turn twelve, which according to Ben is the beginning of adolescence, when all a boy can think about is girls. Tyler's twelfth birthday will be on March eighth, which Mom says is real special as that's International Women's Day. "Best gift I could have given myself, a wonderful, enlightened young man."

Tyler doesn't know about enlightened, but being born on a girls' holiday isn't exactly something he's going to be bragging about anytime soon. Even if he will soon be an adolescent with a mind supposedly wallpapered with girls.

* * *

The day before his birthday is town meeting day, which Tyler has learned in social studies class is something special about Vermont. Once a year, every town in the state meets to talk over and vote on stuff like the school budget and what all needs doing in town: a road to pave, a sign to put up, a new fire-truck hose to buy. A lot of towns hold their meetings at night so that folks who have to work can come. This year Mr. Bicknell gives his class the assignment of attending town meeting and writing a report about it.

Tyler and Mari ride in with Mom and Dad. Grandma has already gone ahead, as she and some of her church friends have made a large sheet cake and cookies and punch to raise money for their youth group trip this year.

Up in the front seat, his parents are complaining about some old guy who always writes letters to the editor. This time his letter was about how a church group shouldn't be allowed to peddle their refreshments at town meeting, as this country believes in separation of church and state. "Grandma sure found her way around that one!" Mom is saying.

Tyler's grandma and her friends agreed not to put up any sign that they were from the church. But in the icing of her sheet cake Grandma traced a church, then stuck a little American flag atop the steeple.

"We're going to be eating a lot of cake this week," his father notes, looking in the rearview mirror at Tyler.

"That's right, Tiger," his mom adds. "Any further thoughts on what you want for your birthday?"

It's a little late to be asking, Tyler feels like saying. Plus his mom already knows. Tyler really wants to go on the field trip to Washington, D.C., that his 4-H club is planning for spring break. But the total cost is close to five hundred dollars, which is more than Tyler is likely to rake in from all the birthday checks he's counting on.

"I know you want to go to Washington," his mom adds when Tyler doesn't speak up. "But, honey, we just can't swing that kind of money right now." She doesn't have to add that Dad's medical bills have stressed the family's budget. Dad feels bad enough as it is. "Maybe we can all go later. Drive down together, camp out—what do you think?"

No, thank you, Tyler thinks. If you strip everything from the 4-H field trip, what have you got left? A family vacation cramped in the backseat with an older brother who doesn't want to be there and a sister complaining she's carsick.

"Never mind," he says grumpily.

"Well, if you think of something else," his mother says cheerily like she doesn't really care. Tyler's birthday wish is just one more item she can now cross off her to-do list.

"I don't want anything else," Tyler grumbles.

Mari looks over worriedly. She and her sisters have been insisting on getting Tyler a gift for his birthday. Tyler couldn't very well ask them for a check. They don't even have a bank account, according to his mother. "I thought you wanted that Red Sox sweatshirt?" she whispers.

"I do from you guys," Tyler says quietly.

Town meeting is being held in their school lunchroom. It's so strange to see all these grown-ups where kids usually sit. The chairs are lined up to face a platform up front, the tables pushed to the other end. At one of these tables, Grandma and her friends are serving up the last of the refreshments. Most of the cake is gone, so if the old fellow happens by, all he'll see is a little American flag flying forlornly above the crumbly remains.

Mom and Dad are detained time and again, saying hi to

neighbors, so Tyler and Mari head for a section where some classmates are already sitting.

Before the meeting starts, Mr. Bicknell motions for Tyler to come out in the hall. It turns out the Boy Scout who was supposed to carry in the flag at the beginning of the program got a last-minute stomachache. Could Tyler take his place and lead the assembly in the Pledge of Allegiance? It's not like Tyler has a choice when his teacher asks him to help out in an emergency. Tyler's just glad that the request came right before the meeting, or he, too, would have had a last-minute stomachache all week long.

On his way back from picking up the flag at the principal's office, Tyler steps into the bathroom. He wants to be sure he doesn't have some cowlick sticking up in the back of his head or his shirt buttoned up wrong. As he's heading out, he spots a folded-up wad just this side of one of the stalls. It's a bunch of money held together with a thick rubber band. Eight crisp one-hundred-dollar bills and sixty-some dollars in smaller bills! Except for when he's playing Monopoly, Tyler has never held this much money in his hands before. And these bills are real.

His first thought is he'll have to report the find so Mr. Bicknell can make an announcement. No one from Tyler's school walks around with this kind of money. It has to belong to someone here for town meeting. Maybe some farmer drove into town and ran some errands, including a stop at the bank's ATM, before heading for the school.

But Tyler has never known any farmer with this much money in his pocket. This is the kind of money that criminals carry around. Probably, the wad belongs to some drug dealer preying on kids who don't know any better. Which makes it dirty money, which Tyler would do well to keep out of circulation.

Besides, there's no wallet, no name, no nothing.

And there's a trip to Washington, D.C., dangling like a carrot on the other side of this choice.

Tyler stuffs the wad in his pocket, telling himself that tomorrow, once he's officially an adolescent, he'll be able to see clearly the fine line between right and wrong that's totally blurred right now. After all, in a few minutes, he has to march up in front of a room full of people, holding a flag with a steady hand, and lead them in saying the Pledge of Allegiance.

Tyler picks up the flag on his way out of the bathroom. For some reason, it feels a lot heavier than it did before, as if a huge stone has been tied to the bottom of the pole.

After the excitement of standing center stage, all eyes on him, Tyler wishes he could be excused. The meeting drags on. Should the town paint new crosswalks or go ahead and bite the bullet and spend a lot more money putting in long-lasting, attractive brick walkways? Should the athletic teams get new uniforms or make do for another year even though the student body voted to change the school colors from maroon and orange? Who wants to look like leaf season all year long?

The motions get seconded, discussed, voted on. But all Tyler can think of is the money in his pocket. What should he do?

Beside him, Mari is scribbling away in her notebook. Tyler better pay attention. After all, he can't just write a report about the first two minutes of town meeting, when an upstanding young man led the assembly in a rousing rendition of the Pledge of Allegiance.

But can Tyler really be considered an upstanding young man if he keeps the money?

Tyler feels confused. It's as if he's lost in some dark wood inside his own head. Seems like a lot of his treasured ideas and beliefs have gone into a tailspin recently. It used to be he knew exactly what was right, what was wrong, what it meant to be a patriot or a hero or a good person. Now he's not so sure. Take his dad, who has to be the most patriotic American Tyler has ever known. But even Dad has had to employ Mexicans without papers to keep his farm. Tyler himself has gotten so attached to the Cruzes that he has even offered to hide them if Homeland Security comes on the premises!

Just a few weeks back, Mari told him how her uncle Felipe was a kind of hero to her family. "He ran *away* from the farm so as not to lead the police to the rest of us," she explained. But doesn't that make him a fugitive, not a hero? According to Mari, Felipe is back in Las Margaritas, but already planning to return to keep helping Abuelote and Abuelota and the whole family. Tyler can't help feeling glad at the thought that his favorite of the three workers might be coming back, even though he knows full well that Felipe doesn't have a legal right to be in this country.

"It's treason's what it is!" An old man's angry voice breaks into Tyler's thoughts. "And it's disgraceful how it's happening right here under our very noses and even our law enforcement people are turning a blind eye to it!"

The old man is standing in the first row, waving his cane. People on either side of him are pulling away. The old guy should actually be using that cane to lean on, since he looks like he's about to keel over with fury.

"Sit down, Mr. Rossetti!" somebody calls out. "You're out of order."

Mr. Rossetti. That's the old guy who wanted to veto Grandma's church group's selling refreshments! The very same fellow who always drives up Mom's blood pressure when he has a letter in the local paper. Every time Mr. Rossetti writes in, it's to criticize one thing or another the young people are doing to America. Since he looks to be about ninety years old, "young people" must refer to most of the folks living in town, if not sitting in this room right now.

"We got laws in this nation and anyone hiring illegals ought to be put behind bars. And I can start naming names if the sheriff's ready to write them down."

Tyler can feel the sweat breaking out all over his body. What if Mr. Rossetti mentions Dad's name? Tyler will be shamed not only in front of the whole town, but in front of all his classmates as well. Wherever Clayton and Ronnie are sitting, they must be gloating! Tyler glances up quickly, checking the rows around him. But it's Mari who catches his eye. On her face is the same stricken look as that time at Grandma's house when she overheard Uncle Larry talking about a raid.

"So I want to put a motion forward that says anyone who's not here legally needs to be rounded up."

The room is deathly still. Up onstage, Roger Charlebois, who's leading the meeting, asks in a croaky voice, "Anyone want to second that motion?" Everyone knows that Roger has a half-dozen Mexicans working on his dairy farm.

A voice comes from somewhere in the middle of the lunchroom. "I'll second the motion." It's only when the person has to identify himself that Tyler makes the connection: Mr. Lacroix, Clayton's father. Beside his dad, Clayton is sitting on the edge of his chair like he's ready to third the motion, even though it's not required.

The floor is open for discussion of the motion. Tyler knows his father's not the type to speak up in front of a whole bunch of people. But his mother is another story. Any injustice or prejudice, Mom is up in arms. Please, God, Tyler prays. He'll forgo the trip to D.C. All Tyler wants for his birthday is for his mom not to get up and call attention to the fact that the Paquettes are harboring Mexicans.

Roger is pointing his gavel in Tyler's direction. For a panicky moment, Tyler thinks he's being called on. The upstanding young man who led the assembly in the Pledge of Allegiance will now weigh in on what he thinks of migrant Mexicans working on the local farms.

"Yes, I have a word to say to Mr. Rossetti and a reminder to all of us." It's Mr. Bicknell, who has stood up behind Tyler.

His teacher's voice has the same urgent-persuasive tone as when he's talking about saving the planet. "First, Mr. Rossetti, I want to ask you where you got the name Rossetti."

"From my father, where else?" the old man snaps back in a smart-alecky voice. A few people snicker, but there's less laughter in the room than Mr. Rossetti seems to have expected, because he gets even crankier and says, "What's your point, Bobby?" Calling Mr. Bicknell Bobby! Tyler feels shocked, even though his teacher's first name is Robert.

"My point, Mr. Rossetti, with all due respect, is that Rossetti is an Italian name." Mr. Bicknell holds up his hands as Mr. Rossetti starts to interrupt. "I know, I know. Your family's been here forever, since the 1880s, when Vermont needed cheap labor to work on the marble and granite quarries in Proctor and Barre. In 1850 there were seven Italians in Vermont, seven, Mr. Rossetti. By 1910 there were four thousand five hundred and ninety-four. What if Vermonters had raised an outcry about these foreigners endangering our sovereign state and nation? Many of us wouldn't be here. Plus we'd have missed out on great builders, hard workers, and terrific pizza."

Now there is genuine laughter. A few people even clap. Roger Charlebois bangs his gavel lightly like he's only doing it because he's supposed to.

Mr. Rossetti has turned pale. He sways a little as if stunned by Mr. Bicknell's flood of facts. It makes Tyler feel kind of sorry for the old man. He has heard his mother talk about how Mr. Rossetti lives all alone at the edge of town in a run-down little house with an American flag on his front porch and a sign that reads TAKE BACK VERMONT on his weedy lawn.

"And one more thing, Mr. Rossetti," Mr. Bicknell goes on. "Not only would we Vermonters have missed out on this rich heritage had we booted out all those Italians, we wouldn't have you here today to keep us all on our toes."

You've got to be kidding, Tyler thinks. Snickers and laughter ripple across the room. But Mr. Bicknell isn't having any of it. "I'm serious. Mr. Rossetti is passionate about his country. Whether or not we share his ideas, we would do well to learn that much from him."

The room goes quiet again. It's as if they are all being reminded of something so easy to forget—how to be a decent human being.

"But the bottom line is that this country, and particularly this state, were built by people who gave up everything in search of a better life, not just for themselves, but for their children. Their blood, sweat, and tears formed this great nation."

Tyler hears a sniffle and looks over at Mari. Her head is bent and there are spots on her notebook where her tears are falling. He wishes he could think of something to say to comfort her. Instead he writes down in his notebook, *Thank you for helping save our farm*, and passes it over so that Mari can read it. Spots keep falling on the page, too late for words to stop them.

*   *   *

Mr. Rossetti's motion is voted down almost unanimously. For the first time ever, Tyler feels he has been part of the making of history. Not because he carried the flag and led everyone in saying the Pledge of Allegiance, but because he has seen democracy in action. People speaking up and reminding each other of the most noble and generous principles that are the foundation of being an American as well as a good person. Mr. Bicknell summed it up best: "We're all born human beings. But we have to earn that *e* at the end of *human* with our actions so we can truly call ourselves humane beings."

As they file out, people come by to congratulate Mr. Bicknell. One of them is Tyler's mother, who throws her arms around Mr. Bicknell and gives him a great big hug. Oh well, at least Mom waited to embarrass Tyler until after the meeting was over.

"You have my vote," she gushes as if Mr. Bicknell were running for some office. "What you said was just so right-on."

"Your son did a mighty fine job himself," Mr. Bicknell responds to Mom's compliments. It's as if he is embarrassed and wants to deflect some attention over to Tyler.

Mom smiles fondly at Tyler. "He never breathed a word about opening the meeting! You know his birthday's tomorrow, International Women's Day." Mom goes into full gear. What a gift Tyler is as a son. How he has always been so thoughtful, sensitive, ready to help out. (He has?)

"You're absolutely right." Mr. Bicknell winks at Tyler. "When I had to decide who should lead us, I couldn't think of a better man."

A. *Better*. *Man*. Wow! Talk about amazing compliments! But instead of a burst of pride, Tyler feels the heavy weight of the wad in his pocket. It might as well be a rock pulling him down into a dark, lost place. He doesn't deserve such high praise from his favorite teacher.

Outside in the hall, a commotion has erupted. Someone's shouting, "I've been robbed! I've been robbed!" Hobbling back into the lunchroom, Mr. Rossetti is waving his cane again and hollering. The story comes out in pieces. He went to the bank to cash his Social Security check before coming to the meeting. Just now when he reached in for his car keys, he realized his money was gone. For the second time this evening he is in such a state that he begins to totter from rage. Arms reach out to catch him as he falls. People are shouting instructions left and right. "Is Dr. Feinberg still around?" someone shouts. But Dr. Feinberg slipped out earlier when he got an emergency call from the hospital. "Somebody call 911." A bunch of people pull out cell phones.

Tyler lunges forward to the old man's side and kneels down beside him. The old man's eyes are screwed shut and his face is pale as death. This is what Gramps probably looked like right before he died. Maybe that's why Tyler doesn't even think about waiting until tomorrow to do what he now knows he should do today.

Tyler shakes the old man's shoulders. "I found your money, Mr. Rossetti," he whispers, hoping no one else can hear him. He's not yet brave enough to confess in front of everybody that he almost kept the money.

The old man's eyes fly open. They are a sad, lonely brown, like Mari's eyes when she talks about Mexico or her mother.

"Really?" The old man's face floods with relief. A small smile works itself like a ripple through the muscles of his face. "There's a reward," he whispers back.

But Tyler has gotten his reward already. It's as if he has cut himself loose from a heavy stone tied around his heart. Maybe he is not a hero, or a patriot, or even an upstanding young man. But Tyler feels older and wiser, as if he has both lost and found himself this town meeting night.

18 marzo 2006

Para toda mi familia en Las Margaritas,

To all my family in Las Margaritas: I hope this letter finds you well!

Abuelota, we are especially happy to hear that you are feeling a lot better. Of course, when you learned Tío Felipe was in jail, you got worse. That is why we did not want to tell you at first. Now we know that there was something you were not telling us! Had Papá and Tío Armando known that you'd been taken to the hospital after receiving the news, they would have rushed down to see you.

Never before have we sent a letter because according to Papá, you don't really have a good mail system. Phone calls to the local store work much better. And of course, we send money to the Western Union office that has opened in town now that so many people from Las Margaritas are working all over the United States. But somehow, it feels extra special to send you our greetings in writing and know that this very same piece of paper I've touched will soon be in your hands.

I apologize for any mistakes in my Spanish. The only time I get to practice writing it is in letters or in my Spanish class with our wonderful teacher, whose family is also from México.

Before I forget, Tío Felipe, thank you for calling to let us know that you arrived safely. You can't imagine how relieved we were! But the one who was the most relieved was the *patrón*'s older son, Ben. It was as if a stone tied around his neck for the last few months had been cut loose. I think I saw tears in his eyes, but I can't be sure.

He was here on Sunday for the party we threw to thank everyone who helped us during those trying months. This was the second gathering in a week, as Tyler had his birthday party on Wednesday. We invited everyone to come in the early afternoon, so we would have plenty of time before the evening milking. Papá and I made chicken with mole sauce, your recipe, Tío Felipe, which didn't taste half as good as when you make it. But everyone was full of compliments, especially your friend, Alyssa, you met at that party.

She drove over with Ben, as they attend the same university. Alyssa repeated her offer of taking anything we wanted to send as she is going to Chiapas to volunteer at a clinic for her spring vacation. Tomorrow she'll come over to pick up this letter along with Wilmita, who is so lonely for you, Tío Felipe.

Señora Ramírez also came to our party, and

she brought her gringo we have heard so much about. Barry is round and fat and jolly with a stomach that he says gets him a job every Christmas at the mall as the Santa Claus. He doesn't know a word of Spanish, but Señora Ramírez is working on teaching him.

That must be why he is so interested in learning the meanings of words. He wanted to know why we call our grandparents Abuelote and Abuelota instead of Abuelo and Abuela, which Señora Ramírez taught him were the names for grandfather and grandmother. I tried to explain how we use Abuelita and Abuelito for one set of grandparents, which is like saying "little grandmother" and "little grandfather," and we call the other set of grandparents—

"Abuelota and Abuelote," Ofie butted in. She always wants to be the one to tell the stories as long as she doesn't have to write them down. "You know why?"

Barry looked very sorry that he didn't know why.

"Because they're fat," little Luby piped up.

"Don't!" Ofie scolded. She was annoyed at Luby for giving away one of the best parts of her story. Now she knew how I felt.

"I still don't get it," Barry said.

Luby puffed up her cheeks to show what she meant by fat.

"They're not that fat!" Ofie contradicted.

"They are too," Luby insisted.

I couldn't believe it! Here they were arguing about what you look like, Abuelota and Abuelote, and neither one has ever laid eyes on you. And they were both partly right. I had told them that you were heavier and taller than Abuelito and Abuelita, not that you were fat.

"Abuel*ote* and Abuel*ota*," I explained to Barry while my two little sisters continued their disagreement. "A lot more of them, get it?"

Barry thought this was very funny and laughed a ho-ho-ho laugh, which must be another reason he gets hired as Santa Claus. Then he patted his big belly and asked if his name in Spanish would be Barrylote? Before I could think how rude it was, I answered, "No, your name would be Barrigón."

Señora Ramírez laughed so hard. Papá opened his eyes at me with a silent rebuke. He must have been surprised. Usually it's Ofie saying the rude things in our family.

"What's so funny?" Barry kept asking.

Señora Ramírez explained that I was making a joke, as *barrigón* means "fat belly" in Spanish. Now my joke didn't seem so funny to me. But Barry laughed his ho-ho-ho laugh again. "You might seem shy, but you are a hot little tamale, aren't you?" I don't know if he was referring to my red face or my fresh tongue. He asked me to call him Barrigón from now on, but no way will I be that rude again on purpose.

Abuelito, these greetings are also for you. You must be missing Abuelita so much! We are sorry that we don't speak to you as often as to our other grandparents. Since you live farther out in the countryside, it is difficult to coordinate when we can call the store that you will be there.

We hear news of you from our uncles in California, who call us from time to time. Always we talk about Mamá. They were the last ones to see her, as they had all traveled north together before they parted ways. My uncles would have accompanied Mamá the whole way, but they already had jobs lined up in California, and Mamá was coming back to Carolina del Norte. I'm not real sure of the way it works as Papá doesn't really like to talk about these matters with me. Depending on where you want to end up and how much you want to pay, you go to one border town or another to be crossed over by a *coyote*. Mamá's coyote had a contact on a reservation, who was going to bring her in an extra-special safe way.

Abuelito, I pray every day to Abuelita in heaven that she look after Mamá and bring her back to us. And I think my prayers might be working! There have been some strange phone calls at the *patrón*'s number next door, a woman speaking in Spanish. Just yesterday, there was another call, but this time it was a man's voice. The *patrón*'s wife only knows a little Spanish, including her numbers up to ten, so she repeated our telephone number slowly several times. She said the guy got real quiet as if he were writing the number down.

I worry that maybe the caller tried to call and we were already gone to school and Papá and Tío Armando were still at the barn milking. The *patrón*'s wife says she herself would have missed the call altogether, if she hadn't forgotten a math test she was giving that day and had to go back home to pick it up. I just hope and pray that the caller will keep trying again and again until he reaches us.

I try not to worry too much. It helps that we have found such nice *patrones* here in Vermont. Tío Felipe can tell you they treat us like we are their family. In fact, the grandmother insists we call her Grandma. Ofie and Luby actually think of her as their only grandmother as they have never met their Mexican ones. I tell them all about you, Abuelito and Abuelote and Abuelota, so they at least know you through my stories. One nice thing that Alyssa did this last Sunday was take all our pictures. She also promised that she'd bring back photos, so we can catch up on what everyone looks like. That will settle it once and for all, Abuelota and Abuelote, how fat you really are!

Ofie and Luby have spoken with you on the phone, so you probably have noticed how they're forgetting their Spanish. Sometimes I even have to translate between Papá and them, imagine! Papá gets upset, but we can't really blame them. All they know is the United States, and they spend their days in school or at Grandma's house, speaking English. Of course, if Mamá were here, it would be different. She always was so proud of México and told us many stories about her life there. Papá works so hard, and when he gets home, all he wants to do is throw himself down on the couch and watch the Spanish channels. It makes him feel happy to be hearing his own language and seeing people who look like us even if they're only on TV. Tío Felipe can also tell you that this state is full of white people, so Mexicans stand out and that makes it easy for *la migra* to catch us.

Besides the grandmother, the wife, and the *patrón*, the family includes three children: one older son I mentioned, Ben, who is studying at the university; a pretty teenage girl, Sara, who is always changing boyfriends; and my special friend, Tyler, who is in my class at school and was my same age up until last week.

I used to feel so alone, neither Mexican nor American. But now that I have a special friend, I feel like I don't have to be one thing or another. Friendship is a country everyone can belong to no matter where you are from.

That's what I wrote about last month for Valentine's Day. Mr. Bicknell had thought up a creative assignment. Instead of sending valentines, he wanted us to write a love story that had happened to us this past year.

He got a bunch of groans in response. "Now hold on, guys," he said, grinning. "I want you to be creative. I mean love in all its dimensions, not just the girl-boy variety!" He stood at the board with a piece of chalk and we had to come up with different kinds of love.

The girls were extra giggly for some reason, and the boys went wild with crazy suggestions, like love for your pet snake or vampire love, where you want to suck somebody's blood!

I decided to write about how we had come to Vermont to help the Paquette family, and what good friends they had been to us. How Tyler had taught me about the stars, and the grandmother had showed us how to bake cookies and given us her extra TV so we wouldn't get bored.

On Valentine's Day, Mr. Bicknell asked us to read our love stories out loud. When I read mine,

Mr. Bicknell asked the class what kind of love I was talking about.

"She's in love with Tyler?" Ashley asked. The girls all started giggling again. The boys hooted. I didn't dare look over at Tyler, but he couldn't have been more mortified than I was.

That day after school, Tyler told me I shouldn't have done that.

I wasn't sure what part of what I had done I shouldn't have done, so I asked him.

"Well, for one thing, telling about your working on our farm. It could get my parents into trouble."

"I didn't say anything about us not having papers," I defended myself. For some reason, I didn't want to keep quiet anymore. "Besides, why do we always have to hide how hard we are working? We are not criminals!"

I should have just dropped it right there, but it felt so good to speak up for once. "You yourself say that if it hadn't been for our help you would have lost the farm."

Now it was Tyler who was angry. I can always tell because his pale face flushes with color. "It's not like we don't pay you."

There we stood, glaring at each other, both mad and hurt and confused. This was happening out in the front of the school as we waited for our bus. Ofie was standing by, all ears, ready to jump in with her opinion. But just then, along come these two bullies in our class, Ronnie and Clayton. The minute they spotted Tyler and me standing together they started chanting a little rhyme:

Tyler and María
sitting in a tree
K-I-S-S-I-N-G.

I didn't think Tyler could turn any redder, but he did! Now I saw another reason why Tyler was upset with me. He had been the only boy in our class to feature in a girl's love story.

Usually, Tyler will avoid a fight, but he lunged at these two guys, throwing his fists around. Meanwhile, Mr. Rawson, our bus driver, must have seen what was happening, as he came bounding out of his bus to separate them. "Paquette, inside," he ordered Tyler, jerking his head toward our bus. "You two, beat it unless you want to go pay Mrs. Stevens an after-school visit."

And that was that. Peace was enforced, but not inside my heart.

Tyler and I soon mended our friendship, especially as his birthday approached. But his words still stung every time I remembered them.

He didn't really appreciate how my father and uncles had helped save his family's farm. It was like we had only done it for the money.

But then Mr. Bicknell gave us another one of his creative assignments. Our class had to attend the town's yearly gathering and write a report about it. At this meeting, Mr. Bicknell stood up and said such beautiful words about people who come to this country because of necessity, and how they are not just helping their families back home, but helping build this great country.

Maybe Tyler's ingratitude had worn an extra-sensitive place in my heart. I began to cry. Tyler must have noticed my tears because he wrote me a thank-you note that made all the difference.

I better hurry up and finish this as Alyssa leaves tomorrow on her spring vacation. Ours won't be until the third week in April. Tyler really wants to go down to this nation's capital with a club he belongs to. But it is very expensive, and although they seem rich to us, the family cannot afford to pay for the trip. The club itself is going to hold a bake sale, which the grandmother is organizing.

But that money has to be divided twelve ways among all the members. Tyler thought he could make up the difference with birthday money, but he did not receive as much as he was counting on. His rich aunt and uncle never even sent him a card.

But then there was an article in the paper about Tyler's club and how they were raising money to go to the nation's capital on a field trip. The picture showed all the members and gave their names. Imagine being famous enough at twelve to have your picture in a newspaper! Right after it was published, Tyler got a call from this old man in town, offering him work for pay. Tyler would go after school a couple of times a week and on weekends and help the old man do things he can't do anymore on account of he's too old, like shovel his walk or help him take out the garbage or carry in his groceries.

This was just what Tyler had been hoping for because his family can't afford to pay him for helping out with the farmwork here, which Tyler will still keep doing, as he is a very hard worker. "You could almost be a Mexican," Papá has complimented him more than once.

So twice a week, after school, Tyler rides the bus to the edge of town and gets off on the block where the old man lives. Then, when he's done, he calls his grandmother to pick him up, as his dad's involved with the evening milking and the mom is getting supper ready. The grandmother has her car back finally; the family had taken it away last November when she kept getting into accidents because she was so sad about her husband dying.

The first time the bus dropped Tyler off, I recognized the old man coming down his front porch. This was the very same old man who had said some not-so-nice things about Mexicans at that town meeting. Tyler had helped him find some money he lost, and the old man offered a reward, but Tyler refused. I suppose when he saw the story in the paper, the old man decided to help out. Still, I would be afraid to work for him, but Tyler says the old man couldn't be nicer.

This past Tuesday, my sisters and I were over with the grandmother when she got Tyler's call to come pick him up. So she invited us along for the outing. She gave me a cake to hold on my lap that she had baked for the old man. Ofie asked if it was his birthday. "Oh, nothing like that," the grandmother explained. "It's just we've got to fatten him up. Poor old Joseph is just skin and bones. No wonder he's gotten so mean."

Well, Ofie was in one of her nosy moods. The whole ride over, she kept asking questions. "Grandma, how old do you suppose Mr. Rossetti is?"

"Oh, I've figured it out from some things he's said. Joseph must be seventy-six, seventy-seven." There was a sweet little smile on the grandmother's face as she spoke. "I remember him when he was a handsome young fellow. There wasn't a girl's heart in the county that didn't flutter when she saw him. Why do you ask?" she said, peering at Ofie in the rearview mirror.

Ofie answered her question with a question. "And how old are you, Grandma?"

"Well, dear, that's not something you normally ask ladies to disclose. But I'm your grandma so you can ask me. I'm seventy-three, or will be this May. You're suddenly very curious about birthdays, aren't you?" She gave a little laugh. "You care to inform me what you're cooking up in that lively head of yours?"

"First, Grandma, how old do people live to be?"

The grandmother suddenly got very sad. "Only God knows that, honey. Look at Gramps." She bit her lip. I turned around and gave Ofie the eye so she would stop before she had the poor grandmother in tears.

But forbidding Ofie anything is like giving her a green light. She stuck her little chin in the air, like she knew better. "I just think you should marry Mr. Rossetti soon before one of you dies."

The grandmother was turning into Mr. Rossetti's driveway, and the old man had come down the porch steps to greet us. Just in time, the grandmother braked really hard. Now I believe what she says about seat belts. That poor cake wasn't belted in, and it jumped out of my hands and smashed against the dashboard and windshield!

The grandmother looked like she was about to die. Meanwhile, Mr. Rossetti had opened the car door and reached in a hand to help her out. "Excellent reflexes, Elsie!" he complimented her.

When we got home, Ofie told Papá that Grandma and Mr. Rossetti were going to get married! I can't believe her imagination. "This must be the month of romance," Papá observed. "The grandmother and her beau, Tío Felipe and Alyssa, and," he added, glancing over at me with a sly look, "the *patrón*'s son fighting for a certain girl's honor." How on earth had he found out about Tyler's fight with Clayton and Ronnie?

I don't know if I figured it out by myself or if I saw the guilty look sneaking across my sister's face. But right then and there, I knew that Ofie had been feeding Papá what Mr. Bicknell calls misinformation! No wonder he has gotten even *more* strict about my going over to Tyler's house even with my sisters.

I tried explaining to him what I wrote for Mr. Bicknell's Valentine's Day assignment. How friendship is a country that includes everybody. All you have to do to belong is be a good friend. But Papá just shook his head like he knew better. "*Más sabe el diablo por viejo que por diablo.*" A favorite saying of his about how the devil knows more because he is old than because he is the devil. I did not want to be disrespectful, but very softly, I asked, "Papá, and what do angels know?"

Just like that, his face lost all suspicion, and he gave me the most angelic smile!

Abuelito and Abuelote and Abuelota and Tío Felipe and *toda la familia*, I certainly hope that Papá is wrong about how you do not allow girls and boys to be special friends. Because if this is so, I hate to say it, but just like my sister Ofie, I would not want to live in México.

Your granddaughter, niece, cousin, and special *amiga*,
Mari

SEVEN
Siete

almost spring

(2006)

INTERROBANG FARM

April is definitely turning into a month of surprises. It's like every day is April Fool's Day. Any moment, Tyler is expecting someone to jump out and say, SURPRISE! APRIL FOOL!

Take all the surprises that have come with his new job.

First of all, who would have thought he'd end up working for Mr. Rossetti? And then, who would have thought that Mr. Rossetti wouldn't be so cranky after all? Or that after losing Gramps, Tyler would find a grandfatherly friend again?

Not that Mr. Rossetti will ever replace Gramps. What

Tyler feels toward the old man is probably similar to what the three Marías feel toward his grandmother. They already have a real grandmother back in Mexico, whose picture Alyssa brought back from her spring break. And yet, all three girls still call Tyler's grandmother Grandma, and they love visiting her. A lot of times, when Grandma picks up Tyler from work, she brings the girls along. Grandpa, they've started calling Mr. Rossetti.

Talk about surprises: Mr. Rossetti with Mexican grand-daughters!

"They aren't Mexican. They were born here, fair and square!" Mr. Rossetti will correct anyone who gets it wrong. No one has corrected him on this point. Ofie and Luby are under strict instructions not to let on that Mari was born in Mexico. For that matter, they're not supposed to admit that their father and uncle don't have the permission papers they need to be here legally. "The least said the better," Mom has instructed Grandma and the girls.

"Nonsense," Grandma says under her breath.

According to Grandma, friendship—and that's what she has with Mr. Rossetti—means you help your friend become a better person. "How else are we supposed to improve ourselves?" she explains to Tyler and the girls. Slowly but surely, Grandma has been working on Mr. Rossetti's improvement, and that involves a lot of baking, visiting, and taking him to church on Sundays.

"It won't kill you, Joseph," she tells him when he grumbles. Mostly, Mr. Rossetti loves any excuse to get to see more of Grandma, whose sad spells seem much improved.

At school, Tyler learns about a new punctuation mark, which Mr. Bicknell calls the interrobang.

"The what?!" Kyle calls out.

"You just used it in your voice." Mr. Bicknell laughs. Now there's someone who loves surprising his students. "An interrobang is a double punctuation mark: a question mark followed by an exclamation point. When you're surprised but you're not sure it's an April Fool's joke. 'The what?!' as Kyle just said. Any other examples?"

Tyler can come up with plenty of them. In fact, April is turning into a whole month of interrobangs.

Mr. Rossetti attending church?! Grandma going to the beauty parlor again?! Tyler headed for the nation's capital after being told by his parents that there was no way they could afford it?!

The girls' mother, lost for over a year, finding her way back to the family again?!

*　　　*　　　*

This last surprise begins one spring evening when Mr. Cruz and Mari come to the Paquettes' back door. Can her father have a word with the *patrones*?

Tyler tags along as they all head for the den. But before he goes in, Mr. Cruz says something to Mari, nodding in Tyler's direction. Mari looks suddenly uncomfortable.

"My father says this is private." Mari shrugs as if to say this is not her idea.

Tyler is not surprised. Recently, he has noticed how Mr.

Cruz—it's not exactly that he's unfriendly, but he seems to be watching Tyler closely as if he thinks Tyler is going to surprise him in a way he doesn't want to be surprised. It makes Tyler feel bad that Mari's father doesn't fully trust him for some reason Tyler is not even aware of.

As soon as he hears the back door bang shut, Tyler heads toward the den, where his parents are having a serious discussion. "This is one time when I do think we should call Homeland Security!" his mom is saying.

"What?! So they can track the husband back to our farm?!"

"Well, what do you propose to do?"

"I don't know." His dad sighs. "I sure can't spare him even if it's just for a week. And how's he going to get there and back? I mean, it's not like he can hop on a plane. And as I told him, I don't have that kind of money lying around to loan him."

"Tyler Maxwell Paquette!" His mother's voice startles Tyler. But she can't very well accuse him of eavesdropping. After all, Tyler is standing in the doorway with his mouth wide open.

"I only came back when I heard them leave," Tyler defends himself. But both his parents are too upset to have the energy to scold him.

Tyler must look worried because his father says, "It's okay, son. Just your mother and I have a private matter we need to settle."

"Up to your room, Tiger," his mom adds.

Tyler interprets the order liberally as his mother just

wanting him to go away and heads over to Grandma's house. It turns out that Mr. Cruz has already been by to ask if the girls can stay in Grandma's care while he travels to Texas. Their uncle will be staying on, but Tío Armando will have his hands full with what used to be a three-man job.

"But why's Mr. Cruz going to Texas?" Tyler wants to know.

Grandma closes her eyes as if she's hoping that it's all a nightmare that will disappear when she opens them again. "You might as well know because María will tell you anyhow. Mr. Cruz has to go buy his wife back from some sleazy guys who are holding her hostage."

"Buy her back?!" Tyler can't believe it. This is the kind of surprise that happens in the violent movies that his parents won't let him watch.

Grandma nods gravely. "I wouldn't go telling your parents, as I don't think Mr. Cruz gave them all the details. He's afraid of losing his job, poor man." Ever since the Cruzes took her in when she ran away from home, Grandma has felt a special closeness to them.

"The little ones don't know, either," Grandma adds. "Except for María, who has to translate for her father. Poor María." Grandma sighs. "What a burden on that sensitive girl."

"How much will it cost to buy her mom?" Tyler asks.

"Three thousand. Dollars, that is." Grandma shakes her head as if she can't believe it.

Tyler can't either. Three thousand dollars is more than the $500 he has put together for his D.C. trip. More than the $860-plus he found in the boys' bathroom. Now he can see what his parents mean about "that kind of money." But then, his grandmother doesn't have that kind of money, either.

"Maybe we can raise it?" Tyler wonders aloud.

"That's more bake sales than I've got left in me." Grandma smiles for the first time this evening.

✳ ✳ ✳

The next day, Mari and her sisters are not at school. As he sits in class, Tyler worries that he'll get home and find them gone. The heaviness in his heart surprises him. It's the same feeling as when Gramps died, compounded by the fact that this is a whole family, and it's not heaven they're going to if they get deported.

After school, as he gets off the bus at Mr. Rossetti's, Tyler's surprised to see his grandmother's car in the driveway. Just inside the back door, Tyler finds Mr. Rossetti and Grandma sitting at the kitchen table. His grandmother has her checkbook open like when she's home paying bills.

Mr. Rossetti is as agitated as he was on town meeting night. There's a kink in his eyebrow and a frown on his forehead. "I disapprove wholeheartedly, Elsie, and I'm not going to be a part of it!"

"Who asked you to agree to anything, Joseph? You're just lending me the money, okay? Let's see . . . I'll need—"

"But I know what you're aiming to do with it." Mr. Rossetti's voice sounds trembly and truly torn apart. "Sit down, son," he says to Tyler. "Your grandmother here's being unreasonable."

"Unreasonable?!" Grandma puts a hand on her hip. "Wouldn't you move heaven and earth to get back someone you love?"

"Elsie, you haven't changed a bit since you were young! Always a dreamer." Mr. Rossetti is shaking his head at her. "And I'm still trying to move heaven and earth to get you to notice me!"

Grandma's face softens with surprise. She sets her pen down and tucks a stray gray curl behind her ear. "Joseph Rossetti. I had no idea."

"Precisely," he says gruffly.

Tyler feels suddenly uncomfortable, like when he happens into the den and Sara is "entertaining" her new boyfriend, Hawkeye. Arms wrapped around each other, they look like they are wrestling.

His grandma sighs, breaking the spell. "So what are we going to do to help out those poor girls and their father?"

Mr. Rossetti agrees with Mom. These smugglers are in Texas. That's American soil under the rule of law. Homeland Security can stand by, and just as Mr. Cruz goes in with the money, boom, they descend on the place. Maybe seeing how he has helped them round up criminals, Homeland Security will reward Mr. Cruz with a visa.

"And you call *me* a dreamer?!" Now it's Grandma shaking her head at Mr. Rossetti.

Tyler and Grandma swing by the trailer on their way home. Tyler has told her that the girls were not at school today. "I haven't seen hide nor hair of them all day long, either," Grandma remarks. "I don't know what we'd do without them," she adds, mirroring Tyler's thoughts. "I know I've become so attached to the whole family."

The men are still milking, but the girls are in the trailer, sitting in front of the TV. Instead of their silly *Dora* cartoons, they're watching a news special about all the protest marches going on in support of immigrant rights. "Papá wants us to tell him in case something is announced," Ofie explains.

Mari accompanies Tyler and Grandma to the door, then slips out after them. "I don't want my sisters to hear," she whispers. There are some new developments. Mr. Cruz phoned back the *coyotes*, which is what he calls the smugglers. He pleaded that he hasn't been able to come up with that kind of money. According to Mari, the *coyotes* lowered the amount to half! Her father and Tío Armando have come up with most of the money. Mari's uncles in California will put in the rest.

"My father thinks that maybe with all the demonstrations, the *coyotes* are all getting nervous to unload their cargo," Mari adds.

Cargo?! Tyler can't believe a human being would think of another human being that way! But he knows what Mari means about the demonstrations. It's all over the news. In cities around the country, there have been big marches by people in favor of changing the laws to help immigrants. Just in Los Angeles, thousands upon thousands of people took to the streets. Then, a week before Tyler's 4-H club is supposed to go on its trip, there's a national strike. People who support immigrants are asked to stay home from work. In D.C. there's a huge protest march. The camera sweeps over the crowd waving American and Mexican flags and chanting *"¡Sí, se puede!"* which Tyler proudly translates for his family. Yes, we can! Yes, we can!

And this makes a whole bunch of people nervous, including the parents of several 4-Hers, who pull their kids out of the trip. What if a riot breaks out? What if there is a paralyzing strike and they can't get back to Vermont? When five kids drop out, the trip is postponed until things quiet down.

Tyler is surprised that he's not more disappointed about not getting to go to Washington. Maybe the freedom-fighting energy of the marchers on TV is catching. Like Mr. Bicknell said the other day in class, the function of freedom is to free someone else.

Meanwhile, Mr. Cruz has allowed his daughters to go back to school. Mari is on cloud nine. "We talked to her last night," she tells Tyler one morning as they wait for the bus. Before sending any money to the *coyotes*, her father insisted on speaking to his wife. After all, it could be one big horrible trick. "She said she loved us. She said she'd see us soon. She said to keep praying hard." Mari is in such a state that even during class, Tyler can see that her thoughts are far away.

But then, one more surprise, and not the good kind. By

evening, Mari is sobbing on her back steps. It turns out that fifteen hundred dollars just buys her mother's freedom to be dumped out on the street in an undisclosed town in Texas where they are holding her. If Mr. Cruz wants a "custom delivery," to North Carolina, say, where the *coyotes* are already sending a whole vanload, that's another five hundred dollars he has to come up with.

Tyler doesn't have to think twice. He has saved that much for his postponed 4-H trip. "Tell your dad I can loan it to him," he tells Mari. That afternoon at the milking parlor, Mr. Cruz comes over to where Tyler is helping feed the cows that are waiting to go in. He reaches for Tyler's hand. "*Gracias,*" he says with emotion in his voice. "*Usted es un hombrecito bueno.*"

Tyler doesn't need Mari to translate her father's words. It's like the compliment Mr. Bicknell gave him on town meeting night. At least this time, he might not be a good young man, but he is getting better.

✦   ✦   ✦

When Tyler comes back inside that evening, Mom is beaming from ear to ear. "Now what?!" he asks. Even he can hear the interrobang in his voice.

"Your aunt Roxie just called. She feels terrible about forgetting your birthday. They were doing a big Mardi Gras party in New Orleans, and then they flew to Brazil to buy this year's used Carnaval costumes for their online store.

Anyhow, we got to talking about your not getting to go to D.C., and they want you to call them, okay?"

Tyler's heart sinks. He can see what is coming. His aunt and uncle are going to offer to take him to D.C. But the money for his trip has already been loaned. He thought he wouldn't even have to tell his parents until Mr. Cruz paid it back.

"It's nothing bad," his mom tells him, but Tyler must still look worried because she goes ahead and tells him the surprise. "Okay, on Friday night, Ben's driving you down to Boston—and then Saturday, you and Uncle Tony and Aunt Roxie and whoever you want to bring along are all going to D.C.! Then they'll drive you back to Vermont before school starts. Isn't that terrific?"

"How much will it cost?" Tyler wants to know.

"They're paying for the whole thing. It's their birthday gift to you." His mom suddenly stops and studies him. "I thought you'd be excited."

Tyler nods eagerly, but his mother doesn't look convinced. "I don't know what's going on, Tyler Maxwell Paquette. One minute you'll do anything to get to D.C. Next minute it's take it or leave it." She shakes her head the way she does over Sara's moodiness. "Anyhow, whatever you decide, just please call Aunt Roxie and Uncle Tony, because I told them you'd be in soon. And please, act surprised, okay? And do thank them, because it was awfully generous of them. Not just the money, but the time—you know how busy they are."

Relief and uncertainty are fighting for ground inside Tyler's head as he dials his aunt and uncle's number.

"Hey, hey, hey, birthday boy!" his uncle calls out. Soon Aunt Roxie is on the other extension singing "Happy Birthday." Uncle Tony joins in. They sing two whole stanzas.

"Will you ever forgive us?" Aunt Roxie sounds like she has committed a major crime, not just forgotten a nephew's birthday.

"He shouldn't," Uncle Tony butts in. "Here we throw parties for the whole world and we forget our own nephew!"

"How shall we make it up to him?" Aunt Roxie wants to know.

Back and forth they talk, like on some sitcom on TV. All Tyler has to do is watch from the wings. When they tell him about the gift they have in store for him, that's his cue. He acts surprised. "Thank you so much," he says gratefully.

"So we'll see you in a few days, buddy," Uncle Tony confirms. He's about to hang up, but Aunt Roxie reminds him, "Wait, we forgot to ask him."

"Tyler, maybe you'd like to invite someone? I thought of your sister," Aunt Roxie suggests. "I mean, there's room. But this is your birthday gift, so maybe you'd rather bring a friend?"

"Yeah." Tyler jumps at the offer. He'd much rather bring a friend. Sara'll want to go shopping. She'll want to go to fancy restaurants where they don't serve hamburgers and Cokes. "Is it okay if it's a girl?"

There is a slight hesitation—an interrobang at both extensions. Then his uncle and aunt chime in, "Why not?"

One more thing. Tyler takes a deep breath. It's been a month of surprises sprung on him, so it's his turn to surprise someone else. "Do you mind if we go to North Carolina instead?"

"North Carolina?!" Uncle Tony makes no attempt to hide the bafflement in his voice.

"What's in North Carolina?" His aunt sounds equally baffled.

"Durham," Tyler tells them. His aunt and uncle burst out laughing, thinking it's a joke.

*　　*　　*

Back at the barn, Mr. Cruz is finishing up in the milking parlor. Tyler tries explaining his plan with his few words of Spanish. His *tío* and *tía* have offered him a trip for spring break. Tyler pretends to drive a car. He has asked to go to Carolina del Norte, where they can pick up Señora Cruz and bring her back to Vermont.

Carolina del Norte, Señora Cruz, Vermont: Mr. Cruz connects enough dots to understand. His face lights up with such joy that Tyler can't help smiling. Mr. Cruz grabs Tyler's arm and gestures toward the trailer. They need Mari's translation help to work out the details of this wonderful surprise.

As soon as he's in the door, Mr. Cruz nods for Tyler to repeat what he said in the barn. Remembering the looks Mr.

Cruz has been giving him, Tyler doubts Mari will be allowed to go on his birthday trip. So he repeats his invitation without specifying which of the Cruzes is to be his special guest.

"My father says thank you." Mari is suddenly talking in English to Tyler. "He says he would like to go, but he needs to keep working to begin paying back his loan. He says it is difficult for my uncle to do all the milking by himself. My father says it's better—if your uncle and aunt would permit it—if I go."

His aunt and uncle driving to North Carolina to pick up Mari's mom?! Her father letting Mari go?!

April is definitely turning out to be a month of inter-robangs. Any moment, Tyler is expecting someone to jump out and say, SURPRISE!

But no one has so far.

22 abril 2006

Queridos Papá, Tío Armando, Ofie, y Luby,

We are already in Boston, and tomorrow we are coming home! I know I will be seeing you before you even get this letter. But my heart is bursting with all the things that have happened since I left you.

Papá, as you are the one reading this letter, you will know what to leave out that my little sisters should not hear. When we've spoken to you from the road on the aunt's cell phone and now from her home, I haven't wanted to say much. I didn't want the calls to cost a lot of money, and also I didn't want to upset Mamá, who was always close by.

Please don't be alarmed when you see her. She is so skinny that I think we could fit into the same clothes. There are marks on her arms and face, but if you ask her what happened, she just cries. That is the worst part, how upset and nervous she is. Any little noise, she jumps. Any little thing, she cries. I don't know what to do except tell her over and over again that she is safe, that everything is going to be all right, that we will soon be together as a family again.

The aunt, Mrs. Mahoney, takes me aside. (She says to call her Roxie, but I just can't get used to it.) She says, "María, bear with her. Your mother has been through so much." It's only now that she and Mr. Mahoney know the whole story.

When we first got to Boston, Mrs. Mahoney said she'd already had three phone calls from Tyler's mom. Mrs. Paquette had started worrying about us picking up Mamá in Carolina del Norte. What if we were stopped on the way back to Vermont?

Sara groaned. "All I can say is I'm eternally grateful to you, little bro, for not leaving me behind to deal with Mom's nerves." At the last minute, Tyler had consented to invite his sister along. But Sara had promised not to bring up shopping or eating at any restaurant with tablecloths.

"Your mother, I love her to death"—Mrs. Mahoney gave her niece and nephew a sympathetic look—"but boy oh boy, is she ever a worrywart. I'm surprised you kids turned out as adventurous as you have!"

"You're telling me." Sara let out a long sigh.

"She wants you to call her." Mrs. Mahoney handed Tyler the phone. "Tell her we'll be fine. We're just picking up Mari's mother and then taking in the sights."

"The sights of Durham," Mr. Mahoney said in the voice of a radio announcer, winking at Mrs. Mahoney.

Tyler gave me a panicked look, then dialed Vermont. "Mom, it's no big deal," he kept saying. "We're just giving Mrs. Cruz a ride home." Afterward, he told me she made him promise, no funny business, which I thought was a strange request as there was nothing funny about what we were about to do.

What Tyler didn't tell her was that I had the envelope with the rest of the money for the *coyotes*. What I didn't tell Tyler was that I was just as worried as his mom! But I couldn't let on. I was afraid that his uncle and aunt would change their minds about picking up Mamá if they knew she was being held hostage.

Tyler assured me that his uncle and aunt would probably love knowing that we were actually rescuing my mother. "They used to have really dangerous jobs," he told me. "My uncle was like a bodyguard in a bar and my aunt had to wear skates to race away from bad guys!"

We drove down from Boston and arrived in Durham late Monday night. Right away, we got a motel with two side-by-side rooms. Don't worry, Papá. One bedroom was for Tyler and his uncle, and the other for us. Papá, I know the custom in México is to be very strict when a girl and boy are together. But as I told you, Papá, it's not like that with me and Tyler. We are just special friends.

Our room had two beds, so Sara and I took

one, and Mrs. Mahoney the other. Once the lights were out, they talked and talked. About clothes and makeup and shopping and huge parties that the aunt and uncle arrange. (Can you imagine throwing parties as your *job*?) Sara told all about her newest boyfriend, who wishes he were an American Indian. The aunt listened and gave her good advice. They even asked me what I thought. Me, who's just turning twelve and won't be permitted to have a boyfriend until I'm at least twenty-five!—right, Papá?

Finally, Sara and her aunt fell asleep. I was tired, too, but I couldn't sleep at all with the anticipation of seeing Mamá the next day.

We woke up to a warm, sunny morning—as it was already spring in Carolina del Norte. After breakfast, we piled into the car. I had stuffed the money in my backpack to hand over to the *coyotes* when we picked Mamá up. But first, we had to find the bus station where they had told us they would meet us when we sent the other half.

The Mahoneys drove slowly up and down the streets. It was a run-down neighborhood, near where our old apartment used to be. I sat in the backseat, between Tyler and Sara, trying hard to act like nothing was wrong. But I was so nervous, I felt short of breath. I was sure I was going to faint. Or worse, throw up.

We finally found the bus station. Before we

got out, Mrs. Mahoney pulled out some balloons and noisemakers and packets of confetti from a little shopping bag she'd brought along with the name Party Animals on it. "To welcome your mother," she explained. She looked so pleased with herself, I didn't know what to say. One thing I knew: those *coyotes* would not appreciate a big welcome scene.

"I think it's better if we just let Mari be by herself with her mom," Tyler spoke up. I felt so grateful to him! "She hasn't seen her for a whole year."

A whole year, four months, and four days, to be exact.

"Oh, okay," Mrs. Mahoney said. She sounded disappointed like a kid told to put her toys away. "You want to go in and check if your mother's already here?" she asked, turning to me in the backseat.

"First I have to call," I explained. It was the politest way I could think of asking Mrs. Mahoney if I could borrow her cell phone.

"Call who?" Mrs. Mahoney asked.

I didn't want to lie to her, Papá. But I also wasn't going to tell her that the *coyotes* had instructed us to call once we were at the station. So I just said, "The people who are bringing her."

Thank goodness that was enough of an explanation. She handed over her pink phone with such teensy keys I kept hitting the wrong ones with my trembly fingers.

You had told the *coyotes* that it would be your daughter who would be picking up Mamá. Still, the gruff voice on the other end sounded surprised to hear a girl calling. One good thing was that our conversation was in Spanish, so I could talk without alarming anybody else in the car.

He gave me the last of the instructions. I was to wait inside the station, keeping a lookout at the glass door. When a gray Chevy van pulled up, I was to come out by myself with the money and hand it to the driver, who would then deliver *mi paquete*. My package! What a way to talk about Mamá!

"Our friend says to wait for my mother inside," I said.

"Are they going to be a while or something?" Mr. Mahoney wanted to know. "We could just take a quick spin and see the sights of Durham." Again, he winked at Mrs. Mahoney, but this time she didn't laugh. She looked preoccupied, like she was starting to suspect something was wrong.

Ay, Papá, I didn't know what to do or say. But for a second time, I was so grateful to Tyler. He opened his door and scooted out, saying over his shoulder, "Come on, I'm getting carsick just sitting in here!"

I followed the others inside the bus station. It

was almost deserted at ten on a Tuesday morning. The Mahoneys wandered around, reading signs posted on different boards. Tyler and Sara got a bunch of pamphlets from a rack about what to do that was fun in the area. They sat down in some plastic seats and started to look them over. Meanwhile, I stayed posted by the door.

The wait seemed endless. But once the van pulled into the parking lot, it had come too soon! How was I supposed to walk out the door and across the parking lot when my feet felt glued to the floor?

"Is she here?" Tyler had come up behind me. Sara and the Mahoneys joined us.

"I better go by myself," I explained, pushing the door open. "I'll be right back," I said in the most casual voice I could manage. I don't know what I would have done if they had tried to follow me.

The bright sunlight blinded me after the dinginess inside the station. The van was idling at the other end of the parking lot, ready to pull out of the driveway. I walked slowly, the money envelope inside my backpack I was holding in my arms. I was hugging it so tight, it was the only thing keeping my pounding heart from bursting out.

When the driver lowered the window, I was half expecting to see a horrible monster. But it was just a Mexican man wearing sunglasses that reflected my scared face. His hair was yanked back roughly into a ponytail like he hadn't bothered to comb it first. His upper lip and chin were covered with black stubble like maybe he was going to grow a beard and mustache but don't count on it.

"*¿Y el dinero?*" was his hello. Where was his money? He needed better manners, a haircut, a shave, a different life.

I pulled out the envelope, and he grabbed it and flung it to an older man sitting next to him. "We count it first," he said, starting to raise the window.

But my eyes had already been drawn to the backseat. There she was, Mamá! Suddenly, I forgot my fears, and cried out, "*¡Mamá! ¡Mamá!*"

"*¡Mi'ja!*" she cried back.

"*¡Silencio!*" The driver had turned around, his hand lifted as if he were about to strike Mamá if she didn't shut up.

My mother's eyes were wide with terror, like when a cow is being loaded into the trailer to take to the slaughterhouse. But beyond the fear, I could see something else. She was taking me in, every inch of my face, with loving amazement, before the window closed, parting us once again.

After the longest minute, I could hear a voice inside call out, "It's all here." The window rolled down again, this time only halfway. "Come around the other side and pick up your package," the driver ordered.

That's when I got really afraid. Up until now, the Mahoneys and Sara and Tyler could see me from the door of the station. But once I went around to the other side of the van, it would be like the astronauts going behind the moon. No one could communicate with them, Tyler had told me. These criminals might grab me and take me hostage as well.

Somehow my feet obeyed. As I was coming around the front of the van, the side door slid open and Mamá was shoved out. She stumbled, and if I hadn't rushed over to catch her, she would have fallen down on the ground. *"Mi bolsa,"* she called out. But the door had already banged shut, and the van was squealing away.

Mamá looked undecided whether to run after it, begging for her bag. But I grabbed her hand and said, *"Vámonos, Mamá."* Soon we were both running across the parking lot just as Tyler and Sara and the Mahoneys were coming out of the station.

"Is everything all right?" Mrs. Mahoney wanted to know.

"Let's just go, please," I begged. I think I was still afraid those horrible men would come back and shoot us or haul me and Mamá away.

I didn't have to ask twice. It turns out that in the few short minutes that I was in the parking lot, Tyler had confessed to the Mahoneys that these weren't exactly friends who were delivering Mamá. We scrambled into the car and drove off. "All I ask," Mrs. Mahoney finally said once we had pulled out of the station, "is that you not breathe a word to your mother or she'll never let you stay with me again."

"Don't worry," Sara promised.

Meanwhile, Mamá was trembling and crying and looking so confused. She didn't know where she was or why she and I were in a car full of strangers. "*Son amigos,*" I kept telling her. "They are our friends." But she kept looking at me with those terrified eyes like she didn't believe it.

None of us knew what to do to calm her down.

"Maybe we should take her shopping," Sara offered. "Buy her something really nice." Even I laughed, nervous as I was.

Tyler glared at his sister. She had forgotten her promise. "I think we should take her to the emergency room and get her some medicine," he countered.

The aunt shook her head. "Last thing we need is for the authorities to be called and for her to be apprehended. Can you imagine?" This last question was addressed to her husband, who looked in the rearview mirror to see if we were imagining it. I sure was. It would kill Mamá if they stuck her in prison after all she had been through!

Suddenly, I remembered all the pictures Alyssa had taken that I had stuffed in my backpack at the last minute. I pulled them out, and one by one I went through them. Mamá snatched them and was eating them up with her eyes: Papá and Luby and Ofie and me standing outside the trailer in our winter jackets. Ofie and Luby and me with Tyler and the grandmother. The grandmother and Mr. Rossetti with Luby between them holding up her two little stuffed dogs. Mamá kept stroking each picture, saying the names she knew over and over.

When she got to the one of Tío Felipe and Abuelota and Abuelote sitting on a bench in the town square, Mamá was surprised. Of course, she had no way of knowing Tío Felipe was back in Las Margaritas. "Oh yes," I told her. "He went for a visit." Time enough later to fill her in on all the upsetting details.

Then, partly for her sake so she'd feel safe, but also for mine, I asked Mr. Mahoney if we could drive by our old apartment building. As the streets became familiar, Mamá started looking out the windows, pointing to the small grocery store where she always shopped for our Mexican food, the Catholic church with the statue of the Virgen de Guadalupe where we used to go to Mass. There were Mexican people on the street. I admit I felt homesick thinking of all we had left behind.

"Why did your father move you?" Mamá asked as if reading my thoughts.

So I explained about the new job, the steady work, how we got to live right on the farm with wonderful *patrones* who treated us like family. I introduced everyone in the car and explained who they were. For the first time, Mamá's face relaxed, and she gave Sara and Tyler the biggest smile. That's when I noticed that several of her teeth were missing. I didn't even want to think how she had lost them.

"We left the new *patrón's* phone number behind at the apartment for you," I went on explaining. I was worried that she might feel that we had run off without leaving a message for her.

"I know, *mi'ja*," Mamá said, nodding. She started crying again, but not agitated and terrified like before. It was a sad, gentle crying as she told about all the things that had happened to her. As if those tears were allowing her story to be flushed out of her. Papá, I am sure Mamá will tell you in more detail. I say this because sometimes she looks at me as if trying to decide how much or what to tell me. But like she says, I have become a young lady in her absence, so she can entrust me with grown-up information.

It turns out that after Mamá left my uncles, she met up with her *coyote* who was taking her through a reservation. But on the way, they got held up by another gang. Mamá now became the property of these new *coyotes*. They brought her to their leader, and—this is where Mamá hesitated and looked unsure what to tell me. "He forced me to be his . . . servant," she said, choosing each word carefully. "I had to cook for him and take care of his clothes and do whatever he told me. He threatened that if I tried to run away, not only would he find me and kill me, but he would track down my family and do the same to them."

She bowed her head a moment, as if just the thought was sending stabs of fear through her. I, too, felt afraid.

"Is she okay?" Sara whispered beside me.

I nodded. I didn't want to interrupt the flow of Mamá's account with a translation. It was important for her to tell her story, not to have to carry it alone inside her.

"About eight months ago," Mamá continued, "this head *coyote* had to go back to his home base in México. He left a brother in charge who was not as vigilant." That's when Mamá started sneaking phone calls. When she called our apartment in Carolina del Norte, she found out that we had moved to Vermont and left a number.

But every time Mamá called the number, a stranger would answer in English. One time, it was a girl, who said something in Spanish, and Mamá was so excited. . . . But by that time, the chief *coyote* had come back, and he caught her on the phone and gave her the beating of her life. "He knocked out two of my teeth," Mamá said, opening her mouth to show me what I'd already seen.

"I began to lose hope," Mamá admitted. "I stopped thinking about escaping. I just wanted to avoid getting hurt or bringing danger to any of you." She stopped and gazed at me with the saddest eyes in the world. Ay, Papá, it just made my own eyes fill, and we held each other for a moment and cried together.

Everyone in the car was real quiet and respectful. Like they could tell Mamá was reliving terrible moments. That is also a reason why I am writing this letter, Papá. So Mamá won't have to repeat this part of the story until she is stronger.

One day, the *coyote* chief's wife showed up all the way from México. For some reason, that woman was furious to find Mamá in the house. It was the only time Mamá saw that *coyote* gangster afraid. The wife made her husband move Mamá to one of his other houses with instructions to contact relatives and collect payment for her delivery. "Get rid of her one way or another," the wife said. Mamá was sure that this was her death sentence. Especially when she heard from her new jailers that you, Papá, and my uncles were having trouble coming up with that much money.

Then, from one day to the next, it was like the Virgen de Guadalupe had been sent to the rescue. (All those prayers I said and candles I lit!) Mamá and some other Mexicans in the house were told to get ready, as they were leaving in an hour for Carolina del Norte. They all had to lie down in the back of the van, covered with a false floor for three days while the *coyotes* drove and drove. From the commentary among the others, Mamá learned why there had been this urgency in moving them. One of the gang's houses had been raided, and the orders from on high were to deliver the cargo as soon as possible.

When the Mahoneys' car stopped at the motel parking lot, both Mamá and I looked up, confused. We had both been so involved in her story, as if we were in that van together, trying to breathe enough air. But here we were, safe and together, surrounded by friends! I felt such a surge of relief and happiness. "Thank you," I said with all my heart to everyone in the car.

"*Gracias, muchas gracias,*" Mamá agreed. "Tell them," she told me in Spanish, "*que les debo a ellos mi vida.*"

"My mother says she owes her life to you," I translated.

"Were they really going to kill her?" Tyler asked in an awed voice.

I turned to face him. "I better tell you later," I said quietly.

Tyler's blue eyes looked directly into mine and I could see he was getting it: I could not talk in front of Mamá, even if it was in another language.

The aunt turned around in the front seat. "I think we should call your father," she reminded me. "I know he must be waiting to hear from you."

We reached you just as you were all sitting down to lunch together. I don't have to tell you how joyful that call was! Very thoughtfully, the aunt and uncle and Tyler and Sara slipped out of the car, leaving us to our private reunion. All of us cried and laughed and talked, taking turns. It was you, Papá, who had to remind us that we must not abuse the generosity of our friends in lending us their cell phone.

Their generosity has not stopped there. That very afternoon, the aunt and Sara and Mamá and me got dropped off at a mall, which made Sara very happy. Tyler was okay because he got to go to the Museum of Life and Science with his uncle. The aunt bought Mamá some underclothes and a toothbrush and little things she had to leave behind in her bag. Mamá kept saying that she didn't have any money, but the aunt shook her head not to worry. Later, the aunt and uncle took us all out to a Mexican restaurant for dinner so that Mamá could have food she might really like. She needs to eat and get strong.

Over the last few days, I've seen her slowly calming down like one of those wild barn cats that you stroke and stroke until it lies in your lap purring. And remember those letters, Papá, that you asked me not to mail to Carolina del Norte? I had brought them along. Mamá has read them half a dozen times already, and each time, she smiles softly, so proud of my stories.

It's only at night that we lose her again. Mamá keeps crying out with a nightmare. We shake her awake, and it takes her a minute or so to realize where she is and who we are. And then she cries again. I feel bad because I know that neither the aunt nor Sara has gotten a good night's sleep the whole way home.

On the drive back, the aunt and uncle had arranged a wonderful surprise for Tyler. They had planned for us to spend a day and a half in this nation's capital after all. I was so glad, because I knew that Tyler had given up his birthday wish to help us bring Mamá home. Now he could get a little bit of what he had wished for.

Papá and Ofie and Luby and Tío, I hope someday all of us can visit this beautiful capital city together! There are so many grand buildings and beautiful gardens and fountains and museums filled with everything you can imagine. Tyler's first choice for a visit was the National Air and Space Museum. We saw the most incredible show in this theater called a planetarium that felt like we were zooming toward the stars. Mamá kept gasping and making the sign of the cross. Afterward, she was full of questions.

"*¿Es verdad?*" she kept asking after each fact I translated. Was it true that the universe began with a big explosion? That those stars were millions upon millions of years away from us? It makes me sad that Mamá and you, Papá, were not able to stay in school past sixth grade, because you are both so eager to learn. You would have been A-plus students!

We even went on a tour of the big white house where the president lives. Mamá could not believe she was inside a president's house, not to clean it, but as a guest! It was hard to pay attention to what the guide was saying, because at every turn I was expecting to bump into Mr. President. I kept wondering if he had received my letter—not that I would dare ask. But we never saw him or his wife or their pretty twin daughters. Later, the aunt and uncle explained that the tours just take you to the rooms open to the public. You never go near the living quarters of the president and his family.

We spent the rest of the time walking around

the city. Even Sara didn't complain or ask to go
shopping. But we didn't see any demonstrators
like we had seen on television. The streets were
calm and full of people enjoying the beautiful
spring weather. Everywhere there were so many
flowers, like Nature was celebrating its
quinceañera.

At first, Mamá clung to my hand, afraid she'd
be picked up. But soon, she, too, relaxed as if she
realized this was not just the capital of one
country, but the home of everyone who loves
freedom.

One of the places we visited was this stone
wall engraved with the names of thousands upon
thousands of soldiers who fought and died in a
war not long ago. The stone was black and shiny,
so you could see your reflection as well as the
blooming trees and the clouds in the sky. We
walked quietly down a winding path beside the
wall, as if into the earth itself, to thank the
soldiers who had died for us. Every once in a
while, a visitor would stop, head bowed, touching
a name, whispering a prayer. It was beautiful in a
sad, solemn kind of way. The same feelings as
when we sing *"La Golondrina"* and think of a
home we might never see again.

Mamá seemed to understand this place even
before it was explained. "Each of those names left
behind a grieving family." She sighed and stopped

to stroke the wall herself. Maybe she was thinking of all those she had left behind. I know I was thinking of how we grieved for her during her absence. But unlike the names on that wall, she has come back to us.

We drove north the next day, and as Mamá and Sara dozed in the backseat, I gazed out the car window. The leaves were retreating back inside their stems, the green meadows were becoming brown, the windy sky steel-gray and cloudy. Spring was turning back into winter.

I kept thinking about Mamá and all she had been through. How we have to be patient with her. How we have her now in our hands but her spirit is not yet with us. How she is like the *golondrina*, still lost in the blowing wind, looking for a safe harbor.

But unlike the swallow of the song, Mamá will come back to us. Please, *por favor*, believe me, Papá, Tío, and my *hermanitas*. All we have to do is wait. Like the spring that has not yet arrived in Vermont. But I have seen it and it is coming.

And so are we!

Mamá sends her *besitos* and kisses
along with mine,
Mari

EIGHT

Ocho

spring

(2006)

RETURN-TO-SENDER FARM

Spring is Tyler's favorite time of year on the farm, but it doesn't arrive until May in Vermont. Oh, there are warm days in April, little crocuses poking up on the south-facing section of lawn around the house. Mom hangs out the wash and the wind blows it dry by noon. Dad starts mending fences, so that he can put the calves and heifers and dry cows out to pasture.

One morning, the air is full of twittering, and when Tyler meets Mari at the mailbox to wait for the bus, they both say at once, "They're back!" The swallows have returned, right on time. "I think they're chirping in Spanish," Tyler jokes.

"*¡Primavera, primavera, primavera!*" Mari singsongs. Spring, spring, spring!

But like the phrase stamped on an envelope with an index finger pointing back to where the letter came from, this is Return-to-Sender spring. A cold front blows in from the north, dumping a snowstorm. Frost beheads the daffodils. The puddles in the fields turn to ice, reflecting the gray sky.

This year, Tyler feels especially impatient for spring to get here. Maybe it's because he already started spring by going south to North Carolina, only to return to winter as they headed back to Vermont.

But finally, really and truly, May rolls in with day after warm day. The only problem is the constant rain, which makes it hard to get the fields planted. But even rain can't dampen Tyler's high spirits. All winter long, the farm is in hibernation mode, only the milking parlor and barn humming with life. But come spring, the farm unpacks its animals and its smells and its sounds and spreads out on all sides. Then a farmer's second job begins: growing the food to feed his cows during the fall and long winter.

School is a drag, because there's so much that needs to be done on the farm. Tyler has to scale back his hours at Mr. Rossetti's. One afternoon a week, he cleans the yard, rakes out the garden, gets the flower beds ready for the bulbs Grandma brought over to improve Mr. Rossetti's property.

Weekends, he helps his dad and Corey and Ben (whose classes have already ended!) out in the fields. Meanwhile, the milking and barn chores are left for Mr. Cruz and his brother. The two groups cross paths at night as one comes from the fields and the other from the barn, briefly exchanging whatever information is needed before heading home wearily to supper, maybe a little TV, and bed.

It's at these times that Tyler notes how sad Mr. Cruz looks, not at all what Tyler expected after the ecstatic reunion a few weeks ago. The minute the car pulled in the driveway that late Sunday afternoon, Ofie and Luby came racing from the trailer and their father from the milking parlor. Tyler thought they'd knock Mrs. Cruz over. They practically carried her back to the trailer, and Tyler and his dad agreed to finish up the milking with Armando so Mr. Cruz could just feast his eyes on his skinny wife.

But according to Mari, the stories Mrs. Cruz has been telling her husband about her captivity must be truly awful, because Mari is not allowed to even know what they are. "I hear them sometimes at night in the kitchen—my mother talking and crying, and my father crying right along." Then, for days afterward, her father walks around with a fierce look in his eyes, his jaw tense, and his hands in fists. Any little thing and he blows up at Mari and her sisters. "It's really terrible at home," Mari admits. "I mean, it's great that Mamá's back, but I thought, I don't know, I thought it would be different."

Tyler nods. He knows exactly what she means. Maybe this is what grown-up life is all about? Sad and happy stuff all mixed together. His old hand-blinker routine no longer works. He knows too much inside his own head. "You yourself said, Mari, you just have to be patient and wait," he tries consoling her.

"I know," Mari admits, but it doesn't seem to lift her spirits in the least to say so.

✳   ✳   ✳

For Mother's Day, Tyler's whole family gathers at Grandma's for a big dinner, cooked by the men in the family. Halfway through the meal, the men start fessing up. It turns out that Uncle Larry picked up his spareribs at Rosie's. ("I knew it!" Aunt Vicky says, licking her fingers.) Dad bought the cake from the bakery at Shaw's, and Uncle Byron special-ordered the pâté from some shop in Burlington. (Everyone wolfs it down until Aunt Jeanne announces it's made of ducks' livers.) Only Tío Armando actually made the refried beans. Meanwhile, Mr. Rossetti brought two twelve-packs of beer and a bottle of champagne that makes Grandma's cheeks turn pink like a girl's.

As they're all finishing the cake, Grandma clinks her water glass. "I have an announcement to make," she says, grinning slyly.

Tyler tenses up. It hasn't been a full year yet. Much as he has gotten to really like Mr. Rossetti, Tyler is not prepared for him to be married to Grandma.

But that's not the news Grandma wants to share. "I'm going to Mexico!"

"By yourself?" Aunt Jeanne asks. Tyler can't tell if his

aunt is worried about Grandma going by herself to a foreign country or worried about her going to a foreign country with a man who is not Gramps.

"Of course not!" Grandma lets out an exasperated sigh. "Martha's going with me. We're taking the youth group to Chiapas. Alyssa's set it all up for us to work at the clinic where she volunteered."

"But when are you planning on going?" Aunt Jeanne asks. Tyler is sure that whenever it is Grandma says she's going, Aunt Jeanne will find some Web site warning that it's the worst time to visit that part of Mexico.

"Summer sometime. We have to wait till all the kids are out of school."

The guests are quiet, digesting the information. Mari whispers to her parents and uncle what is going on. Their faces flood with joy. The grandmother will be the guest of the family. She can stay at their new house built with the money they have been earning in America.

"Well, I think it's exciting and real special for the kids," Grandma says. She sounds a little miffed that no one but her Mexican family seems especially happy about her plans. "I know Alyssa said it was a life-changing experience."

"Who needs to change their life at our age?" Mr. Rossetti speaks up in that ornery tone of voice Tyler hasn't heard since town meeting night. "Elsie, what kind of cockamamie idea is this? I know it's no use trying to change your mind. But doggone it, I'm going with you to keep an eye on you." It's a statement, but Grandma treats it like an application, one that might not be approved.

"Well, Joseph, not so fast there. It's a church trip, so you'd have to join up to go with us."

A long look passes between them. Tyler's not sure how it will go. Mr. Rossetti coughs and takes a sip from his glass. "What's everybody looking at?" he barks at the table.

"Okay, okay. I'll join your darn church, for heaven's sakes," he grumbles at Grandma once everyone looks away. It's not easy eating humble pie in public. And Mr. Rossetti has had to eat several pieces recently. At least Grandma sweetens them with her wonderful baking skills. Mr. Rossetti is looking a little heavier and a lot healthier and happier than he was back on town meeting night.

Now that Grandma has made her announcement, Ofie must feel like it's open season. "Guess what?" she asks the table. "Tomorrow's Mari's birthday! She's going to be twelve."

Before you know it, everyone is singing "Happy Birthday." Mari flashes her sister an annoyed look and bows her head, embarrassed.

Her mother leans over and whispers something in her ear. It must make her feel better because Mari nods, smiling.

"Mamá said Mari could pick anything she wanted for a present." It's Luby's turn to report. Her two little dogs are asleep on her lap. Recently, Tyler has noticed that Luby will sometimes leave them at home instead of carting them everywhere. Maybe now that she's getting older, Luby realizes that two stuffed puppies are not going to protect her from the bad things that can happen. For some reason, this makes Tyler feel wistful for something he can't put his finger on.

254

"Guess what?" Luby continues. Of course, no one knows what they are supposed to be guessing about. "Mari picked a really pretty diary with a tiny key so she can lock it and we won't be able to read it!"

"You can't read!" Ofie reminds her little sister.

"Can too! I can read my name. *L-u-b-y*. *Luby*. I can read *d-o-g*. *Doggie*. I can read—"

"That's not reading," Ofie cuts her off.

Mr. Cruz eyes the two quarreling sisters. Immediately, they stop.

Meanwhile, Tyler is wondering what on earth he can buy Mari at the last minute. He's got very little to spend. Most of his money is still out on loan to Mr. Cruz. But how about a special gift that doesn't cost anything? It's been a while since they had a stargazing session. The winter nights were just too cold to stand outside. But now the nights are mild and fragrant. The stars have shifted, and it's fun to find them reshuffled in the sky. Boötes, the herdsman, tracks the two bears with his dogs. Shy Virgo slips into view. The Big Dipper pours down its light. Leo, the lion, roars, glad to be king of the sky again.

The next day at school, Tyler stumbles upon a Web site where you can actually name a star for someone. And the best part is that it's free! You just print out the certificate.

Tonight, Tyler will set up his telescope on the hill behind Grandma's house and surprise Mari with the certificate. Then they can look at the star now officially named Mari Cruz. It's the coolest surprise ever!

Here's hoping the clouds lift—both for the sake of

planting the fields and for Mari's sake. She needs a scoop of blessings from that Big Dipper. She said as much to Tyler when she admitted it's been terrible at home. Tyler keeps reminding her what Gramps always told him: "Anytime you feel lost, look up."

He'll write that on the back of the certificate, along with *Happy Birthday*. His mind snags on how he should sign off. *Love, Tyler?* All his card-writing life, he has signed that way, automatically. But now for some reason, the word *love* glows, like a star, still unnamed in his heart's sky.

Monday night, the clouds turn to rain. Tyler heads over to the trailer with his star certificate and an IOU for stargazing. He's surprised that today at school, Mari didn't mention any kind of celebration at home this evening. Come over for cake and soda. Come over and celebrate with the family. Come over, period.

But he can understand. Last Christmas when Felipe was in jail and Ben in trouble and Sara complaining that just because her brother was grounded, it wasn't fair to punish her, too, Tyler couldn't stand to be home or have friends over. He loved escaping to Grandma's or to the barn. If Mari's father is that upset all the time and her mother is still jumpy and waking up everyone at night screaming, Mari probably doesn't want to share her troubles with the rest of the world.

And yet, Tyler's not the rest of the world, or so he hopes. They've become special friends. Mari is someone he can talk to about stuff he can't even talk to Grandma or Mr. Rossetti about. Growing-up stuff like how what used to seem so simple is suddenly much more complicated. His mom has told him that being an adult is about navigating your way through choices and challenges using the North Star of your heart and conscience.

"But you're not alone, Tiger, honey," Mom has told him, brushing his hair back out of his eyes like she's been doing since he was a little kid. "Your family, your parents, your teachers, we're all here to help you and guide you, mostly by example."

That's the problem. The examples his parents are giving him are sometimes confusing and contradictory. Like how you can be a patriot and break the law. Or how you can say no eavesdropping and then listen at Sara's locked bedroom door to make sure she hasn't snuck in her new boyfriend, Mateo, a Spanish exchange student. If Tyler points out these contradictions, he gets scolded. "I don't want to hear another word from you, Tyler Maxwell Paquette," his mom says. "You're out of order, son," his dad adds sternly. End of discussion.

One thing Tyler has not mentioned to his parents is the exact details of picking up Mrs. Cruz in Durham. Sometimes when they pester him with questions about the trip, Tyler is at the point of confessing. But then he remembers his promise to his aunt and uncle. Again he feels that welter of contradictory feelings, right and wrong so mixed in with each other that he's bound to do wrong even when he does the right thing. Besides, Sara has already warned him that if he says a word, she will kill him. Just as he thought, by telling the truth he'll turn his sister into a murderer!

But with Mari, Tyler can talk and talk and feel heard. That's the best part. Otherwise it would be just too lonely for words: being a single, solitary human being for your whole single, solitary life!

"Hey, happy birthday," he says when Mari opens the door. The TV is blaring in the background, Spanish news. The rain is coming down, but a small awning extends over the back steps, so Tyler can pull the certificate out from inside his rain slicker without it getting wet. He's put cardboard on both sides and wrapped it up so it looks more special. "The second part of the present comes when it stops raining," he explains. That about gives that part of the surprise away.

Mari unwraps the gift daintily like the paper's too valuable to tear. If she only knew. Tyler found a bag with a pretty floral print stashed in the recycle bin. It does make a nice wrapping.

Mari glances over the certificate. She looks unsure what it is. "Thank you so much," she says politely.

Tyler can't contain himself. "It's a star named after you!"

Mari's mouth drops open. She reads over the certificate carefully this time. Tyler rereads it himself for the umpteenth time, but now with the added pleasure of sharing the surprise.

"But, Tyler," Mari protests, "this must have cost a whole lot?"

Tyler is debating whether to tell her it was totally free when they hear her mother's voice calling from the living room: "Mari?" She wants to know who it is. Mari answers over her shoulder that it's Tyler, then something about her *cumpleaños*, which Tyler knows means her birthday.

"My mother says to invite you. Do you want to come in?"

Normally, Tyler would say sure, but some tension in Mari's face lets him know she doesn't really want him to accept her mother's invitation.

"Maybe we can talk on the steps instead?" Mari offers more eagerly. The awning gives them some cover, and it's kind of nice being outside with a little light beaming a circle of warmth around them while the rain keeps falling. Tyler sits right down, but Mari has to ask for permission first, which her mom must grant, because she closes the door and plops herself beside Tyler with a big sigh.

"Is your dad upset again?" Tyler asks after a moment's silence.

"Well, it's just . . . ," Mari begins. "The president, your Mr. President, was just on TV saying he's sending the National Guard troops down to the border. They're going to build a huge wall." Mari's voice is as damp as the night. What a way to spend her birthday! "My parents are talking about going back before that happens."

"Do you want to go back?" Tyler asks. What he doesn't say is that he doesn't want her and her family to go at all.

"I always thought I would," Mari says, her voice steadier

now. It's as if talking with Tyler also makes it easier for her to face difficult news. "But I don't know. I . . . I love it here on your farm."

That could be the single most wonderful thing a girl could say to Tyler. "I love it here, too," he agrees. "It's like my favorite place in the world." Not that he's seen much of the world: three big cities and the highway out the car window between them.

Just then, the door flies open, startling them both and breaking the spell. It's Mr. Cruz, and he does not look happy. He barks some accusation at Mari, who defends herself by holding up her gift and again mentioning her *cumpleaños*.

But Mr. Cruz just seems to get angrier at Mari for offering excuses. He jerks his head for her to go inside. But before she can, Mrs. Cruz appears beside her husband. She smiles warmly at Tyler, the gap of missing teeth turning her beautiful smile into something broken and sad. She says something softly to Mr. Cruz, touching his arm. But he shakes her off and gestures for her to go back inside as well. Then, glaring at Tyler, he says something to Mari that Tyler can tell she doesn't want to translate.

"*¡Díselo!*" her father commands.

"My father"—Mari hesitates—"he says he doesn't have your money yet. To stop coming around to collect. He'll give it to you as soon as he has it."

Tyler wants to say that that's not what he came for. But the look on Mari's face is begging him not to contradict her father. To please leave right away. That much he can give her for her birthday.

He turns and walks back home, not bothering to put his hood up. If they were not salty, Tyler would pretend his tears were just raindrops washing down his face.

✦ ✦ ✦

Sunday night before Memorial Day, the skies suddenly clear. The stars sparkle as if they've been washed by the rain. Tyler is up at Grandma's with the three Marías, pasting little paper American flags onto pencil-sized rods. Tomorrow, they'll all go to the town cemetery and plant a flag beside each veteran's grave, including Gramps's. All the members of the local VA will be there, giving speeches. Mr. Rossetti will play taps, which he says he'll do as long as he has enough breath in his lungs. Tonight as they work, Grandma has the radio turned on to this station that is playing lots of music in honor of Memorial Day tomorrow.

"Grandma, are you really eloping to Mexico to get married to Grandpa?" Ofie starts in.

Grandma's cheeks again turn pink, but this time she hasn't been drinking champagne.

"Who told you such a thing?"

Ofie looks confused. Every kid in the world knows when they're about to get a grown-up in trouble. "Aunt Jeanne was just saying . . ."

"I knew it!" Grandma says crossly. "That Jeanne! She imagines things and then I'm held accountable. I'm going to give her a piece of my mind!" She marches toward the phone, wiping her hands on a dish towel.

Mari flashes Ofie a look. See what you've done, causing a family fight! "Remember, Grandma, Ofie has a big imagination and a big mouth," Mari reminds the grandmother.

"I do not!"

"You do too!"

Ofie shoves Mari, who shoves her back. That's one thing Tyler has noticed. Mari is learning to stick up for herself.

"Okay, okay," Grandma says, coming between them. She has forgotten her phone call. There's a more immediate fire to put out.

"Mari and I have to check on something outside, okay?" Tyler tells Grandma, who nods, looking relieved. "Thank you, dear," she murmurs, giving Tyler credit for being a peacemaker. In fact Tyler is glad for this fight, since it gives him an excuse to do something with Mari without her usual tail of two younger sisters. Earlier, he set up the telescope on the small hill just above Gramps's garden. It's the only way Tyler will be able to deliver his rain-checked gift. He doesn't dare go near the trailer anymore, feeling so unwelcome.

Out they go, across the backyard, past the garden that Gramps would be planting tomorrow if he were still alive, uphill to the very place where last November they saw the Taurid meteor shower.

"Where are we going?" Mari asks finally. She must not have guessed the big hint Tyler dropped on her birthday about waiting for a clear night to deliver the second half of her birthday present. No doubt the scene with her father erased happier moments from that evening.

But as soon as she spots the telescope, she gives a little cry. "Can we find my star?"

Tyler has the coordinates all ready. They crouch down, taking turns looking through the telescope. Her star is a teensy smudge of light, but the way Mari oohs and aahs, you'd think it was as big and bright as Venus or Mars!

At one point, as Tyler is angling the telescope lower in the sky, he notices a clump of stars he has never seen before. Puzzled, he stands up to orient himself. Those lights are not in the sky but on the dark edge of the horizon and getting closer. As he watches, the glare coalesces. A battalion of cars, lights flashing, is racing toward the farm without a name.

"What are those?" Mari has stood up beside him. Her voice is edged with the worry that seems threaded through everything she says nowadays.

As they look down toward the farmhouse, the swarm of cars comes to a screeching halt. Dark figures leap out and surround the small trailer, where three Mexicans are just now watching a game of *lucha libre* and waiting for the three Marías to come home. Meanwhile, in Grandma's kitchen, peace has been restored. Ofie and Luby finish up the little flags that they intend to plant tomorrow at the graves of patriots who died for their freedom.

Dear Diary,

It's been over two weeks since Mamá gave you
to me for my twelfth birthday. You looked so
official, with a little strap and lock and teensy
key! I couldn't seem to come up with anything
important enough to write down.

But then, after two weeks of nothing
happening, suddenly a lot has happened and
writing in a diary was the last thing I could think
of doing. Besides, it was only yesterday that we
made a list for Grandma and Tyler of things to
pick up for us at the trailer and bring over to our
secret location, which I don't have to keep secret
from you. So until today I didn't even have you
along. It feels so good to have this safe place
where *la migra* can't come and haul my words and
thoughts and feelings away.

We are hiding, my sisters and I, so I don't
have much privacy. And most of the time, I'm too
worried to write. Worried about Mamá and Papá
and Tío Armando, and what will happen to all of
us. I bite my nails so much that at night my
fingers throb.

Friday, June 9, 2006

Dear Diary,

We haven't been to school for almost two weeks now. Mrs. Paquette went over to Bridgeport and talked to Mrs. Stevens. Tyler says nobody except Mr. Bicknell and my sisters' teachers know about us.

But by now everyone in class is asking where I am. Some of them have been asking Tyler if it's true what Clayton and Ronnie have been spreading, that I am in jail! I guess there are rumors all over town about what happened over at the Paquette farm.

So I'm going to write down exactly what happened. If I am finally taken away to jail, I will leave you, dear Diary, to tell the world the whole truth of what we have been through.

Sunday, June 11, 2006

Dear Diary,

Mr. Rossetti went to church with Grandma, so for the first time we are alone in the house. My sisters are downstairs watching television, as Grandma finally brought our TV over. Mr.

Rossetti doesn't own one. He calls it the idiot box and says there wasn't anything wrong with radio that needed fixing. He has a lot of opinions about things, I am finding out.

No news yet about Mamá and Papá, but Mrs. Paquette says that she and Señora Ramírez have contacted Mr. Calhoun, the lawyer who helped out with Tío Felipe.

When I heard Tío Felipe's name, I suddenly thought of our family in Mexico! They would worry so much when they didn't hear from us. I asked Mr. Rossetti if we could call Mexico, but he doesn't have long distance on his telephone. He says he doesn't know anyone he wants to talk to outside Vermont!

So I asked Mrs. Paquette, who asked Ben, who asked Alyssa to call and explain. My whole *familia* was so worried. But Alyssa told Tío Felipe that a lot of people are working on getting my parents out of jail and reuniting us all again.

Just hearing about that reunion, I start crying and can't stop. That just gets Ofie and Luby going, and then it's terrible as Mr. Rossetti doesn't know what to do except give us his handkerchief to blow our noses. That's another thing about him. He doesn't believe in Kleenex. There wasn't anything wrong with handkerchiefs that needed fixing, he says.

Dear Diary,

Today, I am going to write down what happened when Mamá and Papá were taken away. I meant to do it on Sunday, but my sisters called me down for a special program about swallows on TV. They know swallows are my favorite animal because of the song *"La Golondrina."*

I didn't realize there was so much to know about them! How they fly for days and days, eating and even making babies as they fly, so desperate are they to get where they are going. How they bring good luck to farmers when they nest in their barns. (Tyler says his grandfather would never let anyone disturb a swallow's nest, even when the milk inspector said there was too much of their poop around.) Best of all is how, like my own family, swallows have two homes, one in North America and one in South America.

Here is what happened the night *la migra* took my parents away:

Tyler and I were outside looking at my star, which is the most spectacular birthday present I have ever received. I still cannot believe there is a star in the universe with my name on it! I don't know how Tyler could have afforded to buy it, as he loaned all his money to Papá to help ransom Mamá back. He also gave up his birthday trip to go to North Carolina to rescue Mamá and invited me along. That is all the birthday gifts I will ever want from him for a whole lifetime.

Just as Tyler was about to take his turn at the telescope, we saw cars racing toward the farm. Next thing we knew, all these agents had surrounded the trailer and were shining huge searchlights so nobody could escape in the dark. They banged on the door, but when Papá opened it, just as quickly, he slammed it shut. Two agents had to push against it hard, finally knocking it down. Next, they were hauling Papá out, but he was struggling and swinging at the agents. Meanwhile, Mamá was jumping out of the window of our bedroom, but there were agents all around ready to catch her. Two of them grabbed her by the arms and herded her inside one of the cars. She was screaming the whole time. Only Tío Armando came out peacefully, head bowed, his hands handcuffed behind him.

Meanwhile, Tyler's parents came running out of their house. His mother was shouting something, but the agents were not listening. She ran back inside and came out waving a piece of paper, which one of the agents grabbed and put in his pocket.

All the time we were watching, I was sobbing hysterically. When Mamá began to scream, I tore off down the hill toward the trailer to be with her. After all she had been through, I just knew she'd have a nervous attack right then and there. But Tyler caught up with me and wrestled me to the ground.

"Don't, Mari!" he whispered, pinning me down by my wrists. "You can't go, you can't. They'll take you, too." When I finally stopped struggling, he pulled me up and took my hand, and we ran as fast as we could down to his grandmother's house.

When we burst inside, Grandma and Luby and Ofie looked up surprised. I guess they hadn't heard all that commotion with the radio playing. I couldn't talk because I was crying so hard. Tyler explained to his grandmother what we had seen. "They were all dressed in jackets with guns and stuff, not like real policemen in uniforms. The jackets had ICE written on them."

"That's Immigration and Customs Enforcement, oh my!" Grandma's hand was at her chest, her breath coming fast. Even she was in a fluster. "They didn't take your parents, did they?"

The color drained out of Tyler's face. "I don't know." Suddenly he looked as scared as I was.

Luby and Ofie had begun to cry, which made my own tears dry up. Months ago, when Tío Felipe had been jailed and Papá was all worried that he was next, he made me promise that I would take care of my sisters like their little mother. I had to stay strong for them.

Grandma ran to the phone and dialed Tyler's parents, but nobody answered. Either they were still outside, talking to the agents, or maybe they, too, had been taken away for committing the crime of hiring Mexicans without papers.

The grandmother looked so pale, I was afraid she was about to faint. "We're going to stay calm. Really calm. And very calmly we are going to get in my car." It was like she was talking to herself, but we were more than happy to follow her instructions.

Next thing we knew, we were driving in the opposite direction from the trailer, taking the back way into town. It wasn't like Grandma told us to hide or anything, but my sisters and I crouched down in the back. I felt just a taste of what it must have been like for Mamá, riding under a false floor in a van all the way across America.

We pulled into Mr. Rossetti's driveway, and Grandma ushered us to the back door, knocked once, then walked right in. Mr. Rossetti was already in bed upstairs. "Joseph!" she called up. "You got company."

A few minutes later, Mr. Rossetti came down the stairs in his bathrobe as fast as he could with the help of his cane. His white hair was all messed up like a little baby's. "What in tarnation?" he said when he found us standing in his kitchen, all looking terrified.

"We need for you to take us in," Grandma began. Then she sort of raced through a crazy explanation about agents surrounding the farm and us escaping the back way. Before she had even finished her account, she was heading toward the phone mounted on the kitchen wall. It looked like a telephone from when telephones were first invented. No wonder we couldn't call Mexico. Mr. Rossetti probably couldn't get long distance on that old phone even if he wanted to.

"Hold your horses, Elsie," Mr. Rossetti was saying. "Maybe I just woke up, but this isn't making a bit of sense to me. Why would the law be after you?"

"I don't know that they are, Joseph," Grandma said more calmly. She already had one hand on the phone. "But if you'll kindly let me make a call, then I can tell you what is going on."

The phone couldn't have rung more than

once, and then Grandma was talking to Tyler's mom. She repeated some of the stuff she was hearing out loud for Mr. Rossetti's benefit, as he looked like he was going to grab the phone away from her any minute. "Let me talk to her," he kept saying, but Grandma kept holding up one hand and shaking her head.

"They were taken away. . . . You don't know where. . . . They left you a number. . . . You didn't mention . . . Yes, they're here with me. So's Tyler. But you're okay?"

When she was done, she hung the receiver carefully back in its holder and sort of collected herself, then turned around. She still looked worried, but her voice was calm and strong like she was an actress playing the part of the heroic grandmother who saves the day. "I want everyone to take a seat—you too, Joseph."

Mr. Rossetti grumbled about the gall of some people not letting him use his own phone, but he did finally sit down. Once we were all seated, Grandma explained what had happened at the farm. How my parents and uncle had been taken away by Immigration and Customs Enforcement. How Mrs. Paquette had tried to show them the paperwork that proved the Cruzes were paying taxes. How Sara had arrived as it was all happening with her boyfriend, Mateo. How Mateo had translated for Mr. Cruz, who asked the Paquettes to please not say anything about the three Marías as he was afraid they would be taken away. How before they drove off, the agents gave Tyler's parents a phone number that they could call for more information on the status of the Cruzes, and if and when they would be deported to Mexico.

Mr. Rossetti had both his hands on his cane in front of him and now he put his head down on his hands as he listened. Seeing this, both Ofie and Luby began to cry.

"I want my daddy," Luby wailed. "I want my mommy. I want my doggies." All I could think was that just what Luby called our parents—not Mamá, not Papá, but Mommy and Daddy—showed she didn't belong in Mexico.

"That's no way to treat decent folks!" Mr. Rossetti said when Grandma had finished her account. "And what's more, these here girls have rights. They're American citizens!" he added angrily, jabbing the air with his cane. Tyler glanced at his grandma, who flashed us a look to keep quiet. So much for telling the truth to your friends to improve their characters.

There were a bunch more phone calls back and forth, but Grandma said that Tyler's parents were afraid to say too much in case their phone was being tapped.

"That's when they spy on what you're saying without you knowing it," Tyler explained. It sounded just like what Mr. Bicknell had said happens when your government is a dictatorship.

It was very late by the time we piled into Mr. Rossetti's spare bedroom upstairs with pillows and blankets that smelled musty, like they had not been used in ages. Ofie even found this cocoon in her blanket with a little moth folded inside it. Tyler slept downstairs on the couch. I don't know where Grandma slept. Mostly, she stayed up, talking to Mr. Rossetti late into the night. I could hear their worried voices drifting up from the kitchen.

As for me, I don't think I slept a wink. I couldn't bite my nails as there were no more nails to bite. By the time I finally got out of bed, light was pouring in the window. Grandma was gone and so was Tyler. They had driven back to the farm early to help out with chores. That's right! Papá and Tío Armando would not be there to milk the cows this morning.

Later that day when Grandma came by with Tyler, she told Mr. Rossetti she had called someone from the VA to come over and pick up all the little flags we had put together. "I just don't have the heart to celebrate anything today," Grandma admitted. Her nerves had calmed down, but she looked tired and as sad as when we arrived on the farm last August a few months after her husband had died.

Mr. Rossetti was nodding his head. "My

sentiments exactly, Elsie. I called up Roger and told him I couldn't blow for them today, either. And it's a crying shame, because if anyone deserves our gratitude it's our vets."

That's why later that night, once it had gotten dark, we piled into Grandma's car. It is the one and only time we've been out since coming over to hide in Mr. Rossetti's house. We were surprised they were risking it just one day after everything had happened. But Mr. Rossetti said he wanted to be sure we girls saw the proud face of America.

Which was why I was confused when we ended up in a graveyard! There were little flags all around that Tyler shone his flashlight on, the very ones we had put together the night before. We stopped at one gravestone that Mr. Rossetti explained belonged to his older brother, Gino, who had died in World War II.

"These boys did not die in vain," Mr. Rossetti said in a gravelly voice. Then he cleared his throat and said it again. "I'm going to make damn sure of that."

"Watch your language in the graveyard," Grandma reminded him. But she didn't sound that upset at all over Mr. Rossetti's swearing.

Before we left, Mr. Rossetti pulled out his trumpet from the trunk of his car. There in the dark with sprinkles of rain falling on our faces, he played the saddest tune, as sad as *"La Golondrina."*

"God bless America," he said when he was done.

Both North and South America, I thought, remembering the swallows on the TV special.

Saturday, June 17, 2006

Dear Diary,

Mrs. Paquette came by with Señora Ramírez and Tyler today. They've spoken to Papá! He is now in a detention center in Clinton, New York, wherever that is. Mamá is somewhere else as they were separated when *la migra* took them away. Papá is sick with worry about her as well as about us. Señora Ramírez said he pleaded with her not to say anything about his children because he has heard that *la migra* takes kids away from the parents. "I told him I don't think that will happen," Señora Ramírez explained. "Plus, you girls are *americanitas*. You have *derechos* and rights as U.S. citizens."

Tyler and I looked at each other, wondering if this was the time to come out with the whole truth. But Mrs. Paquette whispered something to Señora Ramírez, who quickly glanced over at me and then looked away.

Honestly, I don't know why it has to be such a

big secret that I was born in Mexico. Or why grown-ups can't just tell us what is going on. "They don't want to worry you," Tyler says. But it worries me more to think there's something so awful that I can't be told!

Besides, Tyler always fills me in. Maybe because his ears stick out a little, but he seems to overhear a whole bunch of secrets. Today, he stayed on after his mother and Señora Ramírez went to meet with Mr. Calhoun up in Burlington. It had been raining all day, and so his father wouldn't be able to plant the back field. Tyler had a free afternoon until milking time.

"It's really hard right now," he told me about the work around the farm. "Just me and Ben and Dad." His father has improved a lot, but the fingers on his right hand don't yet work correctly, so doing chores takes a long time.

What Tyler has overheard is that the raid on the farm happened on account of Mamá's bag that *la migra* confiscated when they raided the *coyotes'* house in North Carolina. Inside, they found her Mexican passport and phone numbers they tracked down to a farm in Vermont. But instead of thinking that poor Mamá was a victim of these *coyotes*, the agents assumed she was one of the traffickers! So she is being treated like a criminal. "Your dad, too, on account of he resisted arrest and struck a federal agent," Tyler explained. "The only one who's going to get sent back real soon is your uncle, as he just let them arrest him, then admitted he was here without papers and all he wanted was to go home."

"Mamá and Papá should do the same thing," I said, even though I knew that would mean we would all have to go back to Mexico, and I wasn't sure I wanted to live there anymore. But I'd rather go back and be together with my parents than stay here, all separated, with Mamá and Papá behind bars. "We've got to tell Señora Ramírez to tell Papá—"

"But that's what I mean," Tyler broke in. "They don't get to make that choice, because now they are criminals who broke the law. You know, like when your uncle Felipe ran off. They'll have to stand trial and maybe go to jail before they can go home."

That's when I really lost it. Two or three weeks without getting to see my parents I could stand, but months and months! We had already suffered for over a year without Mamá. Now we had finally gotten her back, and she was being taken away from us again. It just did not seem fair at all.

"Mari, don't cry, please," Tyler kept saying. He looked as helpless as Mr. Rossetti when my sisters and I start sobbing. Only difference is Tyler doesn't have a dirty handkerchief in his pocket to offer me.

Later that afternoon, when Grandma came by to pick up Tyler, she brought us a cake to cheer us up. It was made just for us, I could tell, as the frosting was pink. Stuff she makes for Mr. Rossetti is more hearty and supposed to help him move his bowels. Now, there's a kind of love for Mr. Bicknell to put on the board next year for his Valentine's Day assignment. Old people's love where you try to improve their characters and help them go to the bathroom!

I almost made myself laugh out loud, writing that down. But then, remembering that I probably won't ever see Mr. Bicknell or my classmates, I started crying again. This time, though, there's no one looking on, wondering what on earth to hand me for blowing my nose and drying my tears.

Except you, dear Diary. You can hold all my sadness just as long as I cry in ink here.

Sunday, June 18, 2006

Dear Diary,

Today was the first day in a long time that it wasn't raining, so Tyler's whole family had to get the corn planted. After supper, they all came over with a carton of ice cream in honor of Father's

Day. Mr. Paquette hardly said a word, he was so tired. I suppose it's no way to spend your special day, but then it's a whole lot better than spending it in jail.

All day I felt so sad thinking about Papá. There had to be a way to help him and Mamá get out of jail, but I couldn't figure out how.

"What if we told *la migra* the whole truth?" I asked Tyler, who shook his head.

"They won't listen, Mari, I can tell you that much. Why do you think they're called ICE?"

They were ICE all right, with cold hearts to do what they'd done to my family!

Still, look at Mr. Rossetti. He had turned out to be so nice after all. Maybe if we explained what had happened to Mamá and why Papá would have been so frantic to protect her, and how they had kids who were suffering, and two of those kids were American citizens whose sufferings counted even more, maybe the agents' icy hearts would melt. "Maybe they'd even give us our papers because they felt sorry?"

Tyler crossed his arms. For the second time in two days, he reminded me of Mr. Rossetti! This time it was the same look Mr. Rossetti gets in his eyes when Grandma comes up with one of her grand plans. And the very same words were coming out of Tyler's mouth: "Mari, you are a dreamer, aren't you?"

Wednesday, June 21, 2006

Dear Diary,

Today was the last day of school. Afterward,
the bus dropped off Tyler, who had a letter for me
from the whole class! Mr. Bicknell wrote it on the
board, and everyone contributed a message.
Then, during lunchtime, he typed it up on his
computer.

I'm going to paste it here.

Dear María,

We miss you so much. Today, on the last day of sixth
grade, we decided to write you a group letter, telling you
how much it meant to us that you were in our class. (Mr.
Bicknell here: I'm typing each person's message in a separate
paragraph.)

Dear María, you are the best Earthling on earth! Love,
Maya

I hope you come back to be with us in seventh grade, so
you can help us save the planet. Peace, Meredith

Dear María, are you in Mexico? I hope you are having an
awesome time. Chelsea

María, call me if you can, 802-555-8546, my father is a
lawyer and he can help you out. Caitlin

Have a great summer. Sincerely, Ronnie

Have a great life. Sincerely, Clayton Lacroix III

María, you deserve to stay in our country. It would be a better nation with you in it. Your friend forever, Tyler

I hope Jesus takes care of you and your family. God bless you, Amanda

Here is a joke for you, María: Why did the burglar take a shower? He wanted to make a clean getaway! (I got a whole bunch more, but Mr. Bicknell says everyone just gets to send one message.) Keep smiling, Kyle

María, I've got a joke for you, too: Which state is the smartest? Alabama: it has four A's and one B! Michael

María, Mr. Bicknell says enough with the jokes, so I'll keep mine for when I see you again. *Gracias* for the help with my es-*pañol.* Dylan

Hola, María. Muchas gracias para mi amiga de su amiga. Rachel

María, I really liked when you wrote stuff and Mr. Bicknell read it out loud. I loved learning about the dead people's holiday and how every night for two weeks before Christmas, you party. That's cool. If I could still be American, I would love to be Mexican, too. Love and *amor* to you, Amelia

María, Mr. Bicknell is letting me say my message privately just to him. I am very sad because my daddy just told my mom that he is in love with someone else and is going to divorce her. I sure wish you were here so we could be best friends because Rachel doesn't want to be mine anymore. Ashley

As you can see, María, you left behind many friends at Bridgeport. We hope for the best for you and your family. Always remember that you have a home in our hearts, no matter where you are. Friendship knows no borders! Mr. Bicknell

I've read the letter over and over, laughing
and crying both. I feel so sorry for poor Ashley.
As for Clayton and Ronnie, I sincerely hope they
grow up to be nicer adults than they are kids.
That Kyle tells the funniest jokes, and Michael is
pretty funny, too. But my favorite of all is Tyler's.
It would be a better nation with you in it. If only
this country would listen to its kids!

Sunday, June 25, 2006

Dear Diary,

On Friday, a big thing happened.
The day before, Señora Ramírez stopped by,
and I asked if I could have a private word with
her. We went to the backyard, where there is a
little birdbath and two stones that are big enough

to sit on. I told her the whole truth about how I wasn't a U.S. citizen. "I know," she admitted. Then I asked if she'd drive me over to *la migra's* office so I could explain everything to them.

She was real quiet like she was working it all out in her head, what could happen. A little bird came and landed on the birdbath. When she looked up, it flew away.

"Are you sure this is something you want to do, *querida?*" she asked. She always throws a few Spanish words into her English. It helps connect me to where I came from and makes me feel part of a bigger story. It's one of the special things about talking to her. Plus, she really listens. Not the way some grown-ups pretend-listen, and you can tell they already have the answer and are just waiting for you to finish.

"*Sí, estoy muy segura,*" I told her. Saying I was really sure in Spanish sounded more convincing to her and to me. Sure, I was scared. But I had thought and thought about it and made up my mind. Especially after Tyler told me that he overheard his mother talking to his aunt Roxie about my mother. It turns out that Mamá is in the clinic at her detention center in Boston "under sedation," which Tyler says means they are giving her pills to keep her calm. I can believe that. Meanwhile, Papá has been moved to a place in

New Hampshire. The only good news is that Tío Armando is already back in Las Margaritas. Alyssa sent word that Tío Armando was really happy to be reunited with his family. That last piece of news is what convinced me.

"To tell you *la pura verdad*," Señora Ramírez was saying. The pure truth was that she agreed with me! Having *la migra* see that my parents were not criminals but hardworking parents with kids might help. She was almost one hundred percent sure that my sisters and I would not be taken away to some foster home, since we were being well taken care of by friends of our parents and there were no relatives around to claim us instead.

"So will you take me, please?" I asked.

Again, she thought it over. "Tell you what," she said, standing up and brushing off her pants. "Let me talk it over with Caleb, okay? And I'll get back to you." It took me a second to remember that Caleb was Mr. Calhoun, the lawyer who had offered to help my parents just as he had Tío Felipe.

Later that afternoon, Señora Ramírez called to say Caleb had agreed. It couldn't hurt for ICE to put a face on case A 093 533 0744. He was free to accompany us to the Homeland Security office in St. Albans tomorrow morning. "Barry'll drive us up in his Subaru. The three of you can ride in the back."

The three of us? I was shaking my head even before I explained. I didn't want my sisters along. They had suffered enough without also having to go in front of scary agents who had taken our parents away. "Just me, and Barry, and you," I pleaded with her. "Please, ¿por favor?" Then I thought of one more person who would make it easier for me if he were along.

So the next day, the two of them and Tyler and I drove up to Burlington, where we picked up Mr. Calhoun. Today he was dressed more formally in black pants with his shirt tucked in. He'd also taken off his earring, though you could still see the little hole in his ear. It actually made me more nervous that he was trying to make a good impression.

He sat with us kids in the back and asked a whole lot of questions about what all I would say. The more I said, the more he kept nodding. "Just as I thought." He went on to explain the whole situation. How my parents had been seized during a national sweep called Operation Return to Sender.

"Operation Return to Sender?" Barry was looking in his rearview mirror like he wasn't sure he had heard correctly.

Mr. Calhoun nodded. "Actually, the target was undocumented immigrants with a criminal record. That's probably why they flushed out your mother's smugglers down in Durham, where they found evidence linking your mother to them."

"But isn't that what they stamp on a letter, *Return to Sender?*" Tyler asked. "When there aren't enough stamps on it?"

"Precisely." Again, Mr. Calhoun was nodding. "People as excess baggage." He looked disgusted. "Anyhow, your parents hardly fit the bill. Now we've got to convince Homeland Security."

He was saying *we*, but it was up to me, and I knew it.

We drove up to a low brick building and pulled into the parking lot. I felt almost as scared as that day when we had ransomed Mamá back from the *coyotes* in North Carolina. Now I was going to try to do the same, but instead of money, I was going to offer a story. The story Mamá had told me about what had happened to her.

Just inside the door, we found ourselves facing a glass partition. An officer in a uniform looked up, scowling, from the other side. "Bulletproof so they don't get shot," Tyler whispered. He would know from when he visited Tío Felipe at the county jail. It just made my heart race all the faster.

Mr. Calhoun gave our names through a little speaking hole and explained who we all were and why we were here. The officer picked up his phone and repeated the whole story before buzzing us in. "Go ahead and take a seat." He nodded toward a long bench against one wall. "Mr. O'Goody'll be right with you."

"Oh jeez!" Mr. Calhoun sighed. Right then and there, I knew that despite his name, Mr. O'Goody was not good news.

Before I could get too nervous, a stocky man with a thick neck and a big jaw stood before us. He didn't look a whole lot older than Mr. Calhoun, except for being bald with just a fringe right above his ears. But what he'd lost on his head, he had on his eyebrows. They were real bushy, which made his eyes look sneaky, like they were undercover but ready to pounce on you if you told a lie and lock you up in jail.

He shook everyone's hands. When he got to me, he said, "You must be María?"

I couldn't find my voice, no way, so I just nodded.

"Come along then," he said real gruff like he already knew that I was going to be a waste of his time. Especially if I wouldn't talk. "Your friends can wait here."

Mr. Calhoun quick stood up and said he needed to come along and represent his client.

"Me too," Tyler added. He had promised to stand by me, no matter what. For a second there, I'd been afraid he had forgotten.

Mr. O'Goody turned to face them both. "I know you got your law degree, Calhoun. But what about you, young man?"

Tyler shook his head and his face got even redder than Mr. Calhoun's hair. "I'm Mari's friend . . . and I just . . . came along so she wouldn't be so scared," he stammered. Then, he added, "Sir," the way a soldier might salute some important general.

Mr. O'Goody looked Tyler over for a minute. It was like he was running through a checklist in his head about what to look for in a terrorist. Thank goodness Tyler looked just like who he was, a Vermont boy with a bunch of freckles on his nose and the prettiest blue eyes.

"Come along then." Mr. O'Goody herded us down a long, empty hall without windows or pictures on the walls. Only posters with stuff printed on them. Probably rules and regulations that would trip anybody up.

He opened the door to an office, then stood to one side and let us go in first. A couple of chairs faced a desk with its back to a window, which seemed a shame with such a pretty view of a field with some horses munching on wildflowers. Mr. O'Goody didn't have any pictures on his desk like most of the teachers did at school. It was like he didn't have a wife or kids, so how would he ever understand why my family was suffering from being separated? "Take a seat," he said, nodding at the chairs. It was a trick offer, because there weren't enough to go around. But Mr. Calhoun went ahead and took a chair, and Tyler and I stayed standing.

"You, María, you sit here." Mr. O'Goody moved the other chair to one side of his desk where a machine was all set to go. At first, I thought it was a lie detector, but of course, without wires connected to me, how would it know my heart was in my throat? "I'll have to tape her testimony," he explained to Mr. Calhoun, who nodded his approval.

Mr. O'Goody turned the recorder on. I could hear that tape making little clicking sounds, but I couldn't seem to turn on my voice. Then from behind my chair, Tyler came and stood in front of me. "Hey, Mari. Just make believe you're telling me, okay?" That was the most helpful thing anybody could have said. Even Mr. O'Goody, I could tell, was impressed.

And so I started. . . . The whole story of what had happened to Mamá, of how she'd been gone for a year and four months. How my father couldn't go to the police because he wasn't allowed to be in this country in the first place. How we had moved to a farm so he didn't have to leave his kids all alone for weeks at a time now that we didn't have our mother. Somewhere in there I threw in that my sisters were American citizens. I didn't say anything about myself. I would leave that for the end.

When I got to the part about ransoming my mother, I just wanted to cry. But I told myself this was one time I couldn't give in to my sadness. I had to keep going. So I told how we had come back from North Carolina with my mother always jumpy and screaming in the middle of the night. How instead of my father being overjoyed to have her back, he was angry all the time, losing his temper, mostly because he blamed himself that he hadn't been able to protect his wife.

"That's why when *la migra*—I mean the ICE agents—came to the door, he just wasn't thinking. He would never ever have hit anybody in the world before all this happened. It's like he's turned into someone else with the bitterness and the hurt inside him."

Nobody was saying a word, and I was too scared to look up and see if Mr. O'Goody was even listening.

But now I had gotten to the really hard part, the part I'd been thinking and worrying about for days. "I'm not an American citizen," I confessed, "just my sisters. So I'm turning myself in. I hope you'll take me instead of my mother, as she will go crazy if you keep her in prison. She's not going to run off, I promise, if you've got me in your jail."

It was over. I had said what I came to say. All those tears I'd been holding back just came flowing down my cheeks. My nose was running, but I didn't have anything to wipe it with. I felt someone else join Tyler in front of me. I thought it might be Mr. Calhoun wanting to console his client. But it was Mr. O'Goody, and he was offering me a whole box of Kleenex!

"You're a brave and noble young lady," he said. His gruff voice had softened. "I can't make any promises, but I'm sending this information down to our regional office in Boston, along with my recommendation that your mother be released pending her hearing. I'm also going to add a personal note, commending your exemplary behavior."

I didn't know what exactly that meant, but it must have been good because I wasn't hauled away and locked in a jail. In fact, Mr. O'Goody shook my hand extra long as we said goodbye in the waiting area.

"So O'Goody's not a bad sort after all," Barry said as we pulled out of the parking lot.

This time, Mr. Calhoun did not commit

himself to a yes or no. "All I can say is O'Goody's having a good day today. Either that or he finally got laid."

Another American expression I'm going to have to ask Tyler to explain.

Friday, June 30, 2006

Dear Diary,

We leave tomorrow for Boston! Mamá will be released into the custody of Tyler's aunt and uncle, who have agreed to let us stay with them until Papá's case can be heard. Hopefully, he'll get released real soon, too. It's kind of complicated, but Mr. Calhoun explained it to Señora Ramírez, who explained it to us as best she could.

Mamá agreed to testify against the *coyote* criminals so they can be convicted and not do what they did to her to anybody else. And because she's going to do that, she's getting a special letter in her file that's going to help her when she applies to get into this country legally. Meanwhile, Papá's mental condition at the time of his arrest will be taken into consideration. When it's over, we'll all fly back to Mexico together.

"But what if we don't want to go to Mexico?"

Ofie said, pouting. "What if we want to stay in our own country?"

Señora Ramírez suddenly looked real tired, like she had climbed a mountain, only to look up and find an even bigger mountain ahead. She had worked so hard to reunite us. But that wasn't enough, not for my sister Ofie, anyhow.

But it wouldn't do to scold Ofie. She would just get more stubborn. Besides, I could understand how she was feeling. So I pulled my two sisters aside for a family meeting.

"I want us to try really hard when Mamá and Papá get out. So many sad things have happened to them," I explained. "And wherever we end up, the important thing is we'll all be together as a family. And remember, the two of you can always come back because you are American citizens. So this is just for now. Okay?" Luby nodded, but Ofie was putting that chin of hers up in the air. "And, Ofie, most of all I want us to be friends, okay? Please, *por favor*? Not to argue because we'll need each other more than ever."

Ofie's chin came down. She looked ready to strike a deal. "You'll let me borrow your butterfly backpack?" I nodded. "And use your makeup?" My makeup? The pinkish lip gloss and a sparkly blush Sara had given me when we first got to Vermont. "Sure," I told her.

"How about your diary? Can I read it?"

Well, Diary, I was about to say, No! But then I thought if I could leave this record behind for the whole world, surely I could let my own sister read it.

"Yes, I'll let you read my diary, okay?"

Ofie threw her arms around me and almost knocked me over. That made Luby want to do the same thing. Suddenly, I had two not-so-little sisters hanging on me.

"We're going to Mexico! We're going to Mexico!" Luby and Ofie chanted, jumping up and down.

I sighed with relief, until I looked across the room and saw the sadness on Tyler's face. I felt my heart folding up like a letter in a sealed envelope stamped *Return to Sender*. Tyler would never know how much I was going to miss him, no matter how much fun we ended up having in Mexico. I would never find such a special friend again, one who would even name a star after me!

Before he left today, he asked if there was any one thing I wanted to take with me. At first I said no, but after he was gone, I got to thinking. Yes, there is one thing.

I know Grandma and Mrs. Paquette are packing up as much of our stuff as we can carry in the car. They're also planning to come down one more time before we actually leave Boston to say goodbye. But before we leave Vermont on

Sunday, I want to go by the farm one last time. I want to see it in the early morning when the sun is coming up, how it sits so pretty in the gentle swell of the valley. The two farmhouses with the trailer between them and on the flat stretch behind the houses, the big red barn with the little cupolas that look like birdhouses. I want to watch the cows, black and white like scrambled puzzle pieces, coming in from the pasture to be milked, the swallows diving in and out of the open doors so fast that it's hard to follow their every move. And I want to see a boy coming out of the barn, hauling his new show calf that he is going to name Margarita after our hometown in Mexico.

And then, I can leave, yes I can, because the place and the people I've grown to love will all be stored inside me and here on your pages, my dear Diary.

NINE

Nueve

summer again

(2006)

July 28, 2006

Dear Mari,

It's going to be so strange to see you in
Boston. I know we've talked on the phone, but I
don't know. It's just going to be strange, that's all.
It'll be the real goodbye, I guess, for now. Then
you'll be in Mexico and who knows where I'll be.

What I mean is things haven't been going
well with the farm since your dad and uncles left.
This summer has been so rainy, most of the seeds
have just rotted in the ground. Dad's already
calculating that he's going to have to buy a lot of
grain he doesn't have the money to buy. Anyhow,

that scary word is going around the house again, *sell* the farm, get out from under before the bank comes and takes it away anyhow.

What's funny, well, not so funny, is that a year ago, I just wouldn't have accepted the idea of not living here. It kind of drove me crazy, if you want to know the truth. My parents had to ship me off to my aunt and uncle's just to get my mind off the worry.

But now, I don't know. I still think this has to be one of the most beautiful places on earth—like you yourself said. But somehow, though the idea of not farming still makes me real sad, I can accept it a lot better. Maybe losing Gramps helped me practice losing? Or just knowing what you and your family have gone through makes me feel like it could be a lot worse. Also, I guess I'm seeing other sides that might be fun, like having more time for things I love besides farming. Maybe I'll end up being an astronomer or a meteorologist or maybe I'll study Spanish and travel to Mexico and help out all the farmers there so they don't have to leave their land.

Anyhow, like Mom keeps telling me, life is about change, change, and more change. "When you're born as a child, you die as a baby. Just like when you're born as a teenager, you die as a child." Hey, Mom, thanks a lot! Sounds like our whole lives will be full of funerals, doesn't it?

"But there are good sides even to bad or sad things happening," my mom reminds me. Like this fall, it'll be kind of sad not going back to Bridgeport. But a good thing'll be that I won't have to take the bus, since I can catch a ride with Mom because the middle school is right next to the high school where she teaches math.

"You've got to develop the habit of thinking positive," Mom's always telling Dad and me. That's why she started yoga and meditating, on account of the mind is a puppy we have to train. (I bet Luby will love hearing that!) I guess my mind's more like my dad's. But it's not like our minds aren't trained—they are! They just go after the sad stuff. Like those golden retriever police dogs we saw on TV, remember? They hunt down missing kids and even adults. Just give them a whiff of a T-shirt or a pair of pants, and they're off.

But I'm definitely going to try to be positive in this goodbye letter that I want to give you before you leave. One really positive thing is how good it feels to be talking to you again, even though it's on paper, which I know you like to do, but I'm not so good at it. Another good thing is what Mr. Calhoun told Mom. How the judge at your dad's deportation hearing said he was going to drop all charges and send everybody back to Mexico and if your record stays clean, then in ten more years, when Ofie turns eighteen, she can come first as an American citizen and apply for her parents to get their papers!

Ten years! In ten years, I'll be twenty-two! Old enough to be done with college, if I go to college—which Mom says is not an option: not going, that is. "In today's world . . ." I know your parents are always telling you to study, study, study so you can end up with a better life than theirs.

That's kind of sad, I know. Like your parents will never get to live the life they want. At least, my mom really loves teaching, and even Dad was real happy farming, until he had his accident. But farming's no fun anymore, he says, the way he's having to do it now, scrambling the whole time. Mom tells him how he has many more incarnations to go. Nothing wacky like reincarnation, just how he can live many other lives in this life. Why, with his experience he could be a field agent and help other farmers. He could do any number of things. Dad kind of sighs like Mom is being what he calls New Agey, but I think it does help him to think that his life won't close down if he has to sell the farm.

Besides, what they are thinking of is not selling, but sort of leasing the whole farm to Uncle Larry. (He's like your uncle Felipe, except Uncle Larry isn't lucky and unlucky, just lucky. Like how not one of his six Mexicans was picked

302

up.) Of course, we know what Uncle Larry means to do: turn our farm into part of his whole MooPoo operation. It's pretty amazing that collecting cows' poo can make a farmer rich but milking them won't! Well, Uncle Larry milks them, too. He's got all his bases covered. Nurseries and parks and fancy gardens buy up all his composted manure. Meanwhile, he sells the organic milk for top dollar.

The way it'll work is, if one of us kids wants to farm in the future ("Don't look at me!" Sara says right off), we will be able to get the farm back from Uncle Larry. We'll just have to figure out what we owe him for improving the place. (I can't see how making a "manure product," what Uncle Larry calls it when he wants to sound fancy with people like Uncle Byron, is going to improve anything. But I guess Uncle Larry'll have to build a bunch of storage sheds and buy more equipment and stuff.) The best part about this plan is that we can stay living here. Plus, I'll get to keep Margarita! Maybe that's why it doesn't seem as awful as it once did, the idea of Dad quitting farming.

I'll be seeing you tomorrow when we come down to say goodbye. Mom is driving because Dad can't spare the time off. I feel kind of bad, taking the weekend off, but Dad says, "Son, you've earned it." If I've earned it, so has he, but at least two people have to stay to do the milking, and Dad really only counts for a half with his bad hand. Ben offered to stay, and Corey's now working part-time when he can be spared from his other farm job. Dad's also had to hire two local guys "to almost make up for one Mexican," as he says, complimenting your uncles and dad.

Anyhow, as I'll put on the envelope, I don't want you to read this until you've opened the box I'm bringing as my goodbye gift. By now you'll know what's in it! Yes, really and truly, I want you to keep it. For one thing, I'm asking Uncle Tony and Aunt Roxie for a stronger one for Christmas. They usually give me a big fancy gift then. And yes, I already asked Grandma, since it was a gift from Gramps, and she gave me her blessing, as she calls it. This way, Mari, when you look at the stars in Mexico, you can think of me looking up at some of the very same stars in Vermont. Only they'll be in different parts of the sky, but still.

Grandma also says if the ICE agents won't let you take more luggage, she can bring stuff when she comes down next month with her church youth group. They've raised enough money and they're confirmed to go. Grandma invited me to come, but Mom told me privately that it was a stretch for Grandma to buy another ticket.

Besides, Dad still really needs my help with the farm this summer. But by next summer if Uncle Larry's taken over, I won't have any chores! Another positive thing for my golden retriever mind to concentrate on. And by then, I'll be rich again from working for Mr. Rossetti for a whole year.

That's all for now, Mari. Tomorrow I'll be seeing you at Aunt Roxie and Uncle Tony's. Maybe we can go to the planetarium at the science museum and look at your star through their real powerful telescope. It'll be awesome, a lot bigger than just a pinprick of light.

And, Mari, well, you know how you felt bad that I spent a whole lot of money buying that star? I didn't exactly buy it, because you can't really buy a star, you can only name it. And it doesn't cost anything unless you send away for a fancy certificate or pick a star visible without a telescope, which I'm willing to do for your next birthday. But what will we name it? Maybe instead of Mari Cruz, we'll use your whole name, María Dolores Cruz Santos, to go along with it being a bigger star?

That reminds me. One last thing I want to do before we lease the farm to Uncle Larry: give it a name. Mom thinks it's a great idea. That way when we draw up the legal documents with

Uncle Larry, we can write down an actual name. "It'd be so sad to just call it one-hundred-and-ten-acres-with-frontage-on-Town-Line-Road," Mom says, and suddenly, there are tears brimming in her eyes. I guess there's some in mine, too. But naming it, I don't know, it'll be more ours somehow.

Since you're so good with words, Mari, maybe you can help me with some ideas? Especially because I think a name in Spanish would be really cool. The same name in English wouldn't sound as special. The best I've come up with is *Amigos* Farm, but Sara says it's too blah—this from the one family member who can't wait to get off the farm. I think *amigo* is not her favorite word right now, as Mateo just left for Spain after his year in the States. And this time, instead of my sister dumping him, he told her that now that they were going to be an ocean apart, he just wanted to be *amigos*, friends. So, anyhow, *Amigos* Farm is on hold for now—until my sister finds a new boyfriend.

But whether or not it's named *Amigos*, as long as my family is on this land, it will be a place where you and your family will find friends. One thing I did learn from Mr. Bicknell this past year is that the only way we're going to save this planet is if we remember that we are all connected. Like the swallows. How when they leave here in a month they'll be on their way to where you are.

If it can work for barn swallows, it should work for us. Like we learned from Ms. Swenson, our teacher the year before you came. Something the Hopi elders told their tribe during really hard times: how certain things needed to get done if they were going to survive. How they couldn't put it off. How there was no one else but them to do it. "We are the ones we have been waiting for," that's what the elders told the Hopi people.

You and me, Mari, it's up to us. We are the ones who are going to save this planet. So we've got to stay connected—through the stars above and swallows and letters back and forth. And someday, you will return, Mari. Like Mr. O'Goody said, he's putting a special letter in your parents' file. Meanwhile, I'll be coming to visit you in Las Margaritas. For one thing, I've got to see the town I've named my show calf after.

Adios, amiga, and I guess I don't have to tell you to write back.

Your friend forever,
Tyler

August 19, 2006

Dear Tyler,

I've gotten up extra early to write you, as
Grandma and Mr. Rossetti and the church group
will be leaving in a few hours. They weren't
supposed to go until next week. But when they
found out we are having elections for our
governor tomorrow, they decided to advance
their departure and leave today. Papá thinks it's
best as otherwise they might get caught in the
middle of a lot of strikes and protests, and we
have been having a lot of them.

It started with our big national elections on
July 2nd. (I know, two days before your country's
birthday!) Everybody's favorite candidate here in
Las Margaritas lost, but not by much. Right away,
people began saying the winner stole the
election, and they wanted all the votes counted
again, but the government refused.

"Why, that's just like our 2000 election!" your
grandma said.

"Nonsense!" Mr. Rossetti disagreed. "Our
president got elected fair and square."

Everyone just watches when they have their
arguments. Mostly, people here are astonished
that two old people would come to our town to

work. "*Esos viejitos* should be home taking care of themselves!"

"We're not *viejitos*!" Grandma says when I translate. She does not like to be called old people.

Of course, Mr. Rossetti has a different opinion. "Elsie, you just won't face reality, will you? You'll die young at a hundred—after you've killed us all off, to be sure."

He grumbles a lot but I think he has been having a wonderful time. Luby and Ofie won't let him out of their sight. Meanwhile, Abuelito has come down any number of times to visit *el viejito americano*. He and Abuelote sit around "talking" with Mr. Rossetti, which is funny to watch, because Abuelito and Abuelote don't speak any English, and Mr. Rossetti doesn't understand Spanish. They all just jab the air with their canes and gesture and nod at whatever one of them is saying.

So, on account of our election day tomorrow, everyone is predicting trouble. Big strikes like they are having in Mexico City and in the state next to ours, Oaxaca. Not just protests, like you had last spring for immigrant rights in Washington, D.C. I mean millions of people camped out in the main square for weeks on end, blocking the entrance to government buildings, and even the road to the airport. Papá actually gets very excited and says that maybe Mexico will finally become a place where people like him can stay and work and raise their families.

One of the good things about moving is getting my old Papá back! I was worried when he was released at the airport that being put in prison would make him even more bitter and angry. But finding so many friends who helped him, and your aunt and uncle who took us in and didn't charge us a penny, touched his heart. "There are good people in this world," he said to Mamá on the plane to Mexico. "Angels," he said, sort of smiling to himself. Maybe he was remembering how your mother called us Mexican angels when we first got to the farm a year ago almost to the day—I just realized!

Papá has woken up—most everyone is still sleeping after our goodbye party last night. When he sees me writing, he asks who the letter is for. I hesitate because, well, you know how he is about me and boys. But before I can say your name, he says, "Ese es un hombrecito bueno."

So, you see, Tyler, Papá really does like you. You are the only boy he's called a good young man since I turned twelve and became a señorita. Even my boy cousins he doesn't trust. It's so silly, but Mamá says it's the way she and Papá were raised. And after what happened to her . . .

310

I know he feels bad about the way he treated you after Mamá's return. But like I told Mr. O'Goody, Papá just wasn't himself back then. He also worries about the money he owes you. In fact, he wanted Grandma to take your telescope back to you. "It is too much," he explained.

But Grandma refused. "Tell your father that you don't give back presents!"

I do think it was overly generous, Tyler. Just like I think it was so special of you to name a star after me, even if it was free. I actually feel better knowing I don't own it. Like you told me about the American Indians, how they didn't really believe people could own the land. How can you own a star?! (Don't you love interrobangs?!)

I'm also very glad I won't have to return the telescope. I just love looking through it—and so does the whole town! Papá jokes that if I charged admission each time a neighbor came by to look at the stars through my magic glass, he could be well on his way to paying back his debt to you. Five hundred dollars is a lot of money here— more than some of our neighbors earn in a year. But Papá will pay you back, Tyler, even if it's ten years from now when Ofie can sponsor him. When your grandmother arrived, Papá asked me to tell her that he would return to work on your farm for free till the debt was paid off.

So I had to tell him the whole situation you

had explained to me. "Papá, the Paquettes won't be farming anymore."

Papá sighed. That old tiredness was back in his eyes. "We have suffered the same fate," he said quietly. "Such good people," he added. "Life is not fair."

It's sad to hear your parents say something like that. I guess just like you said about your father (and yourself), Papá sees more sadness in the world than happiness.

"But we can change that," I told him, trying to be positive for both our sakes. We had been watching television, the crowds of campers in Mexico City demanding that the government make their country a place they could live in. "We can make things more fair, Papá. We have to do it because there's no one else to do it if we don't."

A strange look came over Papá's face. It was like he suddenly realized I wasn't a little girl anymore. Oh, I know he's always telling me I'm the oldest who has to watch over my sisters. Or I'm now a young lady who has to be guarded against young men who'll try to take advantage. But right then and there, he understood. I was growing up into someone he might even look up to!

Not only is Papá happier, but Mamá, too. Being around their family and in their homeland has been good for them both. Papá is involved now in the local politics—that's how come he knew so much about the elections coming up on Sunday and could advise Grandma.

Ofie and Luby are doing better, but the first two weeks were very hard for them. They couldn't get used to speaking Spanish the whole time and missing out on all their TV programs. Also, they have to help Mamá with a lot of housework. Here, we can't just have the washing machine do the laundry. We have to gather kindling to cook because electricity costs so much and often there are blackouts. We have to plant the beans if we want burritos and make our own tortillas from cornmeal. After the first week of thinking it was fun to do all these things, now they just say, "I don't want to!" Well, especially Ofie, and Luby copies everything. But I have kept my promise, and I only fight about once a day with Ofie.

"You can't make me," she always says when I ask her to help out. "I have rights. I'm an American citizen!"

Papá overheard this exchange the other day, and he put his hands on his hips and said, "*Americanita,* when we were in your country, we had to work. Now you're in ours, and you have to work in return!"

It was the funniest thing he could have said,

but I tried not to laugh because I didn't want to start another fight with Ofie.

We are all going to be even more homesick once Grandma and Mr. Rossetti leave! Mamá has promised us that we will go back. "When?" Ofie wants to know.

"As soon as we can do so legally," Mamá promises. She paid too high a price for crossing illegally this last time. She has promised me that when I am more grown-up, she will tell me the whole story. "And someday when you are a famous writer, you can put it into a book." She smiles at the future she imagines for her daughter who is always writing letters or writing in her diary.

It's Papá who is not so sure he wants to go back (except to pay his debt to you). He says if this country improves, he wants to stay put. But he'd love for my sisters and me to study and become professionals and live in the United States. For a while, anyhow. Eventually, he wants us to come home. "This has been our land for generations," he says, picking up a handful of soil and sifting it through his fingers.

But it's different for Ofie and Luby, and even for me. Like what you said about the swallows, Tyler. Las Margaritas is our home, but we also belong to that special farm in the rolling hills of Vermont.

Which leads me to your request about what to name the farm. Actually, I've asked the whole family for their suggestions. Papá voted for the name *Amigos* Farm. Mamá pondered for a minute, then said, maybe *Buenos Amigos* Farm, so it's the Good Friends Farm. I was sure that Luby would suggest some kind of dog name, but she voted for Ofie's suggestion: the Three Marías Farm!

"But it's not ours," I pointed out. "Plus, it's kind of conceited to put our names on the Paquettes' farm."

"It is not!" Ofie disagreed.

It is too! I thought, but I didn't say so as we'd had several fights that day already.

Last night, the farm's name came up again. It was after the big farewell party at our house. Papá roasted a whole pig, which is what people here do when they want to really celebrate. We'd invited all the neighbors who've been the host families for the kids in the youth group. We ate and ate and then everyone took a turn looking through my telescope. It was one of the highlights of the party. In fact, as the night wore on, people began seeing the most amazing constellations. Mariano, who is like our town drunk and shows up at every party, claimed he saw the Virgin of Guadalupe in the sky! Everybody was having such a nice time, they didn't want to leave. Finally, Tío Felipe began playing Wilmita, and we sang

"*La Golondrina*" as a way of bidding everyone good night.

Afterward, the family sat outside, looking up at the stars with our own eyes. Mr. Rossetti and Grandma were also there, as they are staying with us, and Abuelito, as it was too late for him to travel home. We were sitting outside, feeling tired, the happy kind of tired, but also a little sad with the goodbyes in the air. "I do believe," Mr. Rossetti observed, "that we can see more stars here than back home."

It was true, there seemed to be more and more stars, the more we looked. Then out of the blue, Grandma asked, "What's the word for star in Spanish?"

"*¡Estrella!*" Ofie and Luby called out together, feeling very proud of themselves for remembering.

"How about *Estrella* Farm?" Grandma suggested.

"I think it's an American farm and should have an American name, Elsie," Mr. Rossetti disagreed. "No offense," he said to his hosts, who didn't understand what he'd said anyhow.

"Oh, Joseph." Grandma sighed. But it was too late for a disagreement, even a mild one.

"I've got an even better idea," Mr. Rossetti went on, encouraged by Grandma's giving in. "How about Stars and Stripes Farm?" Even though I couldn't see his face real clear, I knew

Mr. Rossetti was grinning. "That's our name for our flag in the United States," he told Abuelote and Abuelito. They nodded—"*Sí, sí, sí*"—even though I don't think they had a clue what Mr. Rossetti was talking about.

I thought about what Mr. Rossetti had said, and I kind of respected his opinion. You do have a great country, Tyler, why else would so many of us want to go there? But I got to thinking about all the things Mr. Bicknell had said, about us having to be not just patriots of a country, but citizens of the planet. So why not give the farm a name for the things that connect us?

"Stars and Swallows Farm," I said, trying the name out loud. *"Estrellas y Golondrinas."*

That name sounded perfect right then. But you know how you said your own family will agree on a name and then a few days later think better of it? Well, this morning, Stars and Swallows Farm sounds like a lot of words. So now I'm not real sure what to suggest, Tyler. Maybe your farm is just too special for words—and that's why your family has had a hard time naming it?

Too bad Mr. Bicknell won't be your teacher anymore. He would come up with a creative assignment for everyone in class to suggest a name and write a story why. Then, like in a democracy, everyone would vote.

Last night, I didn't take a vote, but everyone

seemed to like Stars and Swallows. We sat quietly savoring the name like it was a taste in our mouths. Stars and Swallows. *Estrellas y Golondrinas.*

"In a few weeks, they'll be back," Abuelote broke the silence. It took me a second to realize what he was talking about.

"We wait and wait," Abuelota agreed. "And our hearts are not complete till we see those *golondrinas* coming back, filling the sky."

"As numerous as stars," Abuelito observed.

I knew then how much my grandparents had missed us, how a part of their very own hearts had been missing until now. How we were the ones they had been waiting for.

We all grew quiet again, looking up, feeling the specialness of this night before we would fly apart.

Tu amiga, para siempre and forever, too,
Mari

Dear readers, *queridos lectores,*

Although this is a made-up story, the situation it describes is true. Many farmers from Mexico and Central America are forced to come north to work because they can no longer earn a living from farming. They make the dangerous border crossing with smugglers called *coyotes,* who charge them a lot of money and often take advantage. To keep out these migrants, a wall is being built between Mexico and the United States. National troops have been sent down to patrol the border. We are treating these neighbor countries and migrant helpers as if they were our worst enemies.

These migrant workers often bring their families with them. Their children, born in Mexico, are also considered "illegal aliens." But those born here are United States citizens. These families live in fear of deportation and separation from each other.

In 2006, Immigration and Customs Enforcement (ICE, or *la migra,* as the migrants call these agents) raided many workplaces. This dragnet was known as Operation Return to Sender, after the phrase stamped by the United States Postal Service on letters that don't have enough postage or are incorrectly addressed. Workers without legal papers were taken away on the spot, leaving behind children who were cared for by friends, relatives, or older siblings. These children are the casualties of their parents' decision to leave behind their homelands in order to survive.

Caught in a similar struggle in this country are the children of American farmers who are finding it increasingly difficult to continue farming. They cannot find affordable help and have to resort to hiring farmers displaced from other lands. The children of both are seeing the end of a way of life and the loss of their ancestral homes.

When a Mexican dies far away from home, a song known as *"La Golondrina"* ("The Swallow") is sung at the funeral. The song tells of a swallow that makes the yearly migration from Mexico to *El Norte* during the late spring and returns south in autumn. But sometimes that swallow gets lost in the cold winds and never finds its way back. This is the fear of those who leave home as well as those who stay behind awaiting their return. The song reminds us that we all need a safe and happy place where we belong.

With hope and *esperanza*,
Julia Alvarez

A WORD ABOUT THE SPANISH IN ENGLISH
Una palabra sobre el español en inglés

I know it must seem strange that Mari is often writing her letters in Spanish but you are reading them in English.

Just the same, when she reports on a conversation with her father or mother or uncles, these relatives are speaking in Spanish, but wait a minute! You are hearing them in English.

This is the wonderful thing about stories. The impossible is possible. You can read a story about a samurai warrior or two Italian teenagers with warring families or a Danish prince whose father has died mysteriously and be totally at home in their world even though you don't speak a word of their language. It's why I love stories. There are no borders. Like swallows, like stars, you don't have to stop where one country or language or race or religion or gender or time period ends and another begins.

But just in case you wondered, one of the ways we recognize that a word belongs in another language, *otra lengua,* is that we put it in italics. So, whenever one of Mari's letters begins in italics with a Spanish date (*15 agosto 2005*) and salutation (*Queridísima Mamá*) or she writes México with an accent, you will know that it is actually being written in Spanish. But don't worry. Because this is a story, you can understand her Spanish as if you were a native speaker.

Also, whenever I use a Spanish word, I always give you its

323

English translation or make sure you understand what the word means in that scene. I wouldn't want you to feel left out just because you are not yet bilingual! But my hope is that what you can do magically in a story, understand Spanish, will make you want to learn that magic in real life. Being bilingual is a wonderful way to connect ourselves with other countries and people and understand what it means to live inside their words as well as their world.

So, for now, welcome to Spanish in English, and may it inspire you to learn the language of Spanish in *español*.

Acknowledgments

I hereby name the stars on the following pages
after all of you who helped me
write this book.
You know who you are,
my stars.
Thank you!
¡Gracias!

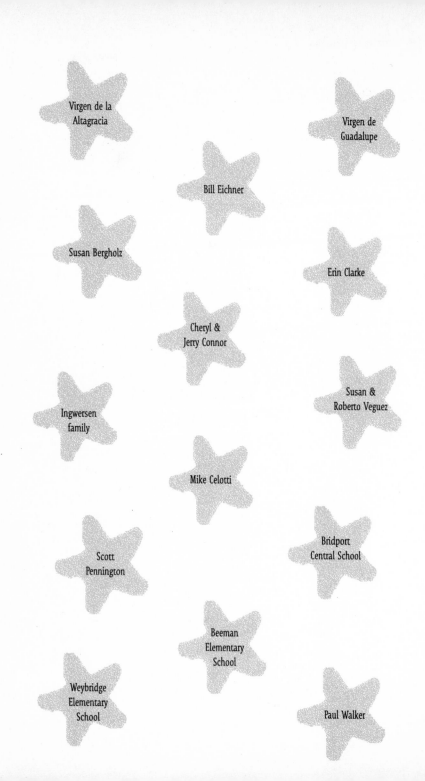

Virgen de la Altagracia

Virgen de Guadalupe

Bill Eichner

Susan Bergholz

Erin Clarke

Cheryl & Jerry Connor

Susan & Roberto Veguez

Ingwersen family

Mike Celotti

Scott Pennington

Bridport Central School

Beeman Elementary School

Weybridge Elementary School

Paul Walker

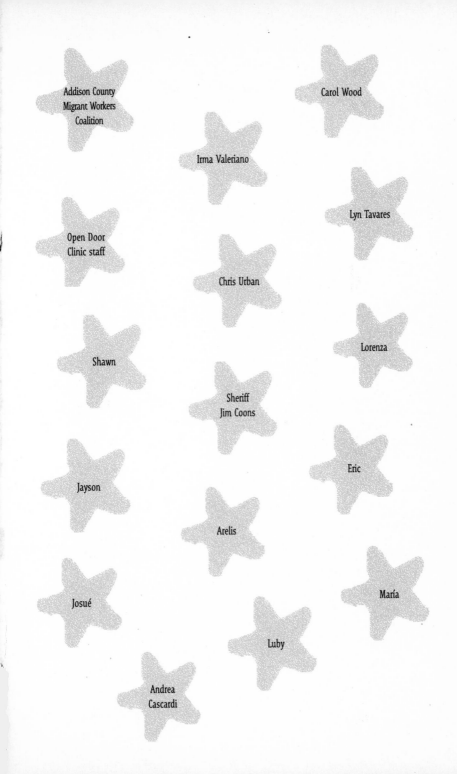

Addison County
Migrant Workers
Coalition

Carol Wood

Irma Valeriano

Lyn Tavares

Open Door
Clinic staff

Chris Urban

Lorenza

Shawn

Sheriff
Jim Coons

Eric

Jayson

Arelis

Josué

María

Luby

Andrea
Cascardi